Draconem Dawn

Maxsimo Salazar

ISBN: 978-1-953805-02-7

DEDICATION

For my wife, Elizabeth. You are my guiding light.

KEY TERMS AND CONCEPTS

This novel includes unique terms and concepts that you will encounter in the chapters ahead. To supplement your enjoyment and enhance the experience, we have compiled a companion website. It will include a comprehensive glossary and other excellent stuff. For the companion website, go to www.DraconemDawn.com or use the QR code below.

ACKNOWLEDGMENTS

I wish to thank my dear friend Roger Rodriguez (*The Long Way To Mexico*) whose encouragement to publish over the last several years and advice on the process have proven to be invaluable. Thank you to Carlos Nicolás Flores (*Our House on Hueco*) who spent countless hours teaching me to write and edit. Without your tutelage, this book would never have left the ground. I must not forget to thank my great friend Gregory Barton who believed in me, and decided to publish this book. You have given my dracons wings to soar. Finally, I want to thank the entirety of the Salazar Clan. Mom and Dad, you gave me life and the will to achieve my dreams. To my brother and sister, you are my best friends. To my children, I do everything for you. But to my wife, I give the greatest thanks for choosing to take this crazy ride by my side for over twenty years.

Audio clip from the Quetz Supreme Chancellor, Her Highness Kiira-Ave Strong Bird to humanity, recorded by NORAD.

You want to know who we are and where we came from? Let me tell you then. We were once dinosaurs, the Quetzalcoatlus, relics of a forgotten world that once teemed with life. The largest of our kind, our ancestors ruled the skies of the great Cretaceous era. While the fate of the rest of the giant lizards was sealed with the Dark Shudder, the mass extinction event, a small group of us survived the blast and, over three hundred million years, evolved into a sentient and highly advanced civilization. We may have remained hidden from you for many millennia, but there was a time when you once knew us openly. In fact, the entirety of your advancement was due to our intervention. We lived side-by-side in harmony, but you had a different name for us then.

Know then, that our assistance in your development is deemed a catastrophic error in our judgment and one that we aim to rectify. We allowed your race to manage Terr, or as you refer to her, Earth. You have failed to protect her, and despite your acknowledgment of this fact, have done nothing to correct it. You choose to blame one another and engage in war instead and further exacerbate her destruction. We were ready to depart for a better uncorrupted world, leaving Terr in your hands, but you brought war to our clans without cause by taking the life of my betrothed. Now, you will be eradicated, for the betterment of all life on Terr, present and future. The planet continues to descend into chaos and we must honor Spirit Terr and fix what you have broken. You will not survive our onslaught, for we are Dracons!

PROLOGUE

Eensul

The gravity of the Quetz's problems weighed heavy on the Supreme Chancellor. Life was slowly becoming normal for the single mother, but not spending time with her daughter became commonplace and increasingly difficult for her. Fortunately, her daughter's assigned guard, Lt. Colonel Akeela, behaved more like an older sister to her young ward. Eensul was not sure if Akeela would surrender her post once Kiira ascended to adulthood at the onset of her seventeenth Stel rotation; but she secretly hoped she would not, due to her daughter's deep affection for her. But of course, Akeela also needed to think of her own career.

Eensul sat her in opulent seat, a shimmery red-hued crystal that was generously padded with the finest synthetic materials. Before her, an ornate and polished marble desk held all the tools she required to lead her race, chief among them, a holo-projector and its seemingly invisible system interfaces. She ruled her people from this perch. She made decisions that affected their daily lives, here in the Americas, as well as in the continents of Africa, Asia, Europe, and even a small contingent on Australia. As for Antarctica, they had not stepped foot on its mass since before its freezing.

Her main concern at the moment; the thing that caused her to fret even before accepting the near-unanimous vote by the Council of Elders to the chancellorship was the state of Terr. Once a resplendent world filled with life and purity, it was now more of a wasteland, dotted with human ceramic structures and oil-based roads that further exacerbated the already climbing atmospheric temperature. Bi-peds spewed toxic fumes and dumped radioactive waste into the very waters that served all life. This was only the beginning of the atrocities that "humanity" committed. Eensul knew that the time of the Quetz on Terr was nearly over. They would inevitably have to leave their beloved world to seek out a new home.

Eensul and three of the elders were in the early stages of designing and building a ship large enough to house their entire populace. Once completed, they could depart for a cleaner and healthier world. *Only three elders*, she remembered. She still had not appointed her replacement as the head of her clan, the Socran. Her brother, Waal, was the obvious choice, but he continually reminded her of this. She well understood that blood is thicker than water; but it was also the very trap by which many a leader had fallen victim to. Waal had always been jealous of her success. There were other royal members of her house that she could choose from, but that could relegate her daughter to a lesser position in the future, and Waal did not have children. Should anything happen to her, he would act as Kiira's legal guardian and as such potentially groom her for the seat as his successor. Still, she was not sure that this was the best path.

Parched, she looked around her cavernous room for a vial of glacier water that was delivered to her earlier in the day as part of her late morning snack. Too busy with her duties, she passed up on the opportunity to have a little something and was feeling peckish. Supper was three hours away, so she decided to replenish her fluids and have a small bite. She walked to the small table by the door where she finally spotted her meal and grabbed the vial. Firmly in her left hand, her inner left talon glanced the top of the tube, opening it up and exposing a straw from which to drink. With one swift sucking motion, the contents were fully emptied. She felt the usual coolness of glacier water course down her throat and felt refreshed. A moment later, though, the refreshing sensation was replaced by something warmer. The shimmering silver robes that covered her full frame felt heavy on her shoulders. Without hesitation, she quickly tore them off, exposing her red feathers. The cool air did nothing to comfort her and perspiration quickly drenched her.

She immediately recognized what was happening. She was poisoned and would die within seconds. She knew who had killed her, but had only enough time to focus on the love of her life, Kiira, her only daughter. The walls were moving and the ceiling was falling down on her. The faux solar light, that glowed from within the walls and ceiling was dimming rapidly. Stumbling over her slippery robe that let fall to the floor, she fell onto her perch, furiously struggling to focus on the holo-screen. The Quetzian characters were a blur to her fading vision, but she managed to locate the transcriber icon and pressed it on the ephemeral screen. She motioned her right hand to begin the recording and blurted out who would replace her as clan elder, just before losing consciousness. But, she forced herself to utter one last thing. "Send last recording to all clan elders immediately."

Kiira

At the tender age of sixteen Stel rotations, Kiira Ave was one of the youngest Quetz to assume the role of clan elder. Though, not unprecedented, it was a rarity. Regardless of the responsibility that was thrust upon her, she was determined to make her mother proud. A gifted student, she was well-versed in Mathematics and Science. Literature was a hobby as well. She needed to brush up on her history and Political Science lessons, though. What was once dull was now weighing heavy upon her scant shoulders. It was also important for her to know how and why her mother died, and wondered who would kill such a benevolent bird. For most things, she relied on her loving and charismatic Uncle Waal. He had already promised to do the heavy bureaucratic lifting until she was older, allowing her to grieve and still have some semblance of ease during her young adult years.

A sharp whistling sound alerted Kiira that someone with access to her quarters was approaching. Kiira quickly turned to see that it was the well-muscled Akeela who entered.

"My detail is leading a clandestine investigation into your mother's death. According to your uncle Waal, his spies have found evidence that General Jaak may be behind this. But, I would not put too much weight on this report. Intel is always suspect, and your mother personally selected Jaak to lead his clan after she ascended to the throne."

"How did she do that? I thought all elders designated their own replacements?" Her small turquoise eyes looked up questioningly.

"Well, per our 'order' you are correct. Though in times of war or great strife, the Supreme Chancellor may appoint an elder as needed. But with the Draconem, things are a little different. Because they are our warrior class, they must serve at the will of the Supreme Chancellor; and thus, their leader is always an appointee. Once chosen, though, they keep that role until they die or are too old to lead us into battle."

"I did not know that. Interesting."

"Yes, it is, and as a member of the Draconem, we are proud to be appointed to our positions. It is a great honor to earn this status. But, little one, please get some rest. Seln is already high up in the sky. Your mother would have wished it. Besides, soon enough, you will enter the world of politics and join the elders in their meetings. And, in a few Seln cycles, you will participate in the formal selection process to determine the new Supreme Chancellor. Your uncle, believes General Jaak is the likely candidate, but there are always political maneuvers that must be contended with. For now, allow your uncle Waal to do his job and sit in your stead. You will lead your clan when the time comes. And leave the investigation into your mother to Waal and I. We will handle it. Okay?"

Kiira's eyes were already lead plates and she needed no further encouragement to rest. She was desperate for her mother and could only find her in her dreams. She wished time would move faster to ease her pain, but did not want to forget either. Kiira's thoughts were filled with images of her mother as darkness overcame her still fragile body.

Kiira

It was close to midnight and Kiira couldn't sleep. Thoughts of her mother's death raced through her mind endlessly. It was expected, but her mother's passing nearly a Seln rotation ago, still took her off guard, and her entire life was in turmoil. As her mother's heir, she was expected to formally sit on the council, but what kept her up was the vacancy of the seat of Chancellor Supreme and the small possibility that she could fill it. She felt that she was still too young and inexperienced for such a role. On the other hand, General Jaak would seek to acquire the position, which in her mind, and in those of some of the other senior Quetz, would spell war for her species. But who would oppose him? He was powerful.

As a Council Member, she was afforded new privileges and could leave her secretive home at will and without question. She was of course not deluded and expected that her departure would be reported and make its way to General Jaak who as the Senior Military Official was also Head of Security. Nothing was ever hidden from him.

Kiira sniffed the air and picked up notes of the granite that was her home. It was an old habit her species had not broken in the hundreds of mega-annum of their evolution. At this elevation, the air was bitingly cold, but after countless generations of living at the tops of mountains, her species was immune to the frigid temperature, their down feather coat well thickened. She glanced out into the distance and through keenly developed eyes was able to discern the twinkling city lights, where countless humans roamed oblivious to the existence of her superior race. Without thinking twice, she walked over the cliff's edge and allowed herself to free fall beak first into the darkness. After a brief moment, she expanded her wings and soared out towards the brilliance and freedom of humanity that she grew to envy. With a flick of her left wrist, she activated an EM scrambler making her invisible to lesser radar technology that gave her the freedom to move beyond the perimeter shield. Next, she enabled a tachyon field giving her the ability to fly with unprecedented speed. *They call it Seattle*, she thought as she soared in the sky. *It means to go beyond but was also the name of the mountain that provided water to the indigenous people. Mother once mentioned a story in which our ancestors lived peacefully with theirs. I will have to read up on that sometime soon.*

Random lights spotted the dense forest. A fiery snake of diseased bi-ped automobiles also speckled the darkness beneath her, winding its way into and out of the populous city.

Although her field generator allowed her the ability to move effortlessly at whatever speed she desired, the chill air still provided her with some needed lift; and it was that feeling of blistery cold that she missed. With the generator on, she could not sense the tingling sensation that the wind provided as it once used to, caressing her skin and agitating her feathers, sending ripples of welcoming pressure all along her sleek body. She reminisced of the days she would spend flying as a young chick with Akeela, her guard. Mother had just been appointed clan elder and time outside became too much of a risk to her safety, something she was ignoring at the moment.

Kiira continued her scan of the terrain below, now moving at a slower speed, and looked down at the electric beauty these people had created for themselves. Another flick of the wrist and she was cloaked in the visible spectrum as well. Peering down, she picked a target to land on that would bring her within forty feet of the black pathways the people used to commute. Satisfied that she found a spot, she swooped down and landed with a gentle thud. She chose a very busy eatery to alight on, whose employees mistook the thumping sound as the air conditioning unit kicking on. Most did not even notice as they were busy sweating away as they bustled about the hot kitchen, preparing dishes from their signature lab-grown chicken protein menu, whose aroma did not escape Kiira's discerning olfactory senses. She shivered slightly as her avian heart burst through her gently sloping chest. Her excitement had caught up with her. She applied the calming techniques she acquired from Akeela and focused on steading her heart.

Remember to find your center and breathe into your stomach, and hold it for four seconds. Breathe out through your mouth for four seconds; and, always remember to relax your mind and release all of your thoughts. Do not think. Just be aware.

Within two minutes, she was back to a normal calm, with her senses focused on observing the scene below through her eyes, ears, nose, and mind. *Tonight, I am a warrior,* she intoned. *This is not a mantra; it is a way of being.*

Kiira knew Akeela was a member of the Draconem clan and as such, a fierce female warrior who happened to rival all of her male clan members. She was a deeply loyal and highly respected member of her clan, which was why Lt. Colonel Jaak selected her to act as Kiira's personal guard when she was born. She listened at length to Elder Eensul's speeches and felt emboldened to speak her mind more often than not, due to her new position as a personal guard to Kiira. But, she also trusted in Eensul fully and in a private ritual gave her complete allegiance with the promise to protect Kiira with her life, outside of the General's knowledge.

Kiira's young eyes caught movement below. People were flopping their flat and noisy feet down the gray ceramic surface. Others were sitting while eating and drinking oddly colored fluids, laughing merrily as they did so. It was odd behavior for Kiira, as her race ate silently and did so quickly. Yet, humans did more than just nourish themselves communally; they also made loud roaring sounds she could not identify as language. She of course, was trained to understand and speak in English as well as many other of their simple languages. It was part of the curriculum young birds of high stature or any member of the Seentia, or Science clan, were presented with. Throughout the evening, she overheard several conversations of no significance. These people related stories that produced spasmodic muscular reactions and sounds that they seemed to derive pleasure from. What they said simply made no sense, yet they all reacted in the same odd manner.

She observed the youngling race for several hours and felt that she learned one key thing: people were social and may not be the warmongering species she was led to believe. Perhaps there was hope for them. General Jaak, however, was adamant of their failures. Whereas her choice would likely be to embrace this sentient group, his was to eradicate them. Uncle Waal, though, was always there to protect her from the senior warrior's rhetoric and assuage it with friendlier tones and ideas.

Satisfied with her little adventure and feeling famished, she lifted off the building's flat roof with assistance from the tachyon field. She flew steadily and after what seemed like too brief of a flight home, she landed by her private quarters to an anxious and visibly upset Akeela, who glared at her as if at her own daughter.

Part 1

CHAPTER 1

Kiira

One Stel rotation since her first flight to the human city passed, and a brisk wind once again ruffled her ruby feathers and pink comb, causing her muscles to tense up briefly in defiance of the sharp chill. Her eyes squinted forming a singular tear. It stayed in place at the far corner of her turquoise eyes. It was the first of its kind for the entirety of her race. Not a single member of the Quetz had ever developed a teardrop. It was not that they did not have emotions. In fact, they were taught almost from hatchlings to control their varied and powerful feelings to the point of seeming devoid of them. The formation of water around her ocular glands, however, was unique. It was another step in their evolution. She would make note of its occurrence and the circumstances around it in her personal log, but would refrain from sharing it for the time being.

Thoughts of her mother barraged her nearly every day, adding to the severe toll the unexpected and unprecedented leadership took. It had been a full Stel rotation since her death, yet time had failed to be the tincture to ease her soul as her uncle Waal had promised. Anyone could be watching, and in particular any one of General Jaak's zealots. She knew that she must steel herself now and forever onward and mute the negative scenes in her head.

Her left foot felt uneasy with the course gravel beneath, that jabbed and tore into it. She turned her foot to force out the sharp rocks that irritated her soft pad, causing them to plummet into the dark abyss. Again, she espied the distant Seattle, whose prosperity and grandeur continued to stir her heart. At night, its bright city lights radiated a deep yellow. But she knew from experience that up close they were a barrage of different hues of blue, red, yellow, green and violet, each with its own meaning. *What a sight*, she thought. *The Quetz must live in quiet seclusion while the bipeds are free to roam about.* As a hatchling, she failed to understand why her mother, heir to the Socran clan, supported hiding in the depths of the mountains, living off of bland, though nutritious synth food, when with their superior technology, they could have ruled over all of Spirit Terr's creatures. In time, she learned that humans, as they called themselves, were deceptively strong and their true power came from their large numbers and dogged determination to ravage all around them in the name of prosperity.

History detailed the first bi-ped machines as clunky, black-smoking monstrosities; but recently, their refinement began to be reminiscent of the Quetz's own earlier tech. Soon, they would catch up and, upon discovering their reclusive neighbors, decimate their inferior numbers. Some of the clan elders felt that Spirit Terr would deal with the bipeds in due time through disease or from some natural disaster, which seemed to be occurring with the spread of several man-made contagions. Either way, the time for a Quetz campaign of power and dominance was gone. The bipedal numbers approached eight billion, whereas their own was limited to only a few thousand, thanks to careful eugenics. They also opted not to overly consume their resources and preferred to live in balance with all around them.

As Kiira remained motionless, her thoughts raced in perfect synchronicity working to achieve the goal of solving the quandary that had engrossed her every waking minute for the last three days. The time had come to make a decision and the answer had finally come. She would lead her race towards a new order, one that would ensure their safety and protect them from being discovered by the bi-peds below. It would, of course, curtail Quetz flights, regardless of the time of day and despite the use of the EM scrambler.

Their scientists continued to develop the tech fastidiously for the past ten years in the hopes of providing all clan members the freedom of flight during regulated schedules and zones. Nonetheless, she feared that the increasing technology of the humans was catching up too quickly, and that their survival necessitated this extreme policy. A few of her most trusted clan members would maintain a highly restricted privilege to fly but only for reconnaissance reasons and only with her express permission. Soon, she would also reveal her plan to all of the

Quetz to vacate Terr and seek out a new world, a planet free of the disastrous bipedal creatures and their filth. She believed that within a few Stel rotations, work on a vast interstellar ship could be completed. Its construction would have to be done on the far side of the natural satellite Seln to prevent detection, though. The scramblers would hopefully be their saving grace. *Damn those creatures*, she thought.

Dealing with General Jaak was another problem she would have to contend with very shortly. Jaak was likely behind the mysterious death of her beloved mother, though the evidence still eluded her and her uncle. Still, as the appointed Minister of Defense, chosen by her mother during her reign, he held great sway when it came to matters of security. He was also the leader of his clan, the Draconem, which gave him a powerful voice in the Council of Elders, which she now presided over, much to his consternation as he coveted the seat of power. His influence as a clan elder also meant that she could not remove him as the highest-ranking warrior without risking a coup, which could result with Jaak as Supreme Chancellor, pushing her towards excommunication. His flamboyant and fiery rhetoric was already beginning to sway the elders towards his side. They could agree with his plan to make their presence known and if necessary, wage war to ensure survival. Kiira saw him as no more than a fear monger and war fanatic. She solemnly prayed to the creator that he was nothing more than a soon-to-be fad passé. Why her mother made him the most powerful minister was beyond her thinking and that of her uncle. It was a political move for sure, but to serve what end? She did not know. It eluded her no matter how much she focused on it. Regardless, a time of reconciliation with him rapidly approached.

In this moment, however, she opted to take one last flight before passing her judgment. The sun was nearly set and she was anxious to test out the new EM scrambler for herself. Her personal guard since birth, LtCol. Akeela, a rare trusted member of the Draconem, had thoroughly tested the new version of the device herself to ensure it was not rigged with any intentional defects. She placed it on her left wrist and activated it by warbling a command. A faint steady hum ensued. Her body began to tingle and soon became invisible to even her own eyes.

Satisfied, she looked down into the valley and allowed herself to drop. The scrambler, which held improved radar-blocking capabilities gave her a sense of newfound power as her fear of detection faded. Leadership had its perks.

The elation of flying invisible ebbed as she stepped into the secret chamber of the Council of Elders, the Sala Eld, and walked towards her seat as Supreme Chancellor, centered in the apex of the stone great hall where, for millennia, her ancestors met. A single bird represented each of the four clans with her clan holding two seats, clan elder and Supreme Chancellor, giving her a tie-breaking vote if necessary. The well-groomed and purple-robed General Jaak represented the Draconem, the warriors of their race, known for their excessive combat and tactics training. Naturally, they tended to be larger and more physically powerful than the rest, giving many of them a sense of self-righteousness, which the others felt was often a trade-off in their inability to think critically.

Elder Lün, in her elaborately gilded golden robe, led the Stora, or historians of the group. They were responsible for the accurate documentation of their entire history as well as its safeguarding. This included all meeting notes from every council meeting for more than a hundred millennia, giving them the deepest insight into the outcomes of countless political happenings and their repercussions.

The Seentia were responsible for all scientific and engineering endeavors. They are arguably the most important clan in the group. They control and can manipulate the advent of technology. Their elder, draped in copper robes, is Libur, an enigmatic bird with growing ties to Jaak. Waal, Kiira's uncle, took leadership of the Socran in her stead when she was voted unanimously to the throne, likely to sway any speculation that the other clans or their members were responsible for the recent assassination. The silver-clad Waal openly opposed Jaak and worked with Kiira to plot against him at every turn. As such, he was her greatest and most trusted counselor. The Socrans were the legalists, whose responsibility was to write and enact all the laws and regulations for the clan. Their strengths lay in the ability to politicize any situation to their advantage.

A small shiver ran down Kiira's spine as she steeled herself from the fierce opposition, she sensed awaited her. The decision was difficult; but the extreme consequences of human detection far outweighed the benefits of evening pleasure flights. Her beak slightly shivered as she spoke. She took quick control over the powerful emotions that came to the surface as she spotted the seat her mother once gave heat to and spoke slowly but with great assuredness with her high-pitched voice.

"I have tested the new EM scrambler and based on the feedback provided to me during the flight and upon my return, I find it more than acceptable. The improvements are well noted."

A momentary ruffling of feathers caught her attention, but immediately subdued itself. This was the moment she lost sleep over.

"Yet, I cannot in good conscience allow for our clan to continue their evening flights, and hereby suspend all personal outings. Only those that I personally deem to be necessary to our survival will be approved. Further, I am green-lighting "Operation Ebon Sky. Construction of our new vessel is to commence immediately. Of course, I understand the elders here can still veto my decree, so I am opening up the floor to further debate and after two clacks, a final vote."

General Jaak remained perfectly poised throughout the announcement and waited for his Supreme Chancellor to be finished. Calmly, he turned to face the rest of the elders before eyeing Kiira directly. The leaders of Stora and Seentia held the General in great reverence due to his many personal sacrifices to their race and as such had always given him the right of first speech. Waal on the other hand, held no awe for the decorated warrior but ceded the floor in hopes the worn soldier would land himself in a trap. He aimed to simply observe and only speak if the need required it. From his granite perch, Jaak spoke with the utmost level of calm.

"Supreme Chancellor," he began his polished address. "There is no need for such a vote. And, may I be the first to openly support your decision? The safety of the clan must come first," he firmly stated. "Further, it is in my opinion that Terr is decidedly lost due to the destruction of the ocean balance. Do not the Seentia clan attest that it is only a matter of a few deca-rotations before atmospheric temperatures are too hot for our sustained existence here?"

The ruffling of feathers resumed more audibly this time, as Libur solidly warbled his agreement with the General. Kiira observed silently. Waal peered towards the other birds and noted their all too eager support of the General, who he thought must obviously be planning something. Another glance towards his niece revealed her well-performed stoicism as well. Together they knew that an internal threat would likely come in the next few Seln cycles, but some sort of negative response was still expected from Jaak. *Was his trap set so soon, his continued vendetta burning that hot?*

The General continued. "We must be united on this issue and give our full support towards Her Excellency. Of course, Your Highness, I would hope, nay plead, that a select few of my warriors be among those allowed to continue night operations." He paused briefly to grimace with a certain level of stern import. "In concert with our defense program and certainly under my direct supervision. No flights will take place without my singular approval," he nodded towards Kiira.

Waal, noting the agreement of the two other clan elders, jumped in. "I believe you mean the Supreme Chancellor's approval General Jaak." Jaak quickly turned to face the Socran elder.

"But of course, Elder Waal. I believe Her Excellency made that abundantly clear just now. I only mean that my talon-selected few will not fly without first obtaining the proper approvals; and I am sure that the Supreme Chancellor would not want to be disturbed by my subordinates. I will of course be the one to bring our daily flight plans for signature." The General's countenance gave way to a near imperceptible grin that Waal immediately caught; but be before he could pry any further, the aging Lün spoke up.

"I agree with the Supreme Chancellor and with the General's request and offer my full support. We should forego any further discussion and vote to end these proceedings, unless the Supreme Chancellor has anything else she would like to discuss. Safety to our clan," she roared.

"Safety to the clan," the rest echoed.

Libur quickly agreed, leaving Waal bound and forced into showing his consent to the General's request. The trap was set and he missed it. He and Kiira would have to meet at a separate time to try to uncover what exact ploys were being set against them. What was supposed to be the shackling of the General now became their own bonds.

Kiira satisfied that her plan was approved, spoke. "So be it. For the safety of our clan, I will review the General's flight plans, which will be submitted one week prior to any dive. I have nothing further to add and consent to ending this gathering." Waal was thundered by his niece's quick footing and felt his pride grow, as she appeared to easily sidestep the ruse. Or, maybe she also had other plans. Maybe she sought to continue her evening flights? As for General Jaak's demeanor, it remained unchanged. Was it a feint, or was there a deeper threat they had not counted on that remained uncovered? Only time would tell, but he needed to act. As rare as they were in their history, a coup still remained a possibility.

Waal walked with his niece towards the invisible door that led to her personal chamber from the Sala Eld and grimaced when he saw her guard, the short-feathered Akeela standing by for her ward. Secretly, he loathed the bird that always seemed to interject between him and his niece. He quickly corrected his grimace and spoke.

"Akeela, so glad to know that you are always prepared to ensure the safety of my precious niece. Oh, but forgive me for using your given name, colonel. An old bird like me is so apt to forget such trivialities," he grinned.

"Elder Waal, there is no need to worry about that with me. I have known you my entire life. But of course, when it comes to the safety of the Supreme Chancellor, I operate with extreme prejudice."

"Certainly, certainly. But you have protected her since she was a hatchling, and you are just a promising young recruit. I have always felt that your clan would be better off with you as elder. Maybe my niece will make such a promotion when the time is right." His brilliant and polished teeth peeked out from his beak.

Kiira, after seeing Akeela, allowed her guard to drop further and lost herself in thought once again, missing most of the verbal exchange. She reached her chamber, stopped, and then allowed for Akeela to do her job, scanning the room with a small sensor that she held in her in left claw. As they waited, her uncle gave her a slight nudge.

"So Kiira, what do you think of Akeela as Minister of Defense?" He grinned at the thought of shifting the balance of power in their favor.

"Uncle, I'm sorry. I was busy thinking of other matters. Though, I am not so sure that now would be the appropriate time. Replacing Jaak could result in a coup. The clan members would resent the change and move to overthrow me, despite their recent vote." Glancing in her direction, she continued. "Of course, Akeela's appointment would give me great joy; but it would also mean finding a new protector, a difficult task for sure. She has cared for me for so long, and who else would give their life so willingly should the need arise? Besides, I greatly cherish our constant companionship."

Although stoic, Akeela beamed internally at the kind words. But, she would never abandon her ward. The mere suggestion seemed a ploy.

"Well my niece, one never knows what can happen. Jaak could fall ill. He is an aging bird after all. Besides so many young female warriors assuredly love you and would eagerly accept a position as your guard."

The irony in this comment was that Jaak was in great health even by the standards of younger birds and a new personal guard could result in a potential weakening of her safety.

"Oh my," Waal spluttered out. "There is plenty of time for one more meeting. I need to speak with Elder Libur on some matters. Please accept my departure, my dear."

"Naturally uncle. Pleasant evening," she bade.

"Yes, of course. Pleasant evening," he replied.

Her quarters cleared, and Kiira walked towards her personal workstation in hopes of quickly clearing up any remaining work before she retired. Akeela approached the chancellor and prepared to speak freely as had been her custom for many years. Noting the wear on her ward's once unblemished facial feathers, she decided to first address her health.

Concerned, Akeela spoke. "Kiira, when was the last time you fully rested? Already, I can tell that you will not perch for more than three hours tonight. Something is wearing on you," she calmly approached.

"Moth…I mean Akeela, there is no rest for us," she retorted. "I deal with the strain of our entire clan as well as the threats on my life. You fret only over me, though, I am not sure which is worse?"

"Truly, I do not know either," she quipped. "Either way, try to rest, for me if you would please. But first, I also mean to ask you about your uncle, Waal. How is he faring as your successor?"

"He's fine, but always fretting over me. I would rather he focus on my clan and not so much just on me. I can't even get a bite to eat without him leering over me. Of course, he has been a great support to me since my mother passed." She paused. "I still can't believe it's been a full Stel rotation."

Akeela frowned. "Oh, I almost forgot to mention that we continue to review the circumstances behind your mother's death, and not an iota of evidence supports an assassination plot from Jaak. Save one bit. A feather was found in these quarters at the time of your mother's death. We just proved this morning that it belongs to Jaak, though, currently that evidence is accessible only to the reviewing scientists and me. They have already been debriefed to not utter a sound about it. But, the feather is also as old as you are, so not an avenue we will likely continue to pursue."

Kiira blinked often and heavily. "General Jaak has been a bane to my family for as long as I remember. But, your previous advice seems more than reasonable now and I think I should rest after all. The work will be there for me in the morning, along with the mystery of my mother's passing."

Akeela hoped Kiira would find rest and was grateful for it as she stepped out to her adjoining but more Spartan quarters. Her aging, hollow bones were ready to rest themselves. As she settled at her desk seat, an idea formed. *If Jaak had a supreme chancellor assassinated, he would be the obvious suspect. He also would lose many of his flight privileges, which he enjoyed so much, and replace them with endless bureaucratic happenings. Besides, Jaak was always more the hunter/warrior than politician. He also knows about Kiira and I, and as such personally selected me to be Kiira's caretaker. So, what would he have to gain by taking the role of our leader? But, if not him, then who? It must be someone else,* she thought. *But who would want Kiira's mother dead?*

CHAPTER 2

Commander, Space Port Operations

Dark side of Seln

Progress report number one to the Clan

Initial construction is underway. All shipments of interplanetary ore and other materiel arrived without incident, including methane from the closest blue gas-giant in our system. Water removal and purification processes are stable. Food stores and energy-to-matter converters are operating well within specifications. Despite the newfound isolation and recent geo-political events, morale is high amongst the engineers and program scientists. Senior staff further assures me that our schedule will not deviate, barring any unforeseen setbacks. We fully anticipate a tithe completion by the end of the solar quarter. Lastly, sensors show nil indication of active probing originating from Terr.

This message sent via prime secure on tachyon wave beta-two.

Long live the Clan.

CHAPTER 3

Dr. Ingrid Morlet, Perth Australia.

Personal log.

Research continues on our tachyon particle detection algorithm. Initial results are very promising as t-test analysis reveals a strong correlation between time delay and what we believe are the generation of tachyon particles. By this time next week, I expect that we will have what we need to publish our initial results and move our sensor to the open field for testing. For fun, we chose the moon as our first target. Although we expect to find nothing there, it remains the most romantic choice amongst my team. If, after a few days, we find nothing, we will aim our sensor at the Orion Nebula. Another romantic choice.

CHAPTER 4

Pulchri

Quarters inside the Seln operations hub were sparse and lacked the familiar quartz or granite furnishings back on Terr. The senior crew was further aggravated with the replacement of natural wood nesting fibers by a fully synthetic polymer weave. Although it was not well-liked, it was necessary due to weight considerations for lift off from Terr. A shallow plastic nest with a built-in warming device was currently occupied by a member of the senior scientist staff. She sat comfortably, working fastidiously on a small piece of electronics, her broad avian shoulders blocking her work should anyone decide to enter without announcing themselves first.

There was a time when the aging Pulchri would have turned down the request from her elder, but after losing her long-time mate, she no longer cared much for tranquility. Although considered to be a very mature bird, her sloping shoulders still caught the attention of many young courters. Her plumage, too, was sensuous with its silky texture and mosaic of tiling red hues. Just one week before departing for Seln base, she accepted one courting offer and spent the night in her quarters with a much younger and subordinate scientist from her laboratory. For nearly half a Seln cycle, she spent her time wrapped in the gentle and still firming musculature of his wings. She didn't care about the stares she got. It was her last opportunity. Soon, everything would change.

Her talons flitted about noiselessly, working on the virtual circuitry of a small piece of crystal. She had access to the communication tower and planned to cause a quick outage by accidentally spilling water over the control panel. One of the maintenance engineers would come by to repair it as quickly as possible, paying little attention to the replacement part, which she would have switched out with her own just prior. Once in, it would take only two short Seln cycles prior to the new faulty circuit to redirect all power to just one comms node. Then she would lay still waiting for her orders.

CHAPTER 5

Jaak

Two senior statesmen sat opposite each other, sipping glacier water through crystalline pipets, their rounded beaks aimed down but their eyes unflinchingly locked on to each other. As they refreshed themselves in silence, Mota, Elder Libur's new aide, entered the large granite room with steps silent enough not to disturb the two elders but loud enough not to raise suspicion. She carefully lifted two small crystal plates from the silver-metallic suspensor tray in front of her, each piled high with steaming synth-protein steaks seared to perfection, and placed them before the two aging friends. Noting that neither elder addressed her, she turned and strode back the way she entered, this time careful not to make a sound. Jaak subtly trained his hearing towards his rear in response and was not satisfied until he heard the automatic door open and then close.

The fresh-cooked meats lasted only a few seconds as razor teeth shredded the food into ribbons. Feeling satiated, the long-time friends relaxed on their wood fiber perches and remained silent as they allowed their stomachs to begin the digestion process. Jaak then looked at Libur and at once recalled why he was visiting. "Libur, my old mate. I believe that we have lost track of time and have covered none of the business we set out to discuss.

The elder statesman feigned indifference in the hopes of eliciting a negative response. He drew in his soft hands towards his stomach and then wrapped his wings around his torso, as if preparing for a long nap. Jaak moved his head slightly, eyeing the room and waiting for his host to respond. When Libur closed his eyes to show his disdain of the conversation, Jaak reached a hand into a small pocket hidden in the folds of his robe and cracked a small vial, hidden within the shell of a walnut, between two of his fingers. He raised his voice slightly.

"Tell me, what is the status of leaching water from Seln's soil?"

"Jaak. You do realize that my report has not been finalized, and conveying any news to you prior to briefing the Chancellor Supreme is a severe breach in protocol?" Libur's voice strained as he addressed his impertinent guest.

Jaak sneered, his eyes looking towards the tip of his battled-hardened beak, a habit he picked up as a young officer. "Of course, but then, what is the purpose of these lunches if not to move around formalities? But, do not strain yourself old friend, as I can wait until tomorrow evening's clan meeting with Her Excellency to discuss lunar moisture if that is your wish." Jaak strained his voice purposefully when he uttered the word, 'Excellency.'

"Well, I suppose you are right Jaak. Why meet if not to bend the rules? In fact, my aide is headed to brief Her Excellency as we speak, so no harm really." Libur paused as he lazily adjusted himself on his perch before tremulously squawking again. "All is well, and extrication of H2O is proceeding with better than nine-hundred and fifty per-mil efficiency. We fully expect that all of our water reserve tanks aboard the ship will be to capacity along with several cases of pre-bottled reusable drink tubes by launch."

The General caught a slight warble in Libur's voice and instinctually retreated to allow his friend to further relax. He did not understand why Libur seemed agitated though. They had been friends since hatching. He pressed on as he calmly took in the scant décor of the resplendent room, well-lit by the emanating amber lights that came from the rock itself, but not so much as to catch every detail. If Libur secreted spy-probes about the room, it would be impossible to detect them. But he deceptively tried to scan the room nonetheless, his eyes shifting from side to side.

"And what of our onboard reclamation capabilities? Surely they will be ready as well?"

"Naturally," he yawned. "Each room will be equipped with vapor filters and our latrines, using the old military term, are already working at one-thousand per-mil efficiency."

Jaak looked up towards the ceiling of Libur's private

quarters, no longer feigning indifference as his black beady eyes scoured the ceiling of the large granite room, continuing his search for hidden probes. He allowed his eyes to flutter to show his host how well he was fed and to play for any recording device but kept his audial passages open. A gentle but long breath escaped his host's lungs signaling him to push further.

"Well, if we can't convince Lün to join our cause, your efforts may be futile."

"Nonsense. Lün was always in the bag," Libur spoke through another lengthy yawn, his eyes nearly shut. "Waal already made sure of that. I mean Mota, my aide."

"Of course, Mota is a terrific young assistant. I am sure she is capable of many things," Jaak encouraged.

Barely able to speak but somehow willing to continue, the statesman continued briefly. "Yes, yes. She is well groomed and being primed to merge with Waal." Waal's name was barely intelligible as the statesman fell into a deep slumber.

Rising, Jaak wriggled his nostrils to ease the pressure from the two invisible filtration plugs he inserted while still in his own quarters and walked away without further regard for his old friend. On cue, his own aide, Major Kiln, opened the door to the room from an exterior panel and produced a crystalline sheet for the General to review as they walked silently down the hallways of the maze-like cavern without much thought.

After walking for more than two minutes, Jaak spoke up, his eyes centered ahead while Major Kiln remained silently astute with his own eyes scanning the rear. "We have what we need. Move ahead with your orders."

"Yes Sir. All preparations have been made and I will ensure their execution once we are back." The old General noted that Kiln's words were perfectly clipped and his tone exemplary, denoting the utmost loyalty. He would make an excellent pairing for my granddaughter. *If I can save her that is*, he thought. *If…I can save her.*

CHAPTER 6

Mota

What an untrained eye would have assumed was that the panel of transparent material was either photosensitive glass or some type of quartz. It was, however, cohesive titanium dioxide. With properties such as controlled optical transparency, durable strength, and photo-catalysis, the Quetz made use of this technology in many aspects for defense and computer output display. What would have been science fiction for the bipeds was ubiquitous in the hidden mountainous caves of these highly developed sentient creatures.

Mota approached the polished walls outside of the High-Chancellor's receiving room, clutching the Seln update report firmly between her left wing and torso. She listened to her taloned feet click on the granite floors of the cavernous halls losing herself to the repetitive click-clack tones that echoed. The sound made her want to fidget, but while on duty, it was important to maintain the utmost level of professionalism. She knew all too well the capabilities of the many sensor types and their quantities throughout the inner workings of the mountain and maintained many of them digitally from her lab when on duty. She knew that she was being noticed. Still, she allowed her eyes to wander disdainfully, unhappy that the very security equipment she was often responsible for, was tracking her. Her feet stopped momentarily as a small hidden nook came to her attention. She did not recall seeing the space that was just large enough to conceal her from the sensors when she led the installation team. She made a mental note and continued another few steps before chirping her access code. At once, a small panel illuminated, and a curt voice ensued.

"State your name and business."

"This is Dr. Mota, aide to Elder Libur, here to deliver the latest Seln report to Her Excellency and Supreme Chancellor." She cringed mentally after squawking the words. They knew who she was and why she was there. The level of formality made her feathers molt.

"Standby," the voice returned.

Two moments later, the wall seemed to melt away giving her access to the room, where two pristine and very senior guards met her. She entered the space, noting the sound her talons made, and again did all she could to keep from shivering. Still, she refrained from looking straight at the two guards, instead focusing on the grandeur of the main entrance. The two oafs, beaming with pride for their assignment and intricately decorated uniforms, moved to take the crystalline-titanium report pad, instantly drawing her ire.

"That is for the Supreme Chancellor and only the Supreme Chancellor!" she rapidly reported.

"We don't care. All items and persons entering these premises must be thoroughly inspected," the more senior of them growled in return.

"I come in Elder Libur's stead with material meant only for Her Highness. You have no right…"

"That is enough," A strong feminine voice boomed. "Guards, we have been expecting her. Admit her immediately."

Stoically and without hesitation, the two guards moved aside and resumed their post, awaiting the end of their shift. Midday mealtime was approaching, and the behemoths had proportionate appetites to satiate, she thought. Mota, though, noticed how rapidly the soldiers heeded Akeela without hesitation. Another mental note. She, too, was respectful of the Chancellor's personal guard and attendant, maybe more than the two oafs that tried to give her a problem. She never did try to play games of rank and stature with the Chancellor's personal guard. Despite her lower upbringing, Akeela was not only in a position of power; she achieved it with much fanfare due to her skill as a formidable warrior and was personally selected for the post by General Jaak many Stel rotations ago.

Akeela received her curtly, while maintaining a higher level of politeness that she resented not receiving upon her admittance into the inner chamber by the muscular behemoths. At this point, she understood that her tablet would be inspected without its contents being reviewed. She expected that much. As Akeela performed her duties, Mota allowed her eyes to focus along the rest of the pristine space, noting the location of the secretary's desk, where a well-groomed and elderly bird sat, seemingly busying himself away with schedules and the sort; however, never allowing his own side-vision off of the visitor. He was to her left. To the right, three razor-sharp tachyon-enabled scimitars rested against the wall, one for each guard and the third for the manicured bird. Despite their appearances as relics, the blades held the ability to fire infinite rounds of tachyonic disturbance quanta, purportedly lethal at any distance, limited only by the accuracy of the eyes of the wielder. Beyond Akeela there was a hidden door. She knew of its location only because it allowed Akeela to step out into the waiting area.

"Wait one moment please, as I consult with Her Excellency. When she is ready for you, I will allow you admittance. Watch what you say and what you do. I will be watching." This last part she uttered with an almost indiscernible growl that sent a chill running down Mota's spine.

"Of course," she replied softly with a modest yet forced bow. *She would do well to serve as my manicurist*, she thought.

After what seemed like an eternity to her, Akeela reappeared, seemingly out of nowhere and bade her enter, remaining close by her side. She balled her fingers into a tight fist but instantly released it, afraid Akeela would take it as a threat. However, she was aide to an elder and a potential candidate to the seat, when Libur was ready to vacate it. She, too, had position. In the meantime, she would address her unprecedented treatment with her clan elder. She felt her initial treatment to be intolerable.

The Supreme Chancellor must have already read the report, so admittance to the chamber meant there were questions. She had anticipated this. The tablet's contents were explosive and would have been delivered by Libur himself, but due to recent internal conflicts, he had opted to inform the Supreme

Chancellor under more subtle circumstances. This was why she was sent. It gave the impression that it was nothing more than a regular weekly communiqué. She began to understand that information was power and whoever kept that information was the one to wield it.

Kiira, though still very young and naïve, was adept in Science and Mathematics, often impressing her uncle Waal. Akeela, too, felt pride but chose to bury it deep inside. Not fully aware of Kiira's intellect, however, Mota found herself in awe of the young leader.

"According to this, there has been a disruption to work on the dark-side. Explain," she demanded.

Mota seethed at the way she was tersely addressed by the younger bird, whose mother's dying hand managed to unwittingly give her the chancellery. Externally, though, she was the consummate professional and answered quickly using her best and most clipped chirps to answer.

"The auto-mols immediately stopped production without warning. When interrogated, they replied that they had detected a tachyon burst emanating from the southern hemisphere of Terr. After careful analysis and consideration, however, Elder Libur recommends that they resume work. As of now, there is no credible threat of detection by the bi-peds."

"Yet, the burst could have been used to detect our operations. So, why is your elder so quick to recommend that we resume our work there?"

"Uh, well, Elder Libur simply believes that the eburst was a 'one of' and that the algorithms required to discern tachyon data, should it detect our base, is beyond bi-ped capability."

"Humans, will surprise you. Do not confuse their barbarity with ignorance. Besides, your elder will better explain himself tomorrow evening at the council meeting."

Kiira's face remained stoic, but noted the continued and unprofessional use of the derogatory term.

"I would like to know the status of water mining operations, production of hydrogen fuel, and the status of our flag-ship. They are not noted here."

Again, Mota stifled a cringe. How this youngling bird, not long coming out from her shell could so easily demand without consideration of the age and experience of her advisors was beyond her. She would never treat a subordinate in this manner, especially one such as her, whose family lineage was once so well respected.

"Of course. Elder Libur intentionally left those figures out in order to de-aggregate the information for security reasons. As of this moment, water and hydrogen production are at approximately nine-hundred and fifty per-mil efficiency. There was a momentary halt due to the frigid temperatures affecting the auto-mols, but solar reflectors were activated to solve the problem. Production has been steadily increasing. As for the ship, it holds at five-hundred and ten per mil. We cannot proceed any further until hydrogen stores and production are at their maximum, which will take six Seln cycles. We do anticipate the auto-mols to move exponentially towards completion immediately thereafter with completion exceeding our original timeline by only one-third of a Stel rotation." She beamed internally as she executed her highly rehearsed answers without pause or error.

"Very well. Oh, and please advise Elder Libur that he will proceed with the full report tomorrow. Thank you."

Before she had time to respond with a thank you, Akeela was escorting her out of the inner chamber, a powerful grip pulling her by her right wing. The two soldiers from the main entrance immediately approached her and escorted her out without uttering a word or squawk. Her muscles tensed at the thought of her insulting treatment. *But, insults are the windows to surprise.*

CHAPTER 7

Jaak

General Jaak sat atop a carved granite seat as he peered at the vast images of the human pestilence that continued to plague Terr, with their buildings, roads, and farms replacing the raw nature of the planet with tar, cement, and refined metals. They knowingly squandered the scant resources of Terr, yet continued to multiply unabatedly without regard to the increasing damage they left behind. The Quetz, Jaak observed, were mindful of the planet's ecology and made use of the bountiful natural domiciles she provided. Child rearing was selective and cautious, and never a burden on their world but rather a means to be a continual caretaker for Terr.

Unfortunately, the ape-men went unchecked. Millennia ago, Jaak's ancestors failed to foresee the anguish this horrific race would unleash. Even as he sat there pondering over their disposable mentality, he knew too of their machinations for a ceaseless internal war, always murdering one another for control of dwindling resources, including the black blood of his ancestors that ran deep underground. For his society, technology helped to unburden their minds of the fear of limited raw materials and encouraged them to further open their minds to new possibilities. For mankind, war was the catalyst to burgeoning scientific and engineering advancement. Yet, despite all of their achievements, they ceased to further evolve and remained genetically stagnant.

If the entire planet was to survive until the next age, the time of celestial enlightenment, humans, as they called themselves, needed to be eradicated. Begrudgingly, he realized that he needed to bring war to humanity and erase their presence for the betterment of all life, fauna and flora. But first, he needed to quietly remove the Chancellor and put himself in her place. All of this could be done without any loss of life. It was a mere political play. Nothing more. His down feathers tingled nervously as he concluded this line of thought.

A second later and his privacy shield began to shimmer signaling a presence outside of his quarters. He looked towards his crystalline monitor and saw that it was Clan Elder Waal draped in extravagant silver robes, probably on a mission of faux diplomacy on the Supreme Chancellor's supposed behest. He glanced at his monitor briefly before closing his eyes. Thoughts of the delicacy of his coup pummeled his mind. *No bloodshed*, he thought. *No loss of life, especially Kiira's.* A full minute passed before he opened his eyes. Waal was still there, standing patiently outside and as diplomatic as ever. But, maybe a little tact was what was needed here. Despite their political rivalry and personal animosity, the two were cordial with one another. Stretching his old leathery legs, he stood up from his perch and vocalized the command to power down the entrance barrier.

"Elder Waal, please come in," he clucked. "I was just about to prepare myself some fermented casaba wine. Would you care for some?" The old General strutted over to his kitchen and reached for two large obsidian-drinking vessels from beneath a polished white granite counter.

"General, it seems that your holo-recorder is activated. Does something worry you about my presence?" Waal, grinned slightly showing his brilliantly polished teeth.

"Nonsense, Waal. I just completed some internal military messages for my senior staff." Another cluck, this one higher in pitch deactivated the sensors and their accompanying lights.

"You see, all off. Wine?" He motioned a well-toned wing towards the extravagant bar.

Waal paused, and for a brief moment, considered if perhaps diplomacy was an option.

"Wine would be lovely at this hour. Thank you very much for your hospitality."

The two elders sat and reminisced for several minutes, each enjoying the drink but also being careful not to overindulge. They both needed their senses honed to a talon's edge. Sensing the evening proceeded well beyond what he intended, Waal changed the topic.

"General, my apologies for this formality, but I er, did come here on business at the bequest of the Supreme Chancellor." He wondered if the official title would ruffle Jaak's feathers, but the General maintained a stony composure. He proceeded. "The Chancellor is concerned about the safety of our nest as well as all those around Terr during the construction of the space vessel, Pterano 1. The bi-peds continue to develop their remote sensing abilities and have begun to refine their hyper-spectral capabilities. She is also concerned about a potential insurrection within our own halls." He stared with stony eyes at the General again waiting for some physical response.

"Elder Waal, please pass on to the Supreme Chancellor that she may rest assured that despite my opposition to our departure, I am sworn to openly obey her wishes and will do my utmost to protect our race." His words resonated with honesty.

"Aah, of course. Loyalty is most certainly bred into you military types, I just..."

"The question Waal, is why is it not bred into yours, eh?" Jaak's words came out like fine silk.

"Well, er, we just don't wear it on our robes as your clan does. We pride ourselves on our refined thinking. The Supreme Chancellor, Kiira, only insists that you fully support her as you said you would two weeks ago at the Council of Elders."

"Her Excellency has never questioned me openly. Why would she start now, comrade," he asked using the old tongue.

Waal, shifted his weight to the left and tucked in his right wing closer to his body as he sat perched in the coarser seat offered to him. "I am not here to ruffle any feathers comrade, only to ensure everyone's safety over the next Stel rotation."

"And what do any of us have to fear? Assassination? After Supreme Chancellor Eensul's murder, the entirety of this hold is set to alert my forces and lock all beings in place should a burst weapon be activated. The culprit would be caught immediately, or have you forgotten that no one can get away with murder now? Our newly installed motion sensors also track everyone's movement."

The Socran's elder statesman moved his well-manicured talons fitfully. "No one has forgotten anything Jaak! We are all aware of our new security measures. Regardless, my sister lays encapsulated in stone, in these very halls as a reminder of the first and what we hope will be the last assassination of a Supreme Chancellor." Waal's voice wavered and his feathers shivered.

And exactly who murdered her? Jaak thought. The imposing military expert thought he knew how, but only his own discarded feathers were found in Eensul's quarters, plumage he molted nearly seventeen Stel rotations ago when he visited her last in her private quarters.

"We aren't sure if it was murder. She could have sent herself to Spirit Terr by her own wing. It is highly doubtful, I submit."

The leader of the Socrans rose from his perch and inflated his chest at hearing Jaak. "I have said what needed to be said. The Supreme Chancellor demands your loyalty. I am done here," he sneered as he turned his beak away from the brutish warrior, his diplomacy fully swept aside.

"Elder Waal. One other thing to pass on to your niece; and I am sure that you will pass it on." He remained calmly seated. "Let her know that if she at any time feels for her safety, that I will personally accompany Lt. Colonel Akeela to add to her personal guard."

"Certainly," Waal spat.

CHAPTER 8

Akeela

Kiira grumbled as she sat before her crystalline terminal, reviewing countless communications from the other elders, all of them hand-selected by her uncle for her convenience. But, at the moment, she only wanted to think of her best friend Saax. She enjoyed the few moments that they shared together and was grateful that her uncle suggested the friendship. But, construction of the giant vessel was entering its next stage after countless engineering reviews and preparations; and she needed to focus. A communiqué from Libur confirmed that progress was on schedule; but for reasons she did not care to investigate, her gut told her otherwise. She dismissed the thoughts knowing full well her uncle had the best interests of the Quetz in mind. He would take care of everything.

The full weight of her responsibilities, nonetheless, weighed heavily upon her. Her back muscles ached as if she had endured a solid beating; and her soft padded feet were just as sore. She needed unimpeded rest, which was forever out of her reach. Her mother had good intentions in wishing her to be a successor, but as a youth, she was ill-prepared to sit as clan elder, let alone as chancellor. If not for the constant guidance of her uncle, she would have already dived off the stone cliff with her wings bound. She prayed for him in gratitude.

A familiar audible beep resonated in the spacious room letting her know that Akeela was just outside the door to her personal chambers. Likely, she was coming in to pull her away from her work and gently nudge her to get some rest. She kept her eyes on her screen as she screeched her signal to allow her entry.

"Supreme Chancellor?" Akeela was standing rigidly at the doorway.

"Daydreaming again," she said softly. Kiira was too tired to look up and glare at her.

"Just as well. You need your rest. Besides, your uncle Waal does well to protect you from the strains of your new position. And, don't worry. I will see to it that you spend more time with your friend. His companionship makes you happy and you are too young to forego that. Even your mother had time to relax." Akeela squirmed imperceptibly as she moved closer to Kiira.

"Come on young one. Let's get you into bed. You've had enough of your administrative duties, and you also have an early day tomorrow. I have decided to resume your combat training. Your uncle disapproves, but as your guardian in life and in health, I think it's best."

The expansive room that once served as her mother's quarters almost one Stel rotation ago, seemed smaller now, the walls closer. Eensul's personal effects remained while Kiira's childish dolls and holo-posters were still in her old bedroom. Waal had suggested redecorating the room to suit Kiira's taste, but she refused it. *It would change the integrity of the room*, she squawked. A few weeks ago, she looked at the various artifacts her mother collected over the years from friends and dignitaries from the other distant clans that served her. Her eyes wandered back towards her guardian as she quietly and slowly rose from her perch and collapsed on her bed with eyes too heavy to remain open any longer.

"Good night Mom. We'll train tomorrow like you want me to."

"Good night Kiira." A shiver escaped Akeela as she crept out of the room unsure of how she felt about the faux pas, mentioning Kiira's mother.

Entering her own simple room, adjacent to Kiira's mammoth quarters, the once warrior bird collected her thoughts and feelings and buried them deeply. Eensul's death was only one Stel rotation behind them but still resonated deeply with all of the clans, locally and abroad. The Supreme Chancellor of all the Quetz was slain in the privacy of the very room that Kiira was sleeping in. By whom, no one knew. How they got away with it, no one knew either. But, this they did know. It was someone the benevolent leader trusted, and that could be anyone.

Rumors flew of Jaak's likely involvement. He coveted the throne for himself, yet loyalty ran in his veins and his appointment came at the hands of Eensul herself. Despite his keen mind and knowledge of defense and humanity, he was not in line for promotion to clan elder. Another bird was, who after failing to ascend to the seat, had left for his home in East Asia.

A small plain obsidian desk sat at the wall by the entrance to her room. On it, a projection of a multitude of images flickered. Some showed her the main halls, others exterior views of the mountain. But at the center of the holo-projection were several angles of Kiira's room. She scanned those first and then quickly reviewed the others. Settled in her faux wooden perch, she leaned back and kept one open eye trained on the images, while the other rested. She alternated her eyes, opening and closing them until it was time to wake Kiira from her slumber and begin her combat training.

CHAPTER 9

Council Use Only (COU)

Memo
From: Stora Clan Elder Lün
To: Her Excellency the Supreme Chancellor
Copy: Council Elders
Subj: Non-Regular Report on Human Occupancy of Terr

Summary: Inhabitability of Terr imminent within 50 Stel rotations. Humanity remains the singular cause behind planetary chaos. While it is certain we will not be able to survive here in 50 rotations, the possibility remains that a human-triggered cataclysmic event could be initiated at any time. Recommendation remains. Depart Terr prior to destruction.

Issue: Atmospheric-Oceanic Health
Ocean acidification increased by one-tenth potential for hydrogen, or 2.5 per mil increase since the human pre-industrial era. Even by human perception, this change is irreversible as current output of carbon dioxide continues to increase at near exponential rates. Over the past Stel rotation, a decrease of 0.96 parts per mil was reported, but due to current human political machinations, this trend is not anticipated as sustainable nor is it enough to prevent catastrophic climate change over the next one hundred Stel rotations.
Status: Imminent irreversibility

Issue: Nuclear Proliferation
No change to report. Development of nuclear weapons technology continues with less advanced states gaining the ability for themselves. Non-state actors continue to glean dirty versions of this weaponology from powerful but rogue states.
Status: Potential for use remains at moderate levels.

Issue: Bio-weapons
Interceptions of human media detail release of genetically altered, yet simple virology-based diseases. Considerable uncertainty remains on whether the release of the virus was by design or accidental in nature. Death tolls are approximately 0.34 per mil.
Status: Based on intercepted communications, there is a moderate risk of a future release of bio-weapons with a strong potential for greater than 9.7 per mil global human death toll.

Issue: Population Increase
A near eight-fold increase in human numbers since the beginning of their industrial age, from one-billion to nearly eight-billion continues to draw serious concern as there are no signs of reaching a steady state in this exponential increase.
Status: Grim. With medical technology continually improving and economic prosperity increasing, natural death numbers will decrease as reproduction levels increase, resulting in a catastrophic reduction of flora resources due to deforestation.

CHAPTER 10

Jaak

The talons on Jaak's feet were honed to a razor's edge. At the moment, they made a click-clack noise on the stone floor as he moved about his office, agitated. Keeping his body prepared for battle at all times was not a necessity, just a habit he learned from his mentor many Stel rotations ago. *He would flog my blue feathers if they were not up to par for a young officer; but, now they just infuriate me when I need my thoughts the most*, he thought.

A crystalline pipet filled with sparkling blue glacier water caught Jaak's attention. His throat felt parched. His will to focus solely on the matter at hand relented again. Maybe the refreshing liquid would ease his mind. His talons continued with their annoying sound as he strode over to the cherry wood desk located at the back wall of the room, where an image of the outdoors was projected giving the impression that the room was open to the exterior of the mountain. He rued the day he ordered the removal of the synthetic poly-fiber matting that once covered the biting cold and expansive floor. It was a security necessity, he felt. Without the matting, no one could enter the room unannounced.

A calloused hand reached for the pipet. Upon touching it, the opening appeared. He emptied the contents into his mouth and relaxed as the cool unmolested water coursed down his throat and into the rest of his body. Feeling refreshed, he placed the empty vial on his desk, its surface protected through a process called temporo-hardening. The end result not only prevented the cellular structure from drying out, it also created a surface layer impervious to liquids, acids, and physical marring. Most of the other Quetz preferred metamorphic or igneous rock for their furniture. Others, if their status did not allow for such expenditure, settled for polymeric materials. Jaak, however, spent most of his life living meagerly and had soon amassed a small fortune. He chose to use part of his hard-earned wealth in Quetzal-credits on this luxury, organic material. He purchased it in the hopes of creating an heirloom that he could pass on to his son, who would pass it on to his heir, and so forth. A rare and soft murmur escaped his beak. Grumbling, he quickly shook off his moment of weakness, thinking there would be time enough for that when he passed on to join Spirit Terr.

Still unable to shake the oxidation from his aging mind, he opted to take a seat by the large desk. Comfortably perched, he chirped code that activated a holo-display, which immediately sprung from the back of the desk's surface. After a few moments of mental silence, he thought of a poem, regaling the tenderness of a rose and its violent defense. Despite his formal militaristic education, Jaak was also an avid poet and writer. The only person to read his works, though, was his beautiful wife, Rob'n.

She was an outcast of the Draconem clan, born too weak to fight and believed to be too kind for politics. But, because his uncle taught him to see beyond the surface of any situation or individual, he decided to befriend her. Though gentle of body, she was fiercely intelligent, and his ministrations towards her were not easily accepted. But, after several Seln cycles, she relented and accepted his proposal for a union. Soon after, clan physicians warned against childbirth which Jaak was not opposed to. If a hatchling lost his or her parents, they could adopt, he argued. But, he relented to Rob'n's dogged insistence on carrying his heir. She passed away after hemorrhaging, as the hard ovum that would be their first and only child, Kaylor, emerged.

His acute eyes immediately took notice of movement on the video feed displayed at the upper right-hand corner of the holo-display. It was a young female bird standing by a dark nook just outside the Supreme Chancellor's suite, turning her body from right to left while holding an unknown tech gadget in her hands aimed towards the visual sensor just around the corner. He recognized her as Libur's new aide, Mota. *But what was she doing? Was she testing the acuity of the sensor? As a member of the Seentia, she should know the sensor's EM-bending capability. Maybe she thought it defective,* he mused. A warble escaped him and the particular visual feed began to record and automatically save data starting from the five minutes prior to activation. At that moment, he felt very fortunate that Major Kiln was able to decipher the encryption key Libur's clan had used to protect the fortresses' security systems. Although, as head of security, he certainly could access all security systems, now he could do so without electronic notice. He could even disable systems if need be.

A chirp rang out. Jaak, eyes were already on the security monitor. He saw that it was Major Kiln and unlocked the door. Kiln waited for the door to dissipate and then walked in, his chest protruding out and his head held high. Jaak looked away from the monitor as Mota finally departed away from the vicinity of Kiira's quarters and gave Kiln his full attention.

"Yes, Major," he intoned.

"General," he said barely able to hide his glee. "All is in place. Clan elder activation codes have been copied to this crystalline sheet. Yours is the only copy of course. I was also able to bug all non-private elder work spaces with audio-visual sensors that will transmit only to the sheet I gave you, which is dark to the network. No one will know that you are capable of listening in on their conversations."

"And, how were you able to bug their spaces without their knowing? Did my suggestion work?" Jaak calmly looked at the subordinate officer waiting for a positive reply.

"Indeed Sir. I was able to hide the observers and transmitters into the crystalline reports I delivered to them just now. Of course, their aides were anxious to learn of the flight schedules, so they greedily accepted them."

Satisfied, Jaak allowed himself a small grin before narrowing his eyes. "Excellent work Major. I trust that you worked alone and have shared this with no one?"

"Yes, Sir. Of course, Sir. My family owes you a debt of gratitude and have forever sworn allegiance to you and your family." Kiln shuddered as he caught himself in a faux pas. "Sorry Sir. I didn't mean…"

"That is okay Major. I am not that soft of a bird." Jaak

dismissed Kiln and pondered a moment on whether he should jump the gun a bit. He decided to wait. One of his Lieutenant Colonels was retiring, and he aimed to have Kiln fill the position. *Better wait just a bit more*, he thought. *But this young Draconem needed to be recognized, albeit only with a promotion for now. He had proven his loyalty as well as his abilities on the field and in the political arena. He very well could be an elder or even rise to the Supreme Chancellorship, if not for his family's lower clan status. What a shame. Maybe I'll be able to fix that if all continues as planned.*

CHAPTER 11

Waal

The clan elder sat motionless atop a polished green marble perch that he had requisitioned from the African continent. By his aging but well-manicured feet, a plump subordinate female from the lowest caste in his clan sat patiently, moving a simple rasp back and forth across each of the elder's talons, removing any potential for a burr and then with a focused light emitter, polished them smoothly. Each listened carefully to the music that emanated from seemingly nowhere, noting the bops and bips, and cracks and bongs, of the ancient form of percussion their ancestors developed millennia ago. The young female was unfamiliar with this form of audial entertainment, preferring the newer melodies that were created during her generation, but nonetheless found herself fascinated by the rhythms she heard. Waal, however, seemingly lost himself to his thoughts, as the complex mix of tones and bangs was on his list of common selections.

Waal was suspicious of General Jaak's visit with Libur. The two were supposedly friends. *Maybe they conspired against him. If so, that needed to end. He needed to take care of Kiira, or the General would. And that*, he thought, *would be unacceptable.* Something needed to be done, but Akeela too, was always in the way. *How could he get to his niece if that infernal bird was always by her side?* Naturally, as she was a member of the Draconem, he knew she could not be trusted. She was middle-caste, but somehow she worked her way to her current rank. *Maybe that sister of mine had something to do with it.*

He had his allies, but in the end, the only creature he could trust was himself. From a young age, he battled being overshadowed by his older sister Eensul who was pre-destined to rule the clan. She was the extrovert, while he was the more pensive and reclusive of the two. She always managed to find herself at the center of attention and he as her aide de camp. She was the athletic one and he the bird who could barely run. But the tables turned, and her mistake cost her her life. Waal recalled a sour situation from his youth.

He had just entered his first feather molting. Soon, he would shed his red plumage for blue, the first sign of masculinity. Eensul was the same age as Kiira is now, about seventeen Stel rotations. But, she always tried to play the role of an adult, always focusing her attention on clan politics, listening in on their parent's conversations with other prominent Quetz. During one particular dinner party, while Waal hid himself from sight, she proudly perched herself across from the adults. Because of her clever intellect and quick wit, no adult deemed her a nuisance and often discussed openly the difficult topics of the time with her present, often allowing her to join in and to opine.

The previous evening over a light dinner, Eensul and the young Waal, debated the topic of certain chemical weapons that the bi-peds used during their World Wars. Mustard gas, they called it. Whereas Eensul felt that it was inferior to any technology of their own and thus harmless, Waal vehemently argued the point that it was only a stepping stone towards more powerful war-time capabilities that should be deterred at all costs. As was her habit, she would scoff at her younger brother and brush his opinions aside.

On this night, however, the appointed military commander, General Princep, argued as she had, touting superior technology that could nullify any bi-ped threat. Eensul having detected a small pause after the General seemingly appeased the fears of his hosts and the other guests spoke up.

"Their burgeoning technology may seem insignificant to our know-how, but over time, their wars will elevate their science and engineering capability to match our own. We should take advantage of our lead and nullify the threat before we no longer can."

Waal lost his breath. The very points she rebuffed not twelve hours ago, she was now taking as her own. And, the adults soaked it up, lauding her as having exceptional insight to such a difficult topic for a bird of any age. To add insult to injury, the General stood beak open before requesting that she spend some time with his clan learning military strategy.

"You very well may be the next Supreme Chancellor!" he roared.

The young Waal, whose blue was just beginning to show, secluded himself to his quarters for a fortnight. The celebration of his coming to adulthood, too, was passed over in order to prepare Eensul for her cross-internship with the Draconem. His parents promised to make it up to him, but due to their demanding schedules and perpetual focus on their daughter, they inevitably broke that promise. Waal never forgot, but instead of allowing himself the privilege of self-loathing, he opted instead to further sharpen his mind and work to shed his fear of society.

There is much to do about the other elders. Will they see reason and follow my lead? There must be a way to ensure our safety. Hmm. Maybe Libur is getting beyond his years too quickly; but his aide---Mota. Yes, Dr. Mota could be of some assistance. She seems ambitious enough and intelligent. Reminds me of myself, he continued. *Maybe she can assist me with gaining surveillance on Kiira. I am very interested in her relationship with Lün's son, Saax, and would like to ensure that a healthy relationship will form there.* If he kept his wits about him, maybe he would survive the turmoil he knew was coming.

The music discontinued as a beady-eyed aide, Fugax, entered the elder's space.

"Sorry to disrupt you Elder Waal," he intoned, trembling. "The Supreme Chancellor, I mean your niece is requesting your presence for supper this evening. She said that you have not supped with her in almost one week and would like your counsel on some, personal matters." Having completed relaying the message, the male attendant, timidly waited for a response from the annoyed clan elder.

"Tell the Supreme Chancellor," he said with perfect elocution, "that I will gladly be in attendance this evening."

"Yes sir, right away sir." The scrawny bird immediately turned and briskly walked away glad to not be on the receiving end of a foot or wing. Other elders would often get physical.

Waal certainly did. Guests who visited Waal saw the cheery and boisterous leader; but Fugax experienced the elder's proclivity for sharp blows to the chest with his bony wings.

CHAPTER 12

Kiira

The oval room that served as the Supreme Chancellor's fitness room went unused. Eensul preferred walking about the network of halls that comprised the Mons-Luz, the name given to the Quetz headquarters. More recently, Kiira imagined the mostly empty room as a place for her and Saax to listen to music and maybe rhythmically move their legs and wings. Akeela, to Kiira's disappointment, had other plans. The little cardio equipment that once sparsely filled the room was gone. On the walls, however, various instruments of battle were suspended with gravity hooks, waiting only to be taken.

Kiira's groggy black eyes were jarred wide awake when Akeela grabbed her without warning and threw her onto the replicated grass mats that covered the cold granite floor.

She cried out disoriented and in pain. "Ouch. What the what? Akeela! That hurt!"

"Good. Now you will learn to never let your guard down or keep your back to a door, regardless of where you are or whom you are with. Get up," she snapped suddenly.

"Or, I will teach you another unwanted flying lesson."

Without having to be told twice, the teenager spryly got to her feet, using the techniques she learned from her attacker many Seln cycles ago. She remained cautiously aware of Akeela but opened her ears to her sides and rear just in case a trap was set for her.

"Good. You're being cautious, but you can relax a bit---for now. I have a scale generator for you. Typically, you would train for one more Stel rotation before practicing at this level of training, but your mother's assassination necessitates you begin training now. You've had enough time to grieve, thanks to your Uncle."

Akeela squinted her eyes as she thought of conducting this training behind Waal's back. She may be Kiira's constant protector, ensuring the youngling's safety, but Waal was her formal and legal guardian. He raved about her being too young and fragile, especially so close to her mother's death. *You must protect her emotionally as well as physically*, he chided her. Fortunately, she sealed the doors from within and instructed the two sentries and the office administrator that they were not to be disturbed. *Kiira was preparing for her monthly cleaning,* she warned.

Akeela strode towards her ward, the movement of her wiry and powerful muscles visible through her red plumage. For scale training, both females stood without robes or coverings of any kind.

"Here, place the wristlet about your less dominant arm. Once it secures itself, you can activate it with a simple chirp directed at its face.

"Why are we training for this? I'm excited about it, but---I thought my uncle forbade you to train me on how to fight with one." Kiira anxiously looked up to her protector unsure why Akeela would disobey a direct order from Waal, a clan elder and her uncle and guardian.

"We never saw your mother's death coming. Your uncle is too much of a politician to see this necessity."

"So, how did you get the scale generators? I thought you could only requisition them from the Draconem clan and that General Ja---."

Akeela looked at her ward with beggar's eyes as she began to shake her wings needlessly.

"Oh, I see. Wow! I didn't think we could trust the General, let alone get his help on anything."

"I think you are forgetting that I am a Lieutenant Colonel and report directly to him, not your uncle."

Kiira looked down at the ground as she shuffled her feet

from front to back and then side to side, thinking about what she just learned.

"Akeela, can we trust him?"

"No, little one. You should trust no one." The warrior bird placed the wristlet on her arm and activated it. "You should activate your armor," she warned.

Unsure of what tone to use, Kiira stared at the wristlet and just chirped the first tone that came to mind. Instantly, she felt a cold chill race about her soft red feathers. It was invigorating. It felt good, really good as if she could punch through stone. Looking about her thin figure, she saw what looked like fish scales covering her up from head to tail. A tail!

On cue, her instructor warbled a familiar sound bringing up holo-reflectors throughout the large room. "Go ahead and get the looking out of the way. And yes, your tail is much larger. It is a weapon that you can slash and beat with, the slashing with the razor tip at the bottom. The weight itself acts as a club. It will be cumbersome on the ground, but in the air, it will help you with tight aerial maneuvers." The young chancellor stared in awe at the visage before her.

"I look like a, like a, like a dragon, Akeela!"

A smile formed behind Akeela's own scales, invisible to her ward. "Yes, in fact, this armor is where the human concept of dragons originated from. They even fought with us many, many Stel rotations ago. Some even had the privilege of riding on our backs. But, those were few and far between."

"Bi-peds, I mean humans," she corrected. "They know about us?"

"They knew of us. To them, our history has been relegated to yore," she corrected. "You must seriously keep up with your history lessons, Kiira. Life is more than Science and Mathematics."

"Yes, Akeela. I will definitely do some catch up studies

now," she beamed.

"The first thing you need to know, is that this armor is as hard as titanium, but we and humans have weapons that can penetrate the scales. You are not invincible."

For two hours, the two female birds practiced defensive ground techniques. Akeela struck, and Kiira parried. By the end of the drills, Kiira felt like the armor was no more than a flapping robe. Both tired from the rigorous training, they headed for a steam clean and then ordered a hearty breakfast of synth meats, fruit, and glacier water.

"Remember, Kiira. Not a word to your uncle if you want to continue our workouts. When you are ready, we will conduct a test flight, with the EM scrambler of course. And, we will be activating the visualizer. With your permission of course."

"Are you serious? You want to fly? And, there's a visualizer? Wow! Oh, don't worry, Akeela. I won't say a word. I love wearing the scales." Kiira looked one more time at the holo-reflectors, admiring her visage.

"You need to learn to fly, and yes there is a visualizer. It will allow you to see in various electromagnetic wavelengths and access visual comms from base command."

Excited at what she just heard she focused on the holo-reflectors once again. "I really do look like a dragon, don't I?"

As the fledgling warrior chancellor continued to stare at her armored reflection, Akeela thought to herself. *Indeed. You are Draconem.*

CHAPTER 13

Quetz Headquarters, Seentia Intelligence Center

The main holo-screen lit up. A young Stora sentry found a bi-ped "news" story of interest and reported it immediately to his supervisor.

"What's so interesting sentry? It appears to be more of the same drivel from those hairless apes over the EM spectrum."

"Not this one ma'am; and our perimeter alarm went off an hour ago. The intruder was destroyed, which could bode poorly." His young eyes looked pleadingly up at his boss, hoping his luck would pay off. If he finally found a good bit of information that was important to the clan, it could result in a promotion and better living quarters for his fledgling family.

"Bring it up on holo-1, and quickly. I have clerical work that will not take care of itself," she replied still disinterested in the sentry's discovery.

With a quick warble, the wall-sized holo-screen was activated, producing video captured from one of the bi-ped satellite networks. In less than two moments, the bored supervisor found herself in awe and felt the need to force her beak shut. Two moments later, and she was running to the communication console to summon Clan Elder Libur. She hoped Dr. Mota would not be responding. She had no such luck.

"This is Dr. Mota. How may I be of assistance this evening?" Her words came across the tel-con receiver unit perfectly clipped in anticipation of hearing from an elder or maybe one of the other aides. Upon hearing the voice of one of the lower sentries, the polish in her tone was replaced with biting acid.

"What do you want Sentry?"

Without hesitation the supervising sentry responded to the venomous bird on the other line, still disappointed. "Dr. Mota. There is 'human' audio-visual coverage that needs attention; and, it follows the protocol for informing Elder Libur."

"I'll be right over to inspect for myself."

"But, this is..." Before she could protest, her line of audio-communication was disrupted. The supervisor began to seethe at the thought of Dr. Mota entering the intelligence center, but quickly steeled herself. Another moment later, and Elder Libur's aide thundered into the dark room, her eyes never making direct contact with the two inferior creatures in the room. The video recording played.

"This is Carol Rae Barton reporting live from Mount Rainier National Park where another military tragedy has struck. A U.S. Navy jet fighter has seemingly crashed into the side of Mount Rainier not more than one hour ago, I am being told. There is no word on the status of the two pilots, but based on eyewitness testimony, the fighter-attack plane was maneuvering around the mountain and exploded in mid-air. I have a Mr. Garcia who witnessed the event himself. Mr. Garcia, would you mind telling us what you and your family saw?"

A tan-complexioned man stood eye level with the redheaded reporter and spoke to the camera wide-eyed and with fear still in his voice.

"Yes, sorry Carol. My family and I were just, we were just out here camping out for the weekend when we heard the jet. I was in the Air Force for four years, so we stopped our activities to look up and just stare at the plane for a while. Fortunately, I had some binoculars with me, and I just, you know, happened to be admiring the plane when out of nowhere it seemed to strike an invisible wall and just explode."

The always-polished reporter dropped her composure for a quick second before interrupting. "I'm sorry, but can you explain what you mean? Did the plane try to go vertical and falter before hitting the mountain?"

"No Carol. That jet never hit the mountain. It seemed like there was you know, an invisible wall. It just stopped mid-air and exploded."

"Ok. Well, I appreciate that you saw what you saw. But, as a military man, right? There must be some other explanation. Planes just don't stop in the middle of the sky and explode."

"No, really. My wife recorded it on her iPhone. It's kind of far off but you can see what happened plain as day."

"Well, ah uh, Mrs. Garcia? Would you like to share that footage with the rest of the world?"

Carol's cameraman peeked a single blue eye away from behind the camera.

"Carol. Not a good idea. Military investigation. Bad idea," he mouthed quietly. The trim and well-dressed reporter in her Manolo Blahniks never flinched. "Dave, let's get a zoom-in on Mrs. Garcia's phone. Mrs. Garcia can you play the video for us please?"

"Oh absolutely. And it's just Lulu."

"Yes, Lulu, can you play it for the rest of us?"

Dave the cameraman wanted to shake his blond shaggy head but knew better than to cross his partner, Carol. *No one crosses Carol,* he thought. *Besides, I don't want to have to carry her shoes again if I do,* he figured. He aimed the camera at the phone, zoomed in as much as he could and then focused it as best he could, which was always stellar. That's how he got assigned to follow Carol all over Washington and sometimes even the country on special assignment. After a quick swipe on the large phone, the video played. He captured it for the entire world to see.

Mota's eyes did not blink as she viewed the bi-ped video.

After seeing enough, she sharply turned towards the lower-caste sentries. "I will pass this up to Clan Elder Libur personally. You will not disseminate this, mention it to anyone, or even discuss it amongst yourselves. Consider this classified at the highest level. Understood?"

It was more of a threat than a question. The two sentries did not miss her tone.

She bored her sight directly into the supervisor's eyes. "And, you. If you would like to see your life improved, you will oversee all activities with regards to this story and report directly to me and only me. Oh, and make sure none of your subordinates open their beaks about this."

Now, she thought; *I have something to help me take the seat of Elder of Seentia clan for myself. With a little luck and a lot of manipulation, the chancellorship could be mine as well. Information is power.*

CHAPTER 14

Akeela

A brilliant orange flame morphed into dark hues of red as the raging fire in the sky, sank beyond the distant horizon. Occasionally, a shimmer from the light-bending field made Stel dance briefly. The two friends sat by each other giggling in a way that is familiar only amongst the young of heart. Akeela reminisced about the days of her own youth and the time she spent with her special friend, the friend who would grow into her lover. Her back to the wall and with two other hand-picked sentries guarding her flanks, she was able to focus her attention solely on the two young birds. Her primary concern, however, was focused on keeping the male's talons off of her ward, should he get too comfortable.

Saax, at the age of seventeen, was nearly three Stel rotations older than Kiira; but he was the son of an ally clan who possessed a sweet disposition. Unfortunately for Kiira, her recent ascendance to the seat of Supreme Chancellor meant constant supervision. Chances could not be taken, despite Elder Waal's protestations that the two younglings should spend some alone time together so that Kiira could maintain some semblance of her youth. *She has been through too much too soon*, he argued. Akeela, felt otherwise.

The two teens sat together for an hour every other night, time permitted, and enjoyed one another's company, reminiscing about their hatchling days, laughing and running around without a care in the world. When they were younger, Kiira and Saax were two of only a handful of children in the Quetz headquarters, and as such were left to do as they pleased. It did not hurt that they came from elder families, those of royal lineage. All areas of the caverns were their playground and their presence was surely felt when they each romped about.

The lights that emanated from the bi-pedal city below them reached their eyes now that Stel was settled and painted their bodies with deep blues and violets. They sat in silence, each to their own thoughts but still connected slightly by touch, his left and her right wing. A gentle but crisp breeze kissed the plumage on their faces. Kiira leaned into Saax. "I miss my mother," she softly clucked.

"I know you do. Whatever you need, just ask. I'll be there for you." Saax kept his eyes trained towards the city, entranced by the magic of the many colors of light that shone up at them, but gently rested his head upon hers. Kiira responded in kind.

The name of 'mother' made Akeela both cringe and feel empathy towards Kiira. Despite the bitterness she had harbored since her hatching, the powers of love and sympathy won her over. She loved the young Supreme Chancellor with all of her being but could not help wanting to turn away from her from time to time. She was, however, duty-bound and never lost focus on her responsibility to protect her ward, until either Kiira was lost, or she herself went the way of the spirit birds. A juvenile laugh silenced her thoughts.

"Ha ha," Kiira laughed out. "You are so funny!" The two birds rolled about pushing one another around gently, Kiira pushing more forcefully than Saax, both of them tipping over onto their backs.

"I'm funny, but you're funny-looking," he blurted out.

"Whatever yellow feather! You look like a bi-ped's butt!" They both roared out loud, still lying on their backs, their taloned feet kicking in the air.

"I may look like a man-butt, but you still like me."

"No I don't pigeon brain."

"Sure you don't."

The banter continued until the two friends finally excised their latent energy. Akeela envied the two and prayed that their playfulness would remain should a political union be arranged. Kiira would need strong allies in the future. Despite their ambition, Saax's family was deeply loyal to Waal.

Akeela's own marriage ended in tragedy, leaving her without her eternal mate and without position. She was fortunate that the up-and-coming Talon-Colonel Jaax had appointed her as protector and caretaker of the newly hatched Kiira Ave. She was eternally grateful then and silently but firmly loyal to him to this day, excepting Kiira, who held her greatest trust. When Supreme Chancellor Eensul died, under highly suspect circumstances, she melted for the youngling.

"Time is up you two. Saax, Kiira needs her rest now. You can see her in two days, if possible."

"Yes Colonel," he politely replied. And to Kiira, "pleasant dreams--- turkey foot."

"You know you like me, weasel face," she retorted before elbowing his side with a bony wing sending him yowling and laughing his way past the two sentries.

CHAPTER 15

Saax

Saax loped into the hall of his family's main quarters. His mother and clan elder, Lün, noticed that his golden robes were covered in dust and debris. As was their custom, he approached her and knelt until she acknowledged his presence. Satisfied of his subordination, she addressed him again.

"Those robes are very delicate and cost me many credits. Why are they filthy?"

Rising from his knees he retorted. "Just doing as you asked. I'm having fun with Kiira. I mean the Supreme Chancellor."

"Fun! This is not a game child. If you wish to ascend to the seat of clan elder one day, you will need to have her at your beck and call, not the other way around."

"Well, I believe that will require the two of us having fun. You want her to love me don't you?"

"But you had not better fall in love." She jabbed at his chest with force. "Your father was my conquest! She must be yours."

"And, where is my father? Off on another mission for you at one of the other clan sites, sucking up for you? Oh wait, that's right. He is living in on that floating desolate rock."

Lün grabbed her imposing son by his wings without trepidation and lifted him off of the carpeted floor glaring at him with reddened eyes. "Do not question my orders young one." Spittle flew out of her mouth and onto his now trembling face. "Your Father does what is necessary for our future. Your future! And you know exactly why he is on Seln base!" she thundered. But, she only told him a half-truth. She told him that he was there to work in an administrative capacity. She kept the rest a secret, to her son and husband.

Saax thought of telling her that in his future, he was simply in love with Kiira, supporting her as Supreme Chancellor. He would not forcefully usurp her seat after marriage. He remained quiet. His mother was accustomed to getting what she wanted and demolishing anyone that got in her way. He looked down at his royal blue plumage, noting its unkemptness, opposite of the stately and well-kept red feathers of his elder.

"Yes, Mother." Back on the ground and submissive once again, he begged his departure.

"Go clean yourself up and prepare for supper. And, don't bother with formal attire. Elder Waal has cancelled his visit with us tonight. You have been reprieved for one more night. His niece, the Chancellor," she scathed, "will be joining him here tomorrow evening. I expect you to behave like a future elder, not a lovesick boy. Go now."

Dejected, he went to his personal room, his shoulders sagging. He cleaned with UV-far lights and pressurized air baths and then selected an appropriate yet formal robe to sup with his mother. It was, per her liking, a costly acquisition, though not his finest. Thoughts of Kiira flooded his mind as he dressed, thinking of the fun they shared and her innocence through it all. Their families had been allies for millennia, always working side-by-side, supporting and protecting one another when one of them held the chancellorship. And, here he was, his mother's pawn. She wanted him to deceive his friend, the friend he was growing very fond of. She was the friend he knew he would fall in love with. He could never openly betray her, but his mother's influence was powerful.

A high-pitched chime sounded, informing Saax that his mother was ready for his accompaniment for their repast. Just like his father, he promptly succumbed. His father, Meetus, was his best friend and mentor. When he was around, that was. At his mother's insistence, he spent more than three-quarters of a Stel rotation away from him. Saax often thought this was a punishment for him. Meetus, was gentle with him and used logic and love to nurture and educate him. He never struck him or even threatened him with punishment, let alone violence. Instead, he spoke to his son and taught him the way of their world. With Meetus gone, Saax's education was left to his mother's strict ministrations.

As the clan elder, Lün sat at the head of the table, as was her custom. On her son's arrival, her eyes gleamed and her beak opened slightly in the way the Quetz smiled. Saax took the seat by her left side and with one swift but gentle motion, pulled it in towards the massive and gleaming obsidian dining table. Once seated, several servants erupted into the room behind a suspensor cart loaded with crystal plates piled high with delicately cooked meats and fruits. They scurried like ants and within a few seconds, they placed the food by each of the aristocratic birds and then departed. Crystalline pipets filled with glacier water had already been served.

"Venison? I didn't think we synthesized it. Too difficult to get the texture and taste right." He remained optimistic that the problem had been finally solved. Deer meat was highly prized and difficult to acquire without detection.

"Of course it's venison, Saax. And no, it is not synthesized," she warbled. "You should know better." As was the Elder's nature, she carefully plucked her food with a well-manicured talon and gently deposited it into her mouth, where she allowed it to sit and slowly envelope her taste buds. Saax, typically, reciprocated her actions when in her presence. But, for the first few bites of the tasty meat, he gorged it down.

"Thank you for the treat Mother. It's always nice to have such a delicacy."

"It was meant for Waal. He cancelled so that he could sup with the Chancellor." Again, she scathed at uttering the word. "Tomorrow night, he will have to endure synth meat. Just as well, your young friend, Kiira, deserves as much."

Under the table, Saax balled up a feathered fist and thought of slamming it down on the hard black surface. But, he was hungry and an outrage from him would result in missing out on a very costly and delicious meal. And it would cost him more than that.

"Absolutely Mother. As always, you are correct. She is nothing more than a child. I will have her under my wing in no time."

Satisfied at her son's change of heart and with her food, as it was extraordinarily tasty, she warmly smiled at Saax. "I am glad to hear that. Your father has a lot to learn from you."

The utterance of the word 'father' sent Saax reeling emotionally. Of course, he would never willingly harm Kiira. His dad would have been disappointed in him if he did. But, he had to steel himself. If he meant to protect Kiira, he would have to gain his mother's trust first.

CHAPTER 16

Waal

The palatial dining room was filled with antique furniture and expensive dining ware. Artwork from ancient but celebrated Quetz artists as well as a few human painters from various ancient civilizations, such as the Mesopotamians, adorned the walls. Beneath the opulent table, hand-woven textiles covered the frigid floor, various shades of silver and ocher meticulously interwoven into fractal patterns. Above them, a chandelier was suspended by anti-gravity fields, perfectly steady and illuminating the room with warm and gentle light. The chairs, upon which Kiira, Waal, and Akeela sat, were made of the finest marble and then covered in delicate synth-straw. In contrast to the opulence, and placed before each bird, was common gruel, served in simple synth-wood bowls.

Delicately seated on his luxurious perch, Waal stared down at his food and with perfect conviction, spoke.

"Aah. Synth-gruel. My absolute favorite," he beamed. He was missing out on what was reported to him as fresh venison and seethed at the thought of his present meal.

"Mother always ensured my sister and I were properly nourished. Good for the mind and excellent for the body. Your mother was never quite fond of it, though. Bless her poor spirit, wherever it may be."

"Thank you Uncle. I personally don't care for it, but I must live like my people. And, of course you are right. It is good for me."

Akeela beamed from her soul at her charge. She knew that she would grow into a formidable yet loving Supreme Chancellor, given the chance. Between Waal's ministering and Lün's recent and poorly timed insistence on setting up a marital union with Saax, she prayed that Kiira would be her own individual self, free to think and rule as she saw fit. But, such was the way of the political world.

As he dined, Waal made sure to keep Akeela in the conversation. He kept mental notes of all of her reactions, or lack thereof and in order to test her, he pushed the conversation to difficult topics.

"Tell me Kiira," he said through brilliant teeth. "How do you like seeing Saax on a regular basis? I hear that the two of you are spending plenty of time together."

"We have lots of fun, Uncle Waal. And, he is so funny. I wanted him over for dinner tonight, but I have to get my rest. There are so many reports to read, it's exhausting."

"Aah. My dear, and I already separated the truly important from the drivel for you. Maybe I should cut them down for you again. You are much too young to be wasting away with bureaucracy."

Akeela turned a sharp eye towards Kiira, reminding her to not cede too much authority to Waal. Despite him being her uncle, she risked never getting the power back. Waal with perfect grace and inconspicuousness, caught Akeela's look.

"Thank you Uncle. But that's okay. I need to learn so that I can eventually assume more responsibility."

"But of course. Just do not be afraid to lean upon your uncle. I am here to help." He paused momentarily to sop up some more of his less than appetizing food with all the aplomb of an elder and aristocrat. He looked at Kiira with one eye with the other well trained on Akeela.

"I almost forgot to mention that I plan on dining with Saax and his mother tomorrow evening. It is a rather informal event, but it would warm my cold-blooded heart if you attended with me. I am certain that your friend would appreciate it as well. What do you think?"

Kiira nearly burst out of her seat upon hearing the invitation. "Uncle, yes! Yes, I would love to attend." For a moment her eyes became downcast. "But, I need to prepare for the council meeting the following morning. I'm so sorry." Her elation subsided at the thought of losing out on seeing Saax, at dinner, with his mother.

"Nonsense, my darling child. I will take care of it for you and prep you the hour before. Besides, it would be nice for you as the Supreme Chancellor to visit Lün on a more personal level. Having her as your ally is very important, as I know, you are quickly learning."

"Oh Uncle Waal, what would I do without you?" Upon hearing his counsel, she smiled again as her thoughts rushed towards Saax. *He was funny, and smart, and so cute*, she thought.

"Excellent!" he roared. "I will inform Lün of your intentions to join us. And, Akeela, do not worry. I will take excellent care of my niece."

Akeela did not hide her displeasure at hearing her poignant dismissal. Waal may be Kiira's uncle, but he was not a Draconem. She did not know if he could truly be trusted. Waal took notice of her disagreeable, yet expected response. She was a purple-blooded Draconem after all.

"I will make the appropriate arrangements so that she will be properly escorted by your own guards, Elder Waal."

"Certainly. Certainly Lieutenant Colonel." He flashed his polished teeth again, perfectly feigning delight. Waal changed the subject as he addressed his niece. "You know, you did not mention why you asked me over for supper this evening. Is everything okay?"

"Uncle Waal. Everything is fine. It's just that you have not dined with us in some time. I was beginning to think you forgot about me."

"Forget my only niece? Darling. How could I ever? You are the sole reminder of my sister."

Akeela caught a quick blink in Waal's left eye that she had seen only when Waal came across as deceptive. But, in those moments he was involved in political musings. *Was he covering something up? What does he know that he is keeping to himself?*

Waal, on the other hand, felt joyous that his niece was playing into his plans. Soon, she would be married to Saax, and together with Lün, he would control the future of the Quetz.

CHAPTER 17

CLASSIFICATION: TS (AUS ONLY)

University of Perth, Perth, Australia.
Internal note:
From the Senior Tachyon Researcher
To the Dean of the Physics Department

Initial tachyon detection from the moon has not been replicated. Three subsequent attempts have proven futile. After careful analysis, we still cannot determine why our initial results have not been replicated. We have enough funding for one final attempt, which we project will take place in one month's time. If we fail to reproduce our findings from two months ago, we will focus our attention on the Orion Nebula.

After careful analysis by my team, the readings we received can be only one thing, tachyon emissions. What is their cause and why have we not been able to replicate it, is unknown. However, we feel that if the detections are indeed tachyons and if they are indeed irregular, based on recent non-detections, then it is possible that they may be evidence of intelligent life well superior to our own. We remain optimistic.

CLASSIFICATION: TS (AUS ONLY)

CHAPTER 18

Akeela

Thoughts of Kiira's beauty, gentleness, kindness, resilience, her Draconem nature enveloped her mind... Tired and leathery feet hung limply in water, as she sat by the edge of a massive ebon pool of pure mountain water that had collected over thousands of Stel rotations, but artfully maintained by Quetz technicians without the use of harsh chemicals. The vacant room served as the Draconem water survival training facility. As it was suppertime, it was empty which was a perfect place for Akeela to be alone with her thoughts. For seventeen Stel rotations, she guarded and loved Akeela. Stel rose and set; and she did not know how much longer she could keep her feelings bottled up inside. Every moment she spent with her, which was nearly the entire day, she wanted to scream out how much she loved her.

Her young ward was currently in the lion's den, enjoying a succulent meal, more than likely, with creatures that wished to entrap her via political machinations. But who was she to intervene? Even as a Lieutenant Colonel, she held no sway in comparison to the clan elders who controlled all of the Quetz populations. Despite her tight relationship with Kiira, she could not meddle in her affairs unless it was a matter of life or death. But, it was a matter of her life. Or could be.

With a quick slip, the warrior officer was in the chill water moving across to the other side with slow and gentle movements. For thirty minutes she continued to swim from one end to the other, hoping that the pain would subside through exercise. It failed to ease it, but the aerobic activity would tire her to the point of physical exhaustion. Of course, that was reckless in and of itself. She needed to remain fully alert for Kiira's sake. After finishing her final lap, she glided out of the soothing water with a short thrust from a pair of well-toned legs followed by a singular powerful burst of her wings.

Waddling over to the warm air dryer, Akeela thought for

only a brief moment that one day she would tell Kiira how she felt about her. *If only that day could be today my love,* she wished. *I would wrap you up in my wings and fill you with my all. Of course, it would only serve to confuse you and maybe even hurt you, something that I would never do.* Akeela's well-toned legs wobbled momentarily at the thought. She needed to bury her feelings again, even deeper this time. *But, I will think about it one more time. Kiira, you are…*

The door to the room opened up allowing harsh light to invade the gently illuminated space, as several soldiers strolled in for an after-dinner swim. Spotting the Superior Officer, they began to turn around. Fully composed again, she faced her subordinates.

"All done here. Come in for a dip. The water is amazing."

Settled in her quarters, Akeela stared at her monitors in anticipation of Kiira's return to the safety of the Supreme Chancellor's spaces. A communiqué popped up on her screen. It was Waal. He and Kiira would be another hour at Clan Elder Lün's quarters. The younglings were having so much fun together; they saw no need to end the engagement so quickly. "Do not worry, Lt. Col., Kiira is well taken care of."

A shiver ran up Akeela's back, causing her feathers to stand up for a brief moment. After acknowledging Waal's message, she reclined deeply into her perch and closed her eyes. Behind them, Kaylor was smiling as he always did, always full of life and happiness.

She found it ironic that a young military officer and one of great historical lineage such as he could be so reckless and carefree. Lt. Col., Jaak was his father. But, Kaylor seemed fit to be more of a Socran, a philosopher, than a warrior. Although physically gifted, she pummeled him in every combat simulator and hand-to-hand training sessions. *He didn't even try*, she thought. *Maybe he was allowing her to win, but that was not likely. He was in the royal class, and she in the overseer. What would he want with her?*

"Stop letting me win," she growled. "You are not serving either of us if that is what you're doing." His green eyes locked on to hers before he smiled broadly.

"Did you ever stop to consider that maybe you are just a really good combatant?"

She looked away towards the edge of the mountain and into the clear celeste sky.

"You make it too easy. Every simulator and sparring session, you seem to give up on me. But, you never have a problem thrashing the other males, or females for that matter. Am I that good, that I am your only weakness?"

"Hmmm. Maybe."

"This is not a joke Kaylor. I need to be the best so that I can bring honor to my family. You are royalty. I am not. I need to earn my position." She caught the slight that she paid to a royal class member and immediately went to bow and ask forgiveness.

"Don't bow to me, Akeela! Fight me instead. This time, I will not hold back," he firmly stated.

The two birds were alone in the exterior combat ring, the rest having retreated for their midday meal. Each of their steps was precarious around the loose stones that covered the ring. He would not make a mistake. She would not err either. He feigned to his right and then shifted his weight to the left to make for an attack. It was a basic move that Akeela did not fall for. Aware of his tactic, she shot a rapid stinging jab with her right-wing towards his middle torso. She saw her wing, moving in slow motion, a technique she learned from controlled breathing, approaching its target. *Got him*! she thought. *That will teach him to not go easy on me.* But, Kaylor was only smiling. Her thrust missed at the last moment. Before she could get over her shock, he was kicking her legs out from underneath her. He allowed her to stand up by herself.

They circled each other again, with some shock and fear now taking firm hold of Akeela's mind. *He surely was holding back before this*, she squirmed. Afraid that she would be trapped again, she hesitated to take the openings he mockingly flaunted at her. He made another feint but seeing it for what she thought it was, she did not react. A second later, she was on her back again, a jagged rock sharply jutting itself into her muscles.

"Damn it," she roared as he continued to smile.

"Come on Akeela. Lunch is getting cold. Take me down."

Back on her feet, she decided to take the initiative and recklessly leaped at him. The move was made out of anger and frustration, something that Kaylor would easily dodge, if not for the loose stones just behind his right leg. He acted to step back and allow her to fall forward but lost his footing instead and fell onto his own back. Akeela, the opportunistic fighter, pounced immediately and submitted him, by placing her left wing onto his throat. Unable to speak, he acknowledged his defeat by closing his eyes. She removed her wing satisfied with her victory.

"Hungry, yet?"

Akeela looked at him. "Yeah," she said. "I guess I will see you back in training later."

He looked at her with incredulous eyes. "Why not during our meal?"

"Er, you know that we cannot sit together. So, why ask?" she glared at him questioningly.

"You can sit with me if I invite you. And, I most certainly invite you. So? Hungry?"

Stupefied at what was transpiring, she relented and the two of them made their way to the dining hall. Upon entering the large room, all eyes were upon them. To assuage their thoughts, Kaylor immediately spoke up about being bested by Akeela in the ring, leaving out that it was an accident. Lieutenant Colonel Jaak, who was seated in the Senior Officer section saw and heard his son, his eyes steadfast. But, in his heart, he secretly hoped his son would court Akeela. He knew her to be very intelligent, hardworking, and a very determined warrior. If his instincts served him, she would make him a terrific partner and wonderful mother. Rob'n would have approved of her.

All of the Draconem warriors-in-training finished their meal and headed back to the ring for the rest of the day. Afterwards, Kaylor approached Akeela and asked if she would take a stroll with him. The night air was crisp and perfect for a leisurely walk.

"Besides," he stammered, "supper would not be ready for another thirty minutes." Because she did not have an excuse to reject him, she relented; and because he did not have an excuse to stay quiet, at the end of their walk, he told her she was beautiful. Every night since that day in the ring, they took a walk before their evening meal. Every night, they fell more in love. And, on one magical day, before his father, Lieutenant Colonel Jaak, and with permission from the then Supreme Chancellor, the two birds wed.

CHAPTER 19

Waal

"Dinner was exquisite. Of course, I have come to expect nothing less from such fine hosts," Waal quipped.

"Spare me, Waal. Of course, you are aware that the fresh venison was served last night? This evening, we only had time to prepare synth-meats."

Despite the ease in the conversation throughout the evening, both Waal and Lün were waging a mental war of wits. Kiira and Saax because of their age and lack of experience did not catch on. The young couple were also busy eyeing one another and hooking talons underneath the opulent table.

As host, Lün looked towards the two younglings, and then focused on her son. She and Waal had something to discuss. "Supreme Chancellor? Has my son mentioned that we have a human classics library rivaling that of any human one? Your uncle mentioned to me just the other day that you are fascinated with their writings?"

Kiira politely stopped her discussion with Saax. "Absolutely. My uncle knows me well, but Saax here has not mentioned it to me at all. Haven't you, my friend?"

"Aah, Saax. Well, we must show her our collection at once, if that is okay with you Supreme Chancellor?" She spoke to Kiira but gave a hidden intonation towards her son, that only he could have picked up on.

"Mother. In fact, I was hoping to give the Supreme Chancellor a tour of our spaces. The last time she visited, we were both in our first feathers. Kiir…I mean, Your Highness. Would you like a tour? We can start at the library."

Anxious to relax the formalities, Kiira gladly accepted and in two moments, the two were gleefully off.

Alone, the two elders decided to forego their own dance of pomp and circumstance and got to the meat and bones of securing a marital union. They each understood what they had to gain once Kiira was wed. She was three Stel rotations from full adulthood; but political marriages could be on paper only. *What transpires once she is of age is another matter,* they mused.

"Do you smell that?" Kiira asked sincerely. Her eyes squinted as if burning from sort of acrid vapor as she looked directly at Saax.

"No." He turned about the room taking in deep breaths through his nostrils, attempting to detect what was disturbing her. He was afraid his family would embarrass itself with a dead rat lying about somewhere.

"There it is again. I can hardly breathe. What is that?" she begged. "I wonder if…yup it's you! You smell like cattle farts!" she roared.

The look of despair on Saax's well-groomed face was replaced with exasperation and delight. "What ever pigeon wing. She who smelt it dealt it, even when it's fake."

They walked about the library, Kiira taking in the details of the large collection of human-penned books. The Quetz were able to remotely monitor human technology and ascertain the rate at which it increased. As such, they had no need or desire to collect their technical literature, or even their history, which was never accurate. All of the human books in the Stora family library were either fiction or philosophical.

"The greatest works of human literature are gathered here. My family has been entrusted with collecting and maintaining them. When they kill themselves off, a new species will likely take their place; and these books and scrolls will serve as a record of the rare beauty they were capable of producing."

"Saax, this is amazing. I've always wanted to study their artistic writing. My mother…," Kiira looked down as she momentarily lost her voice.

"My mother recited so many stories for me when I was little. Tales such as, *The Old Man and the Sea, Frankenstein, The Hobbit, and Winnie the Pooh.* I rather liked that one. It's about an anthropomorphic toy bear. A child's plaything. I must have asked her to recite it to me a hundred times."

Saax stood quietly, staring at his friend and future betrothed, listening to her innocent voice talk about stories and childhood. His mother and Elder Waal were in the other room making the necessary arrangements for the union. He wondered if she even knew. No, he thought. She doesn't. I should tell her. What type of a relationship will we have if she found out that I was a part of the plan to subvert her power?

"Kiira. I…I."

"What is it, Saax?" she inquired.

He hesitated and then decided that he could not say what was on his mind. And, just as well. His mother's wrath knew no limits and at least he could offer Kiira some protection. "Oh, I just wanted to tell you that I recall that our mothers spent countless hours in this very room reading books. It's probably where your mother learned all of those stories. And to think, here 'we' are."

"Okay, gorilla face. No more sappiness. Didn't you mention scrolls? What's that about?" A pair of brilliant turquoise eyes broke through his reservations and put him back on track.

"Yeah, the scrolls include a large number of works published before people invented paper. They are pretty delicate, but we have them digitally stored. There are a few crystalline tablets around so you can read them without worry. Here, let me get you one."

For almost a full hour the young birds sat and read tales to each other about pirates, soldiers, and a group of people called cowboys. Their eyes scanned the text at lightning speed and their chirps allowed for a rapid transmission of the material that humans could not match verbally. They were exhausted by the time a plump and polished Waal came in requesting Her Excellency return to the main hall of the home.

CHAPTER 20

Eensul

Kiira slept deeply snuggled in her small nest. The beautiful young chick, now five Stel rotations in age, rested peacefully, her small chest rising and falling gracefully. A small shiver ran across her body and it was instantly gone. Her breathing resumed its steadiness. Eensul looked down at her, proud to call herself mother, but still felt for the young Akeela, Kiira's birth mother. Her husband's unforeseen death at the hands of a jealous warrior from one of the other mountain fortresses shook everyone, including the once enigmatic Jaak.

Akeela's beauty was considered legendary amongst the warrior clan, and Kaylor's slayer was upset that a member of a royal bloodline took the middle caste looker to be his bride. The killer was immediately executed at the hands of Jaak, but fearful that other middle caste members of that clan may seek further reprisal, he approached Eensul. His daughter-in-law was preparing to give birth, and the hatchling's life was still at risk. He asked if she would consider raising the child as her own. He met her when she was his uncle's intern and learned to respect her wits and sense of humor. She was a wonderful creature, if ever he met one.

In their teenage years, Jaak and Eensul, despite the rivalry between their clans, had formed a deep, yet secret friendship. During lectures, Eensul helped Jaak with his academic courses, to which he earned a great love for. Jaak, on the other hand, helped Eensul with her martial training, something she loved to practice only with him. Despite their close bond, they both understood that it was only a friendship. Still, they grew to trust and rely on each other implicitly, albeit only clandestinely. It would work towards their political advantage, they argued.

Eensul had been too busy to find a spouse and nest mate, but had on occasion taken on a few lovers. As they were currently on a mission to the African fortress, she could claim to have birthed the infant while on her return home. As for

Akeela, she would be appointed as the child's guardian and, covertly, as her wet nurse. In this way, Akeela could ensure the safety of her baby and still remain close to her. Eensul, however, never lost sight of the pain Akeela must have felt for the past several rotations. Regardless, she and Jaak kept their friendship a secret even from her and Kiira. On a few rare occasions and on the premise of clan business, Jaak would visit with Eensul to inquire about his granddaughter. As for Akeela, to ensure secrecy, any discussion of Kiira was only in the form of a status report. Of course, as he formally appointed her to the position of guardian, with his uncle's blessing, she reported directly to and only to him on that matter.

She resented having to wake up her daughter, but her first day of lectures was set to begin in one hour. A tone signaled and Akeela entered the room. "How is she," she asked.

"Resting so peacefully, it pains me to disturb her."

"Oh, go ahead and lift her up. It would be nice for her to wake up in your wings. Besides, she loves you very much."

"It would not be proper. You are her mother." Despite her stoic appearance, her heart was visibly broken.

"Akeela," she softly spoke. "Let us not pretend. Please---hold her." Eensul stepped away and allowed the warrior to approach her daughter. Gently, Akeela lifted Kiira up and brought her to her breast and wrapped her wings around her. Eensul, now standing next to Akeela enveloped both with her own wings. This is how the young Kiira woke up, with her two mothers loving her.

Beady little eyes peeked open to see the two grown females. Instantly, Kiira was smiling. "Momma. Akeela." She let out a small yawn and began to stir. "Why are you holding me Akeela? I'm a big girl now."

Akeela answered. "Would you like me to put you down now?"

"We can leave you alone to get dressed too," Eensul followed.

But, the young bird was happy to have the love of two beautiful females and was not quite ready to grow up so quickly after all. "No, you two can keep holding me. I like it."

After another minute of being held, Kiira finally asked to be put down. After sifting her feathers and then dressing her, the lot of them sat for their morning meal and discussed what she could expect for her first day of academy. The other students would be visible via holo-projection, but a few birds would accompany her physically. Saax was going to be there as well.

"I don't like him," Kiira retorted. "He smells."

"Kiira Ave, you will not say any such thing to him. Besides, it is only for one Stel rotation. The two of you, because of your parent's positions, will receive individual tutoring, thereafter."

"I guess." The young bird looked down at her meal, eyeing the blueberries on her plate. With a quick plucking by one of her talons, they were all down her throat. She looked up and laughed, happy that such warmth surrounded her.

CHAPTER 21

Saax

The joyous mood of the dinner had dissolved. Saax looked up at his mother as he awaited his dismissal. The bright dining room was now a mellow amber, Lün's preferred ambient setting. The dim mood repulsed Saax. Several house staff members busied themselves about, cleaning as quickly as possible. The aging mother still had much to say to her young son but refrained until they were alone. Saax remained at her feet. The staff finished faster than usual, aware that their polite master was cringing while holding his position. They left abruptly.

A pair of hazel eyes rolled now that she was satisfied that they were alone.

"There are audio/visual sensors throughout this entire complex, as I am sure you are well aware of Saax. So, I pray to Spirit Terr that you did not attempt to undermine me in any way. I have very little patience, even for my closest family."

Saax thought of his father at that moment and wondered what he did to deserve spending time on a frigid satellite with little comfort or amenities. "Mother, I did as you asked and only that. She is falling in love. I am certain."

"I don't care how you feel about her in return, so as long as your loyalties remain with this house. Are we clear on that point?"

"Yes, Mother. Crystal."

"Very well, my love. Please head back to your quarters and get some rest. I am sure you need it after tonight." A smile formed across the politicking mother. As he rose, she reached out across him and brought him in for a full embrace with her large but delicate wings. "Good rest my son."

"Good rest Mother."

A collection of various holo-images of different creatures from across Terr decorated the room. His father, a naturalist, captured several images of the bountiful life and saved them for his son, whom he knew would love and be fascinated by them. Perched by his desk, he felt the sorrow of not seeing his favorite parent. He hoped that he could reunite with him soon. His thoughts rushed back to Kiira. Her mother was taken away from her, never to be seen, heard from or held by again. The mere thought of what she was going through, what she had to and needed to endure weighed heavily upon him. He desperately wanted to rush to and comfort her, receive comfort from her. They were friends, but he knew that deep in his heart that he loved her. If the marriage arrangements went through, he would do everything in his power to protect her from her uncle and his mother.

She was still only seventeen Stel rotations in age and far too young to be married. He understood what his mother was gaining. *But what about Elder Waal? There was nothing in it for him. Kiira would remain Chancellor Supreme and I would be her princeps. But why so soon? Is my mother concerned of other possible suitors? There must be something else?* Before he could continue down his thought path, his holo-display lit up. There was a coded incoming call from Seln. His father!

Saax quickly muttered his cypher code and Meetus' face instantly formed from coalescing liquid crystals. "Hello Son. How are you holding up?"

Saax barely able to contain his glee, nearly shouted but instead kept his voice low so that his mother would not barge in.

"Father! I'm so happy to hear from you. Are you coming home soon?"

"No, your mother needs me to stay a bit longer. Aside from being a member of the Seentia clan, I am the only other royal member there. Pulchri is there to keep me company but she tends to spend most of her time busy with work. She hardly ever leaves her room. Enough of that, though. How is your mother?"

"I figured you would have called her first, being your wife and all."

"Well, I figured I would speak to you before she prevented me from calling you. So, how is she?"

"Controlling as ever. She and Waal are negotiating my marriage to Kiira." Saax's lowering of his eyes, caught Meetus' attention.

"What? Your mother hasn't mentioned this to me at all; and you and the Chancellor are far too young to even consider a betrothal."

"Yeah, I don't understand why Waal is even considering this. He doesn't gain anything."

Meetus remained quiet for a few seconds before responding. "Not necessarily. I think I know."

"What is it?" Saax asked.

"Nothing you need to worry about. I will discuss this with your mother as soon as I am back, which will be in another two Seln phases. So, don't worry about it; and get some sleep after we disconnect."

The father and son continued their conversation for a few more minutes, discussing Saax's true feelings for Kiira and the fun they had together every two days. They also spoke of the morose nature of the natural satellite and some of the less confidential information about the recent starship developments. Noting the time, Saax's beloved father decided to end the call.

"I love you, Son. Don't ever forget that."

"Never, and I love you too Dad. Hurry home, will ya?"

Meetus disconnected the call from his end. Saax's holo-monitor immediately went dark. It was wonderful to hear his dad's voice and see his face for a while. Exhausted from the toils of his day, though, he settled into his perch and closed his eyes. Two more Seln phases and he could be with his father again. Maybe he would stay around longer, considering his future marriage.

CHAPTER 22

Mota

A large holo-reflector floated in front of the young scientist. From it, a large pair of orange eyes stared back at her. The rare color was her point of pride. She knew that she was attractive and could mate with any bird she chose. She wasn't dating at the moment, though. She stared at the reflector and carefully groomed herself for over an hour. Her mother taught her at an early age that even if she did not want to be physical with anyone, that she could still control others with her wiles. She already used her physical appeal to convince Libur to appoint her as his aide; and now she caught the attention of another elder, Waal. He asked if she would like to dine with him. Intrigued by the request, she accepted.

Satisfied with her grooming, Mota walked towards a panel by the door of her cleansing room. She uttered a lazy squawk that made a door appear. Inside were several robes. She found her finest copper garment towards the back. The pseudo light reflected off of it emitting dazzling metallic patterns. It was made from materials fitting for royalty. It was a gift from Libur upon starting her role as his aide. She wrapped her robe about her shoulders and walked over to the front of her quarters, just as a chime announced a visitor.

She walked daintily over to the entrance. Sensing her presence, part of the wall disappeared. On the other side, Waal's aide, Fugax nervously eyed her. As aides to elders, they spoke on occasion, but the young male nevertheless found it difficult to converse with her. His beak chattered loudly.

"Hello, Mota. Elder Waal asked me to escort you. He is waiting for you at the planetarium."

Typically, Mota disregarded anything Fugax said, if he said anything, but maintained a certain level of decorum due to his position. "Aah. Hello Fugax. I certainly did not expect you to act as my escort, you being so busy and all. What a pleasure."

Fugax did not expect any warmth from Mota. In fact, he expected her typical dry nature. Emboldened, he slowly extended a shabby wing past his shabby silver rags. "Shall I escort you, then? I am sure Elder Waal is anxious to meet with you."

The vain aide gingerly accepted the scrawny bird's wing, fearful that his meekness could rub off on her.

"Yes uh, certainly."

For the five-minute stroll down the halls of the cavernous mountain, Mota slyly played her tricks on Fugax, asking him questions and laughing at his feeble attempts at a sense of humor. Growing more comfortable with her, he opened up and revealed more about his relationship with Waal and the inner happenings in his clan.

"So tell me Fugax," she cooed. "You must be aware of so much that happens around the fortress. You have been Waal's aide for what five Stel rotations now?" The tone of her voice was warm. Fugax's chest continued to expand as they continued on towards the planetarium.

"Well, only three rotations, but it certainly feels longer. Time moves quickly when you're an aide. You'll see," he noted.

"But don't worry. You're turning heads. I have heard Elders Waal and Libur speak well of you. I even believe Elder Waal intends to ask if you will accompany him to the wedding. Such an honor."

"Wedding?" Mota looked confused.

"Yes, you know. The Supreme Chancellor and Saax, son of Elder Lün. It's not official, but the two elders continually meet to discuss the arrangements. I am not sure when they intend to perform the union, but that will be resolved soon enough."

"Oh, yes, of course. I simply assumed there was another marriage proposal. I'm like you. For now, an organizer, maybe. But as a guest, no."

"Mota, you need to trust me. All of us males swoon over you. You will be a guest!" he exclaimed.

The ambient hallway lighting grew dimmer and the air cooler as they approached their destination. Because of the high-energy photonics used for their displays, the Quetz lowered the temperature of this part of the mountain by two degrees Celsius. Chilled, Mota pulled her cloak tighter around her body, but did not allow herself to shiver. Fugax's thin body and thinner garment could not withstand it; and his body began to shake. He moved to offer his robe, but Mota sensing his intention, motioned him to stop.

News of the wedding confused Mota, as Kiira was still young. She needed more information and getting it from Libur would break protocol. She wondered if he even knew. Maybe Fugax was mistaken on that one bit. Either way, she needed to know more, and the chatty little bird still holding on to her wing was exactly what she needed. Fugax was loose-beaked, but someone whose confidence she could hold. He was also an aide to the Supreme Chancellor's uncle, their heralded leader's closest advisor.

Fugax continued to ramble on about her beauty and the many wagers he and his friends made on who would court her. The odds he would succeed were astronomically low, so he never considered trying.

"Fugax," Mota implored with her orange eyes blinking with concern. "Why do you put yourself down so much? You are a powerful aide, and any female here would just die to be courted by you. In fact, I know I would. But, you need to ask me out first."

The wiry bird stopped walking and guffawed at her words, his mouth open and about to drool, before Mota leaned forward and nudged it closed with her own.

"But Elder Waal seems to like you and he would kill me..."

"Fugax, darling. He's old and I'm only a distant royal. He likely just wants someone to warm his nest; or, more likely he wants to speak business. Nothing more. So, how about tomorrow night after we wrap up our administrative duties, we go for a short evening flight," she asked hoping he would get the hint.

"Uh, but the EM scramblers…"

"I have access to a few un-detectable devices. Don't worry. Besides, I've always liked you and would like to get to know you better." An obvious lie. She detested his wormy appearance and at the moment, felt like jumping into a vat of scalding water to clean herself of him.

"Okay," he stammered. Tomorrow night then. I will stop by to pick you up."

"No. I'll be busy at the other end of the mountain. Just meet me outside the training compound. It's easier for both of us that way." A large smile formed on her face and Fugax thought he was about to topple over by the knees.

"Oh, will you be escorting me back tonight?" She prayed he wouldn't.

"No. Elder Waal said he would do that personally."

Noting their arrival, Mota gently nudged Fugax's faded beak before activating the door panel to give herself access. She felt her lunch regurgitate inside of her. Fugax saw the walls spinning.

"Good evening," he sputtered as she walked into the dark and chilly room. Waal was perched by a table sipping casaba wine. The door sealed itself, Fugax on the other side, looking after his new love.

CHAPTER 23

Kiira

Kiira woke up dreaming of Saax. It was a stark difference from the nighttime visions she had of her mother almost every time she closed her eyes, not that all of the dreams were bad. Many were good; but waking up to pain was wearing heavily upon her soft shoulders. No matter how hard she tried, she failed to shake away her recent dream. There was never any doubt her mother would want for her to move on. But, she was unsure if enough time had passed.

Leg muscles still stiff from being folded under her torso, she cantered away from her nest to freshen up her feathers and stretch a bit. She had shield practice again. Normally, the thought of suiting up got her feathers in a tizzy, but the heavy dinner at Saax's did not settle well. Regardless, Akeela would expect nothing less than her best, and she aimed to please her instructor. She had almost five minutes before she needed to report to the training field but left early to continue her warm-up stretches.

Akeela was already there. Saax was with her.

Stel was beginning to rise, and the air was brisk. Down below, the leaves were changing color from dark green to orange, red, yellow, and the myriad of hues in between.

"Someone is the early riser," Akeela gently jeered as she stood by Saax's side, coyly staring at Kiira.

"Funny me. And, I thought I would be early." The Chancellor Supreme's eyes grew suspicious. "No offense monkey brain, but why are you here? Feeding time for primates is not for another hour."

"Kiira!" Akeela shot out, embarrassed for her ward.

"That's okay. She's just upset because I had to help her read last night." Saax's dangerous smile formed through his polished beak.

"No you did not, you little man-bird!" Kiira exclaimed.

"Enough, the both of you. You would think you were raised by humans and not members of royal houses. And you Kiira! Supreme Chancellor. Fortunately for the two of you, I had the exterior sensors shut off while we train."

"Sorry Akeela," she muttered. Now addressing her young male suitor, "but why are you here?"

Before he could answer, Akeela spoke up. "Kiira. Saax was here earlier this morning preparing for his morning exercise routine. I saw him and figured that since you two are good friends, it might be a good idea for him to train with us. He will be your inflight combat partner, allowing me to act solely as an objective instructor. And before you even ask, I've already shown Saax the basics of shield use. Fortunately, he happened to be carrying his own EM scrambler." Akeela gave him a warning glance.

Not fully confident that the sensors would remain off, Akeela cautioned the two friends to activate their scramblers on her cue. Satisfied, the three birds approached the sharp mountain cliff and plummeted. Three seconds later, the warrior activated her wristlet and went invisible. The other two followed.

A mechanical voice erupted over their built-in audio sets. Akeela was roaring at them. "Now, activate your visors!"

Seconds later and Kiira was able to see both her guardian and friend no differently than before they went invisible. Akeela's digital scales were red just like her own. Saax wore a shimmery deep-ocean blue. Below them, the trees were a mosaic of fall colors, slowly passing below them. Occasionally, a small human campsite would pop up, or a deer would scamper, frightened at the natural predator that they sensed but could not see. The young Supreme Chancellor was in awe of all the life and activity below her. Ahead, she discerned a river and beyond it, a crystal clear lake, still free from the poke-a-dot huts built by man.

"Kiira. You seem impressed, but try switching through the different EM bands," Akeela advised. Not needing to be told twice, she quickly complied, with Saax soon following.

"Don't dip any lower in altitude than you already are. We are going to go 'otic' soon," Akeela's voice instructed.

Comfortable that they were beyond most of the human population, their instructor barked a few orders, telling them how to position themselves into a natural formation. Kiira led with Akeela to her right and Saax to her left.

"Okay young ones. Continue on this heading. Go to otic one in: three, two, one, now."

The beautiful forest was immediately transformed into a tapestry of infinitely changing colors as they reached the speed of sound. After a minute, they shifted to otic two. The two friends felt their hearts race at the thrill of moving at such a speed.

"Wow, everything looks like one giant rainbow!" Kiira sputtered gleefully.

"For sure," added Saax. "It's like a Pink Floyd album."

"A what monkey-bird?"

"Kiira!" Akeela roared. "Remember your decorum."

"Pink Floyd is a human musical group. They were far out. Of course, you would know that if you read anything, little chickpea."

Frustrated and ready for combat training, Akeela bumped Kiira's left side forcing her into Saax. The two began to tumble in the air but quickly corrected themselves. "Now Saax! Attack Kiira the way I showed you!"

Saax wasted no time and shot right, straight at Kiira. But,

the young bird saw him coming and shot up straight into the clouds and away from his visual sensors.

"What are you waiting for?! Pursue her!" Akeela demanded.

As he aimed to follow in her direction, Saax suddenly felt a heavy thump on his back. He dropped himself and looked up to see a red blur chasing him.

"Excellent Kiira. A perfect sneak attack. You could have killed him with a shot to the neck from that position. Saax, now I want you to race ahead. Kiira, go for the kill."

Saax wasted no time in moving ahead, as Kiira was already aiming to shoot him with a training projectile. They chased one another in that way for an hour, sometimes getting a successful shot and sometimes not. The forests beneath them moved as a myriad of rainbows, never ending, never ceasing, always a blur.

Ready to return, Akeela then directed Kiira to loop back in the direction they came by going beak up and rolling her eyes until she was on her back. Settled, the trio gently turned themselves right side up. Akeela continued with verbal lectures on combat flight theory for the trip home.

"Okay, you two! Here we go. Shift to otic three, now!" Kiira and Saax were busy looking down while Akeela kept her attention focused on her visor display. Mount Rainier was just two clacks away. "Sub otic on three, two, one, now!" she roared. Their mountainous home was just ahead, and five seconds later, they were beyond the protection field.

"Oh my Spirit Terr, that was amazing," Kiira yelled with glee.

"We need to do this again!" Saax chimed in.

"And you most certainly will. That is of course, that you keep our little secret Saax. Kiira's safety means that she must be prepared for combat. If you are her friend, you will honor her and remain quiet, even to your mother, as you already promised."

Saax focused on his trajectory but spoke with sincerity. "I gave you my word Lt. Colonel Akeela. I offer my blood bond to you and to Her Excellency Kiira Ave, the Supreme Chancellor."

"Saax, you don't have to." Kiira knew the pain that came with such a bond and did not want to see him suffer at her own talon.

"It is my bond to offer. I beg you not to rebuff me. Please Kiira, it would be my honor."

Akeela felt the heartfelt emotions that poured from the young bird and immediately thought of her husband, Kaylor. Two minutes later and they were back on the training grounds, which per her order was still empty. They made their way quietly back to Kiira's interior spaces and quickly prepared for the blood ceremony.

"Kiira," she pleaded. "Do not remove the feathers. It is traditional, but no one must know of his gift to you."

Kiira nodded in ascent and carefully lifted the layers of feather from the left side of Saax's face, as he kneeled before her. With her right talon, she dug deep into his flesh and carved a symbol that permanently marked him with her name. Akeela administered a coagulant to stop the blood that seeped out. Rising, Saax was met by Kiira's wings as a thank you for his sacrifice, and because she wanted to comfort his pain.

Saax was discreetly escorted back to his part of the fortress, but not before running into Waal, who was quietly waiting with two sentries in the waiting room.

"Aah Saax. I'm surprised to see you here. I must have had my days mixed up. I assumed it was Kiira's cleansing day again. My mistake of course."

"Not at all Uncle," Kiira interjected. "I decided to have my friend over for breakfast instead. Sorry for not informing you."

Waal noted the depression of feathers about Saax's left wrist. He did not recall hearing of the young bird going out for a flight this day or any other. But it looked like he was just wearing a wristlet.

CHAPTER 24

Jaak

Jaak's legs thundered across the hall. He had decided to take a walk along the many corridors before settling in to perform his various office duties. It was important to show his face and interact with his sentries. His presence, while domineering during important business, was received as warm and uplifting by his warriors, who openly admired him. Many casual conversations about him amongst his clan ended with: "he's tough, but fair, and never willing to make us do something he hasn't or wouldn't do." But they also respected him enough to never cross him.

On his way back to his administrative room, he happened to come across Fugax, who was pacing outside his door. The young aide promptly stopped and stood rigidly, a slight shiver steadily running across his entire body. A nearly indiscernible chip from his lower right beak was present.

Jaak addressed him as he squinted to see him better. "You are Elder Waal's aide, aren't you?"

"Ye, yes, General. Elder Waal sent me over to hand over this request from the Supreme Chancellor herself. He deemed it urgent, Sir."

"Why didn't you just hand it over to my aide? He is sitting just on the opposite side of this entrance. If it is urgent, he would have contacted me immediately."

Fugax straightened his back further to the point he felt it would break. "General, I was given explicit instructions to hand it only to you."

Jaak raised a bushy eyebrow. A muscled wing reached towards the diminutive bird, who instantly shrunk away, shaking more violently now.

"Kind bird, there is no need for that with me. Come.

Follow me to my office."

Jaak chirped quietly and the opening to give them passage appeared. Major Kiln was perched with his back straight, fastidiously taking care of much of his superior's business. "Major, no one is to know of Elder Waal's aide entering these premises. Please ensure that all audio/visual footage reflects him only having stood outside with me for no more than ten seconds."

"Yes General. Understood." With that, the elder warrior and Fugax entered into a private room.

"First thing dear bird. You are safe here in my presence, so there is no need for you to continue worrying. Are we clear?"

Jaak's compassionate stare was met with disbelief. Apparently, not all elders abused their aides. Major Kiln seemed fine and Mota, well--- Mota was Mota. Feeling more secure, his trembling subsided.

"I understand General and will remember it."

Jaak peered at the encoded message for a few seconds before lifting his eyes to meet Fugax's, which remained locked on his. "Tell me, Fugax. It is Fugax, correct?" The aide responded in the affirmative.

"Did the Supreme Chancellor draft this?" The tone of the message seemed childish, but despite her age, Kiira was not a fool. It seemed contrived.

"Yes, so I was told." Fugax closed his eyes and took a deep breath and then spoke with greater conviction. "In truth, General, I don't believe so. But, it is not my place to contradict my elder."

"No. It is not. Young bird. I will shortly release you to your elder, but recall my earlier note to my aide. You were never inside my office."

"Absolutely General," he affirmed, still at attention.

"One last thing. If someone is going to strike you with a wing or leg, lean into it. It will soften the blow a bit. And if you desire some self-defense lessons, feel free to ask my aide. The Major is an excellent instructor. Good day."

"Sir, yes, Sir. I mean General and thank you for the offer."

Jaak saw Fugax disappear through the now closing door and thought how such a small bird could endure such trials and remain at his position as long as he has. He was going on nearly four Stel rotations as Waal's aide now. Jaak was, of course, more troubled by the phony request from Waal. He could have requested the flight logs himself in her name. Why go through the trouble of the deception? He looked at his desk and decided to sit down. Maybe he needed to review the sensor logs himself. With his new access, he could see anything and everything. Nothing was a secret to him.

So Lt. Colonel Akeela is teaching my granddaughter how to fight with shield armor and fly with it. Interesting that she drags Saax into it. The teens spend a lot of time together and from what I can tell, they will likely be betrothed if not married soon. He did not trust Waal, but the thought of Waal and Lün was not good. Those two had been cohorts for years on end. It surprised him that Lün opted to marry Meetus. He was a fine bird if ever he met one; but Waal and Lün were definitely birds of a feather. Whatever they were planning, he knew it would not serve Kiira. He needed to intervene. *Maybe it was time to fight for the throne*, he thought. *As for the audio/visual records, they could wait for this evening's council meeting. He would openly hand them over to Waal then.*

CHAPTER 25

News Coverage

"Carol Rae Barton reporting here at Mt. Rainier National Park, where just one week ago tragedy struck, when an F-35 jet fighter exploded in mid-air, seemingly ramming into an invisible wall. The Navy has identified the pilot as Lieutenants Jake Lyon and Suzanne Dawd, both veteran combat pilots and graduates of the Navy's elite Top Gun school.

We spoke with their commanding officer, Captain Pam Jensen, who noted their exceptional service to the country. Both were loving spouses and parents whose families are still reeling from what unfolded eight days ago. Senior officers, though, are remaining tight-lipped about the circumstances behind the incident and have yet to give a formal determination as to what happened.

However, they would not rule out that it was operator error.

Both families think otherwise, claiming that LTs Lyon and Dawd were always very careful aviators and meticulous people in and out of work. They also claim that the jet was still experimental, and that they feel the military is covering up possible mechanical or electronic malfunctions.

It is still too early to tell, but based off the footage seen, something out of the ordinary happened here by the mountain. And, if you take a look behind me, there is a team of military personnel preparing several drones to fly towards the mountainside. Stay tuned."

CHAPTER 26

Jaak

Time was running out. Jaak suspected that if Waal was preparing to make a move it was rapidly approaching, and delaying too much could be costly. But if he moved too early, he could be caught in any of Waal's potential traps. It was time to begin his coup to usurp the throne; but his intelligence gathering left him feeling assured that not a single clan would back him up. He would have to force them to support him. The lives of his race and the very heart of planet Terr depended on his strategic moves.

Major Kiln announced his presence at the door. Jaak checked his holo-screen to verify. After carefully glancing at his unperturbed aide, he gave the young soldier admittance. Kiln formally presented himself by standing at attention, wings tucked tightly by his side, his gleaming taloned feet together, and his eyes trained on a non-existent point directly ahead of him. Jaak just barely raised an eye to look at him, and instead maintained his avian focus on the report he was reviewing. After a quick five seconds, he addressed the warrior.

"Major. It's as you've said. There is unification of the clans in support of Waal. Even Libur conspires against us." Kiln heard the name of Clan Elder Libur leave Jaak's beak with an overtly stoic tone. Kiln then paused before responding thinking of his first lesson from the General.

"Sir, you always said our allies and friends pose the greatest risk. Has anything changed?"

Jaak sighed deeply, exhausted from the long day. He looked Kiln directly in the eyes.

"Young bird, as Spirit Terr as my witness, I would name you as my blood heir if our laws allowed it."

Humbled, Kiln answered. "All that I need, I already have because of you Sir. My family lives because of you. I have already inherited a great gift, larger than any royal title. I gained your trust and confidence."

"And that you will deservedly always have, my young friend." Touched, Jaak paused momentarily to study his aide's face before resuming his work.

"I noticed that Libur's new aide---Mota? She's been ruffling some male feathers lately. What do you know of her?" Jaak asked with a raised feathery upper eyebrow.

It was Kiln's turn to let out a deep breath. "She's a faux feather, sir. And, currently, she's been making several overt passes at Fugax. Unfortunately, he's falling for it. And, if you recall, she supped with Elder Waal a few nights ago. Interestingly, she ignores me. Either she detests military or just my humble origins. I could care less either way. I'd rather have my feathers plucked than speak to her."

"Naturally, but do not lose sight that this is Quetzl chess. Every move and every word has ramifications years beyond, no matter how blind we may be to them," he admonished.

Jaak continued. "Still, I would not trust her either. Her father Ajax was a similarly natured scientist. He even came close to taking the clan leadership of Seentia before Libur made his play. Thanks to my uncle of course."

A brisk air filled the room as the air purifiers kicked on, ruffling the feathers of the two warriors, who relaxed upon feeling the chill breeze. It was a comfort of life that was not removed from their species in the hundreds of millions of years of evolution they had experienced.

Relaxed, the two Draconem birds continued on. Jaak had accepted the report from his aide with his typical deferential mood. Mota was a threat, but just how much, he did not know. He continued onto a different more mundane topic.

"Have we had any shield infractions as of late?"

Kiln's eyes widened as if a thought just occurred to him.

"There was one disturbance last week. I thought nothing of it and figured it was due to an atmospheric anomaly, due to lightning, maybe. What I just realized is that Seentia did not provide a report; and there have been a few interruptions to our bi-ped EM wave feeds. Oddly, the outages can last for hours on several frequencies."

Jaak looked at Kiln perplexed.

"Which frequencies are we seeing interruptions in?"

Kiln experienced an atypical moment of physical agitation as a thought came to light.

"Sir. It's their media outlets. I asked Seentia for an explanation and they passed it off as poor human tech. But, I, I could never, would never think they would withhold information from the other clans. Not Seentia. Wait. General, I have grievously erred."

Jaak quickly eased the soldier's mind. "At ease, Major. I don't think any of us would have suspected that level of play here. Have you checked our sensors in their intel center?"

Kiln trembled but quickly controlled himself. "Sir, that is one of the few rooms we don't have sensors in, for obvious reasons."

Jaak looked down at his desk before raising his eyes again to face Kiln. "I have seen plenty of footage of Mota entering that space. Even as Libur's aide, it does seem excessive. You're going to need to befriend her. And, we may be able to gather something from Fugax. Just be careful with him. If he is falling in love with Mota, it could backfire on us."

"I have an idea," Kiln replied. "You asked me to train Fugax in self-defense. So, why not stage a demonstration with him in such a way that Mota will notice."

Video feed continued to draw the General's attention away from the conversation for brief periods. On his screen he saw Mota leave the Seentia Intelligence Center. His eyes were bemused as he pointed out the feed to Kiln.

"I am not quite sure I follow you. How will this help us learn about Mota?"

With renewed confidence after having felt as a failure just prior, Kiln spoke with a slight smile on his beak. "Sir I believe that Mota has gone rogue."

"So," Jaak retorted. "What does that have to do with anything?"

"Sir, if I may. If Mota is making her own play for power, then she is likely relying solely on her wits. We just need to hint at Elder Libur about her activities. Assuming he applies some pressure, that could force her to trust in Fugax more, especially if we can make him seem stronger and more popular."

It was Jaak's turn to widen his eyes. Indeed, young Kiln was as formidable as he imagined he would be.

"Major, that is an excellent plan. I will handle Libur. You work on Fugax and make sure to boost his confidence with regards to Mota. He needs to feel as if he deserves to court her. As for the demonstration, I know exactly what to do. Plan on shield fighting with him. I am certain the Supreme Chancellor would love to see two warriors test out the latest shield iteration. The event will take place in one-half of a Seln cycle. You have your work cut out for you."

CHAPTER 27

Waal

Synthetic wood fibers from Waal's perch stabbed at him all night, hurting his sleep. He shifted his body in his nest and tossed about. His left wing draped down to the floor. Then his right replaced it, in a sinusoidal rhythm that lasted for hours. Well-manicured talons shuffled endlessly without respite, as sleep evaded him. Images of Eensul soon invaded his closed eyes. More than one full Stel rotation passed, and her ghost had not left him.

As fully mature birds, their parents now deceased, they were alone with just one another for companionship. He too, was an educated royal, yet she still failed to heed his counsel, often ignoring him altogether. She had forgotten that it was he that had succeeded in ensuring her appointment as clan elder. It was he that pulled the necessary strings that got her elected as Supreme Chancellor. Yet, she delayed in appointing him as her successor for reasons he was not aware of.

She also seemed distracted, mooning over that daughter of hers. Her parentage was questioned as Eensul refused to name the father. He figured it was some clandestine affair with a poor warrior bird out in one of the fringe territories. Despite her blue blood, she preferred to mingle with the servants rather than those of her own station. *Despicable*, he thought. If not for him, she would be nothing more than an arrogant aristocrat fawning over the rabble she loved so much. At least Kiira spent her free time with Saax, a veritable specimen of the best of the Quetz. Still, she was too much her mother's daughter. He would have to clip her wings as well when the time was right.

Now if only he could move on from Eensul. Why did her memory have to plague him so? She was a nuisance as a child and now more so as his personal spectre-tormentor. He shifted again and felt a piece of his nest jab the center of his back. He thought of that confounded nest of his. Everything was synthetic nowadays a product of his sister's ridiculous policies.

He longed for the feel of real wood fibers. He deserved as much, he felt.

Exhausted from the constant barrage of thoughts, Waal rose from his nest and dragged his feet across the warm floor rugs towards a plethora of medicines. After searching for a few seconds, he located what he was looking for. It was concentrated melatonin. One small pill and he would sleep for the next several hours. He plucked one of the small glowing tablets and popped it into his beak. Satisfied, he trudged back to his nest and plopped down unapologetically.

It would take at least ten minutes before he would feel the effects of the drug he just ingested. He feebly attempted to think of his breakfast, hoping not to see his sister any further, but she remained a resolute fixture in his mind.

"Waal, you always were such a little tail feather. How did you even ascend to your current station? Our maintenance workers are better qualified. I should go to tell Mother and Father that you wet the nest again. You are so immature."

Waal fidgeted slightly. "I am not listening to you Sister. You died, at my hands. Bet you did not even know that. Oh, and I will rise to be Supreme Chancellor, at any cost. Any cost."

"Wall you cannot rule a measuring stick let alone a race. Who are you fooling? Look, Mother is here to chastise you again. How many times is that now? Oh, who knows. I even lost count."

"She is not here," he replied softly. "She's not here. You aren't either. Leave me alone, red feather."

"Waal, there is no need for a sexist tongue. Don't blame me for your failings."

"I made you, and you are not that smart. You always relied on me for information and knowledge. You just passed it off as your own." His eyes grew heavier, and his words slurred slightly.

"Waal. Please. Do you really believe that? You were always

such a jealous little soft-feathered bird, afraid of his own shadow. Of course, I'm not surprised that you never mated. Probably afraid of subordinate little females, too."

"No!" he roared only his mind now. "I was not afraid of you, was I? I killed you!"

"Yes Waal, you did. But you could not even do it with your own hands. You chose to poison me like the coward you always will be. You are a coward."

Eensul continued to jeer at him as she was joined by his parents and even Kiira. "Kiira! She ignores me too. And, I am not afraid of females! I started dating the most beautiful bird in all the caves of the Quetz."

"She's using you Waal. She's chosen your own weakling aide as her mate. Over you, Waal. Over you…"

Waal tried to fight the cacophony of voices and succeeded when the drug he consumed finally won over. The many colorful faces that ridiculed him were replaced by the tranquility of an ebon abyss.

CHAPTER 28

Akeela

"Everything will be just fine," Akeela said aloud to herself. As Kiira's guardian, the safety of the Supreme Chancellor was on the forefront of her mind; but today, a feeling of despair gnawed at her. She conducted system checks, security protocol assessments, and sensor reviews. But, nothing satiated her unease. She even spoke with Major Kiln via a secure channel for his own assessment. For the moment everything seemed normal. Kiira was only a few meters away and did not have any plans to be apart from her. Akeela's wings flicked about as if trying to swat an invisible gnat. Her talons even clicked on the hard floor of her office every few seconds. It was all in her head and probably just her subconscious brain acting out. She calmed herself with metered breathing to ease her worries.

The warrior's red wings fidgeted slightly as she reviewed the security concerns brought up by Waal for the shield demonstration that was to take place the following evening. Non-royal Quetz were granted permission by Kiira to be in attendance. Kiira figured they could use some much-needed entertainment, considering the stress put on them to depart Terr in the following Stel rotations. Waal wanted to ensure that all members of the royal court flank his niece just in case a rebellion would occur. "What rebellion would that be, Waal? There has not been an uprising since the Middle Ages," Akeela muttered to herself. Still, the elder Quetz had a good point. Kiira needed to be protected at all costs. She would, of course, ensure that Kiira wears a hidden armor-bearing wristlet.

Waal's plan included a detailed sitting arrangement for the royal court. Kiira's allies would immediately be on either side of her, with the Socran to her left and the Stora on her right. To the far right were the Draconem, and the Seentia to the far left. Oddly, each of the remaining elder's aides were given spots just behind the Supreme Chancellor. "The logic," Waal argued, "is to provide resolution to any immediate request Kiira may have of any of the clan elders, without pressuring her with any potential political discussions they may want to have with one another." It was another of Waal's preposterous ideas. But, only two of the aides, Mota and Kwentas, Lün's gorgeous mase aide, would sit by Kiira. Kiln and Fugax were going to be the center of attention in the armored battle. What Akeela further did not approve of was her appointed station more than ten meters away, standing by Waal. That was not acceptable. She quickly modified the plan in preparation for Kiira's approval. She would sit by her ward's side. Period.

Feeling a bit more settled, Akeela's mind went to the demonstration. It would be good to see the combat from a distance and learn from the techniques they would display. She did not know why Fugax was participating, or how he even obtained permission from Waal, but the idea of a fledgling combatant intrigued her. If Fugax could learn to fight, then so could any of the members of her race.

A loud grumbling noise erupted from Akeela's stomach signaling her that it was time for her supper. With the security plan in her taloned hands, she stood up and smartly walked over to Kiira's office, where she found her napping by her desk.

"She was young and needed her sleep," she thought. "Besides, stress can tire out the strongest amongst us."

A muscled wing placed the plan down on Kiira's desk before gently nudging her awake. "Hello, nesting head. Are you hungry yet?"

A pair of crystalline eyes peered up from a pool of bird drool that rested on the ornate desk.

"Gross," Kiira slurred out as she wiped the moisture with her left wing. "Yes, I'm hungry. What's for supper?"

Akeela retorted with a large smile. "So you do always think of food?"

"I'm seventeen, Akeela. Expect anything different?" she snorted a bubble from her beak as she laughed joyously.

"Teenagers. Nothing but trouble. As for supper, I think the chef prepared a mushroom consommé with roasted new potatoes and a fresh salad."

"Who needs salad if can poop on your own?"

"Always the comedian, you are? You don't know what it's like when the replicators begin to fail and can only produce synth bean-protein, their default setting. I hope you never learn."

The two beautiful birds giggled as they walked side by side to their dining hall, just around the corner. Fortunately, they did not have any planned guests. Even Waal was off to dine elsewhere. It did not matter to Akeela what old male statesmen did with their free time. They each needed to rest and privacy would go a long way to help accomplish that. Tomorrow, after the show, they would sup with the other royals inside of the great hall. The selected non-royal, would also enjoy an uncommon fare that night with large baskets of meats and roasted vegetables strategically placed about their side of the cavernous room.

The simple meal arrived shortly after they sat down. This is what Akeela preferred to eat, clean nutritious and wholesome foods. The sauces and spice rubs the elites preferred were not good for fortifying the body.

"Kiira. For tomorrow's event, I would like for you to wear a shield armor wristlet. We can try to conceal it as best we can. Something feels off and we should not take any unnecessary risks." Akeela's eyes pleaded.

"Akeela, I appreciate your concern, but what precedent will I be setting if someone spots a wristlet on me? When I'm surrounded by my royal court?" Kiira looked confused. "Is there a reason that I should be so cautious? What is it that you suspect?"

"Kiira, it's just a hunch." She thought of telling her ward just how squeamish she felt around Waal but refrained. Kiira thought Waal was her uncle. Telling Kiira about her suspicions concerning him could tarnish their relationship and that could spell disaster with regards to her safety.

"I just worry. You will be exposed to many souls all at once and that is always a safety concern. Regardless, I will be sitting to your immediate right, with ever a watchful eye," she admonished with a warm smile across her beak.

CHAPTER 29

Jaak

Jaak positioned himself in a finc marble seat that was several meters away from the Supreme Chancellor. He scoffed at the seating arrangement and wondered who decided to move his clan so far away from Her Highness. It was without a doubt Waal and his rusty gears that made that call. The Draconem, although not political allies with the Socran, were loyal to the crown with regards to physical protection. Still, he espied Lt. Colonel Akeela sitting by Kiira's side. But, he also saw the vain Dr. Mota standing next to Kwentas and behind Akeela. His eyes rotated back to the front where he expected Kiln and Fugax to soon emerge for the simulated battle.

He approached Waal three weeks ago to discuss Fugax's training. "It is nothing more than a bit of shield training. Your aide is a good friend to Major Kiln, and I thought it's a good idea for him to prepare to better defend you should some unforeseen event take place."

Waal, curiously, had slowly warmly to the idea and readily accepted the offer. What he did not tell Waal was that Fugax was secretly being indoctrinated by Kiln, and confiding in them both.

The internal lights from the ceiling of the large cavernous room dimmed only around the spectators, giving the appearance of a well-lit center stage, where two warriors would soon appear. On the opposite side of the room, voices called out asking for the battle to start. Others crooned out ancient battle dirges. Birds also courted one another, lifting and dropping their feet rhythmically, while their torsos twisted from side to side, beaks bobbing in the air. The thought of a battle, simulated or not, stimulated their hormones. He prayed a scuffle would not ensue. Males tended to get worked up over available females, even though mating rituals could not result in hatching, unless approved by an elder. Still, it was another trait their long evolution had not driven away.

Jaak's eyes circled back to Kiira. She seemed happy as she chatted away with young Saax. Akeela, however, seemed overly distracted with the two young lovers and nearly knocked over her drinking chalice. These vessels were seldom used and appeared only during extravagant occasions; but Waal had insisted that his niece's first public appearance was a good enough reason for the formal eating and drinking ware. Jaak only saw Mota's robed upper torso, but she was also busy flirting with Kwentas. *She should watch out with that one. I believe that he is more than just an aide to Lün*, he pondered silently. Fortunately, the love-sick, Fugax was not there to witness it. What he did not understand was why Mota was so close to Kiira. She was Seentia. Maybe it had something to do with her dalliance with Waal, which he was aware of.

The music that played in the halls came to a stop, and the commoner's voices were instantly clearer and louder. Down two separate pathways, two armored Quetz warriors emerged and made their way down to the center of the arena. Voices cheered them on and erupted into a cacophony of grunts and ruts to almost barbaric levels, shouting "kertamen, kertamen, kertamen!" The smaller of them, who showed no signs of nervousness, was transformed into a fierce soldier, with dark blue scales shimmering across his entire body, save his head. Jaak, turned and saw an expression of awe on Waal's face. He would no longer think of laying a wing or blunt talon on the once fragile aide. Though, Jaak deemed that Fugax would likely loose his status as an aide, he had a use for him and would grant him asylum in his clan. Despite his small stature, he possessed other talents.

Kiln stood firmly in front of his opponent and signaled with a slight lowering of his head that they should both don their visors and begin the demonstration. A moment later and they circled one another with faux wariness. Kiln jabbed powerfully with a bony right wing joint, that Fugax easily deflected and then countered with a circling leg sweep dropping the Major to the ground. The crowd roared to life as Fugax sprung to the air aiming to subdue his opponent with a foot stomp. Just as the razor-taloned foot was about to make contact, Kiln rolled aside and shot up into the air with his wings flared out. Fugax slid back several meters defensively and waited for Kiln to drop to the ground.

Both back on their feet, they circled again, looking for an opening. Everything was rehearsed, but the audience was oblivious to it. Kiira, Jaak noticed, was captivated. He retrained his back to center just in time to see Fugax remove a hidden bladed weapon. He shot forward in a flash as Kiln brandished his own curved sword. The two blades crashed into one another sending flashes of enhanced electro-sparks into the air. Again, the spectator birds roared with excitement.

Jaak was correct in his assessment, as was Kiln. Fugax was not a weakling. With a little encouragement and personal training, he became a formidable warrior. He had already endured physical abuse for five years. All that was left was to learn how to strike on his own. Swords clashed as the two combatants danced about the floor and in the air. Over and over, they struggled as each sought to achieve dominance with their metal weapons as well as their appendages and beaks. Suddenly, Fugax feigned a slip and dropped to the ground. Kiln used his powerful wings to shoot up in the air, high towards the ceiling as Fugax regained his footing. First, it was a flicker and then a complete shut down. Kiln's shield deactivated without warning. He plummeted to the ground with one winged hand still gripping the dangerous blade attempting to fly and not lose his grip on the weapon at the same time.

Kiira and the rest of her court looked in silence as Jaak's aide plummeted down towards the hard cold floor. But, Fugax was prepared and swooped up and circled behind the warrior and grabbed onto him, slowing their descent until they landed with an inaudible thump. The room erupted with shouts of relief and chants of *eroas*, *eroas* Fugax. In their eyes, a new champion was amongst them.

Akeela could not believe what she had seen. Even though she reported to Jaak, she was not aware of the ruse he had coordinated. She, too, was in awe of the once fragile aide. Her throat dry, she reached to her right and grabbed her chalice and emptied it.

CHAPTER 30

Kiira

Saax walked with Kiira until they reached his family's residence and upon insistence from his mother, left Akeela and Waal to escort her to her own home without him. Kiira's jubilant demeanor was quickly replaced with exhaustion. It was well past new day and she needed to rest. Tomorrow promised a heavy schedule of meetings that she already resented. Akeela's eyes, however, seemed dimmer than usual. Kiira was well aware that her guardian did not sleep much, but the spark in her eyes was clouded.

"Akeela, are you okay?" Kiira asked cautiously.

"Yes, Lt. Colonel. You seem out of sorts," Waal interjected.

"The both of you should stop worrying. I'm just fine. I just need to rest a bit. It's pretty late and well beyond our sleep time," Akeela whispered past several yawns.

The trio reached the entrance to the Supreme Chancellor's quarters and immediately entered. Akeela did not conduct her usual inspection and instead went directly to her perch and collapsed.

"Akeela!" Kiira shouted. "Uncle, something is wrong." She looked for Waal and saw that he spoke rapidly and briefly into his communicator, requesting assistance.

"Lt. Colonel? Can you hear me?" he questioned. "Come now," he continued as his uncalloused hands grabbed the warrior's wings and began to gently shake them.

Kiira's eyes filled with salty water for the second time in her life. At only seventeen Stel rotations, she did not know how to respond and began to murmur softly as she stood paralyzed with fear for her dear friend. Uncle Waal was tending to her but as of yet was unable to revive Akeela's limp body. At once, images of her mother raced back to the front of her mind. From her hatching, she had bonded with only two birds, her mother Eensul and Akeela, with whom she had formed an unbreakable bond of trust and love.

Now, it appeared she would lose her as well. First, her mother and now the bird she had loved as an older sister was apparently gone. The ambient lights of the room dimmed as she heard the rushed sounds of rapidly approaching medical staff. Her knees buckled as she dropped to the carpeted floor and lost consciousness.

Physicians poured into the spacious room and at Waal's orders, first attended to the Supreme Chancellor. He demanded that the Supreme Chancellor's health be tended to first. After a steadied scan with a holo-imager, she was cleared, but a sedative was administered as a precaution. Waal next instructed the crew to care for the Lt. Colonel as he personally lifted his niece from the floor and carried a groggy Kiira to her room.

The senior physician, a face Waal was familiar with, cautiously approached. All physicians were members of the Seentia clan, but this particular doctor, attended only to royalty. As such, Waal had made his acquaintance on several occasions and found him to be, competent.

"She is in a coma, Elder Waal. We do not know the reason yet, but our initial scans tell us that she will likely not survive. We can upon your permission continue to provide her comfort of life until such time as you wish to end her sleep." The doctor's eyes were heavy with exhaustion, he himself having spent his evening at the contest of warriors.

"Very well. I will leave the decision to end her life up to the Supreme Chancellor, once she is ready to say her…" Waal was interrupted by heavy footsteps.

At once, several armored warriors entered the Supreme Chancellor's spaces unannounced and without ceremony, General Jaak at the lead. Waal spotted them and began to sneer before reclaiming his lost composure upon their unwanted entrance.

"What is the meaning of this," Waal demanded. "You and your soldiers were not requested, General!"

Jaak did not refrain from imposing his dominance. "If you recall, Elder Waal, it is protocol for security to accompany physician staff whenever a medical emergency is made within the vicinity of the Supreme Chancellor, or have you so easily forgotten?" Jaak spat his words out towards his nemesis. He decided to ignore Waal and instead questioned the highly respected medical doctor.

"And where is the Supreme Chancellor? What is her status," he roared. But, before the aging bird could respond, Waal interjected.

"She is fine. I personally carried her to her private room and put her to bed. The shock of losing her guardian so suddenly caused her to pass out. The good physician has already cleared her," he spoke through gritted teeth.

Jaak trained his attention back to the doctor who had administered to him as well in the past. "Doctor," he began. "How is the Supreme Chancellor?" He leveled his steel eyes on the male bird and instantly drew his respect.

"It is as Elder Waal claims. She is fine and needs only her rest. She was also administered a sedative to help with her sleep tonight."

"And what of Lt. Colonel Akeela? She is one of my trusted warriors." Jaak was careful to hide his real concern over her.

"We don't know what happened to her. Some sort of toxin or virus. As of now, we only know that she will likely not survive and will remain in a coma until such time that the order to terminate her life is given."

Jaak kept a stoic appearance. He looked to his reaction team of very capable warriors and gave an imperceptible signal. Immediately they rushed the area and began a thorough safety inspection.

Waal seethed. "What is the meaning of this General? You and your group of brutes have no authority in here."

"Doctor." Jaak turned first to the physician. Attend to the Lt. Colonel in your hospital and ensure she has your best doctors ministering to her. On your way now."

Waal's feathers shivered as his anger rose, but Jaak paid no heed. "Elder Waal, I have every right. Ultimately, I am in charge of the Supreme Chancellor's safety. Per edict MCMLXXIV, subsection alpha V, if any attempt, successful or not, is made on the Supreme Chancellor or any of his or her immediate staff and family, the head of security, which is me, shall make all attempts possible to protect His or Her Excellency's house until such time as he or she sees fit that all is safe."

"I assume," Jaak continued, "that you would be well aware of these protocols since your sister was possibly murdered just one Stel rotation ago."

"You are a brute that cannot be trusted and an enemy to my clan and family."

"Aah, yes," Jaak retorted. "Again you forget that despite our political disinclinations, my clan is sworn to protect Her Excellency's life at any cost. Our loyalty has remained intact."

"You are no more loyal…"

Jaak's eyes burned as he interrupted his political foe. "You are dismissed from these premises, Elder Waal. You can leave of your own accord, or one of my subordinates will escort you out. Your choice. But either way, I will act as the Supreme Chancellor's personal guard until I appoint another one."

Waal thought of striking the General across the face. He would likely miss and be painfully subdued, he thought, so instead mumbled his concerns for Kiira and said that he would return first thing in the morning to check up on her.

"Well as she is your niece, and you are her legal guardian, I will see to it that you are allowed admittance, under watchful eye, of course. Good evening, Waal."

Part 2

CHAPTER 1

Quetz Headquarters, Seentia Intelligence Center

Subj: Intercepted U. S. Navy classified message to the Secretary of the Navy

Status: Guarded. For Dr. Mota only.

Secretary,

Perimeter scan of Mount Rainier completed via autonomous drones. Our suspicions proved correct. An invisible barrier of unknown origin fully envelops the mountain from its base to its peak at a distance of one-half a nautical mile. Drone sensors indicate that the field is impenetrable at high velocities but passable at lower speeds.

With your permission, we would like to activate project Trochilidae. The test pilot for this class of Fighter/Attack jet has volunteered to execute the mission. With his knowledge of the avionic systems as pilot and development engineer, he is the most qualified person to fly the aircraft. An NDA has already been signed along with acknowledgment that any mishap will be treated as human error.

Mission execution will commence in one month's time, on the second of January, in order to ensure minimal civilian presence in the vicinity of the mountain. As a precaution, we would like to have all road access points under our control. Highly recommend that local law enforcement not play a role other than assistance with any trespassers at the forest perimeter.

Very Respectfully,

Admiral K. G. Korn

CHAPTER 2

Kiira

Every bone of her body ached, and her muscles were like gelatin. Despite her exhaustion, she felt a strong urge to open her eyes and face her reality. Akeela would be upset if she slept in and missed practice. Without hesitation and despite her soreness, she sprung off of her disheveled nest and onto her tender feet. There beside her, partially awake was General Jaak. Fear entered her body as she felt for a wristlet. *Where was her uncle? Why was the General here instead?*

"Kiira. You can relax. You are safe with me, so please calm yourself." The aging warrior's eyes showed concern, something she never anticipated seeing in him. Akeela held great faith in him, so maybe she should as well. She remained cautious.

"Where is Akeela? How is she?" she managed to utter. Jaak looked at her with a heavy beak.

"Lt. Colonel Akeela is in the medical ward under the strictest security protocols and with the best medical care. She is, however, in a coma and not anticipated to recover. I am very sorry."

Kiira reeled backwards on her feet but remained footed as her nest prevented her from falling. She quickly steeled herself. She would not dishonor her guardian and combat instructor. "What happened to her?" she asked more collectedly.

Jaak found himself in awe at how the young Supreme Chancellor fought to maintain composure.

"We do not know; but it seems that whatever took your mother's life, may also be at play here. The difference, though, is that whereas your mother instantly lost her life, Akeela," he said with a high level of compassion, "seems to be fighting it. How long she can resist, we do not know. But, it is only a matter of time, unfortunately."

"This is no coincidence then. Who is responsible for this? Why don't we know who killed my mother and possibly my guardian? I demand answers!" she roared uncharacteristically.

Jaak, who remained as calm as ever, looked almost defeated for a brief moment. He perked up his shoulders, though, and answered his chancellor.

"We reviewed all sensor footage from last night's event, as well as before and after Akeela fell. We found nothing other than aberrations in the video feed in your immediate vicinity. What caused it, we do not know. Elder Libur had his scientists working throughout the night to determine the cause, but as of early this morning, they have found nothing. It is being attributed to a random anomaly and nothing more."

Incensed, Kiira asked, "and you believe that?"

"Unfortunately, no. Libur and I have been friends since our hatching, so to receive that report is troubling to say the least. Supreme Chancellor, I would caution you to not repeat any of this to anyone. Feign ignorance as much as you can. Something is afoot; and I am afraid for you."

In that moment Akeela's words came to the front of her mind. Keep your enemies close and friends closer. Trust no one except yourself.

"General, thank you for your candor. But now, I must go see Akeela," she stated. "Before she passes."

"Of course. Your uncle and Saax are waiting for you. I told them to hang tight until after you awoke. Oh, I will be acting as your guardian until such time that we have found someone else for you. If my duties demand my presence elsewhere, I have already blood-sworn both my own aide, Major Kiln, and your uncle's, Fugax." Jaak paused momentarily before continuing unsure if he should press forward with the last bit of information. Instead, he opted to give her only a modicum of hope.

"Supreme Chancellor. With regards to Lt. Colonel Akeela.

It is my humble opinion that you allow her to remain alive with mechanical assistance. It is possible that she could awaken."

"Really?" Kiira asked.

"Hope must remain, Your Excellency. For without it, then what are we?"

Kiira swung a common robe about her shoulders while Jaak looked in the direction of the door. After she was finished, the pair walked out into the main hall and then proudly stepped towards her receiving office. Saax was perched, his feathers astray, as Waal puffed steam from his nostrils. The sight of the pair together, though, brought relief to Kiira.

"Kiira, my lovely niece. How are you feeling? Did the General overly frighten you? Just say the word and I will make him disappear."

"Uncle, he doesn't frighten me at all. You forget that Akeela held him in the highest regards and thus, so do I."

"Yes, of course my dear," Waal muttered.

Saax approached his friend slowly, and then, with her invitation, fully embraced her. Waal, surprised by his niece's comment guffawed with a broad smile as he told her what a fine leader she was to place trust in her political opponent at such a difficult time. On her command, the quartet made their way to the medical ward that resided by Seentia headquarters.

Although afraid to see her guardian in a state of weakness for the first time in her life, she pulled her shoulders back and strode down the hall with the air of a warrior. At the door to Akeela's hospital room in the intensive care unit, stood two resolute sentries. Kiira noticed they wore the robes of Jaak's elite group of soldiers, the Razor Claws. Beside them, Dr. Mota stood flustered, her tail feathers in a bunch.

Jaak spoke first. "Sentries. Stand aside so that the Supreme

Chancellor may visit with the Lt. Colonel."

At once the two muscled birds moved aside. Kiira nodded at each of them in gratitude for their service. She turned about and faced her uncle and Saax informing them, much to Waal's concern, that she would visit with Akeela privately. "She was a sister to me. I need to be alone with her."

Once the door closed, the unapologetic General continued. "Dr. Mota, what is the meaning of this? You are not a physician and have no need to enter these facilities."

Mota looked briefly to Waal before responding. She managed a wink at Waal as the two had entered together.

"I represent Elder Libur in these matters and understanding what almost killed our Supreme Chancellor's guardian is his greatest concern," she replied.

"I already spoke with Libur and he is fully aware that only a select group of physicians and nurses are allowed admittance. Are you telling me that he has reneged on his agreement? If so, please allow me to contact him at once."

Waal stepped in immediately. "General, there is no need for such as that. Dr. Mota is simply as concerned as we are. In fact, I asked her earlier this morning to accompany me so she could ascertain the Lt. Colonel's condition. We only want to protect my niece, er I mean, Her Excellency, something you seem to be failing at."

"Point taken Waal," Jaak muttered without emotion. "But no one, other than the medical staff that I have already approved of, will enter that room. Unless of course, the two of you want to convince the Supreme Chancellor otherwise." The General said through a large smile.

"That is preposterous. My niece is still a young girl who needs guidance. Who is she, I mean who are you to tell me about convincing who does what?"

Mota stood firm by the two sentries, not wanting to budge,

and occasionally glanced over at Saax, who, at no time acted put out. "I grow weary of you General. Fortunately for you and your grunts, lunchtime is approaching."

"Oh maybe you and Waal would like to dine in the planetarium then. I hear the ambiance is quite lovely. And, never forget 'Aide' that you are addressing an elder. Do you require a more formal reminder?" Jaak pressed.

Saax caught on to the slight and realized that something was maybe going on between Libur's aide and Elder Waal. That would explain why she was standing behind Kiira last night, he wondered. She would have been close to Waal. Oddly, he had on occasion seen her rubbing wings with Waal's aide. He did not like what he was learning and wished that his father were there so that he could openly discuss the matter. At the moment, he could not even communicate with him. Every time he tried to reach out, there was a communication error.

Mota left with ruffled feathers, as Waal and Saax remained waiting for Kiira. Unable to hold off his frustration any longer, Waal turned and faced Saax, ignoring Jaak's presence. "I have matters to attend to young bird. Please inform my 'niece'," he strained, "that I will meet with her for supper from here on out. If there is anything she needs, please reach out to me. She has my deepest condolences on her loss. And, give your mother my regards."

As Waal turned and left, Saax felt more perplexed. Even he understood that despite the grim prognosis, Akeela had not passed yet. He looked up at Jaak and spoke with sincerity. "Lt. Colonel Akeela always spoke highly of you."

CHAPTER 3

Saax

A political war raged in the black halls of the mountain's interior. A Supreme Chancellor dropped dead one Stel rotation ago, likely an assassination. Now the new chancellor will likely lose her guardian under similar circumstances. Saax thought of the uptick in visits by Elder Waal to his home and the many private conversations he held with his mother. Waal was the head of Socran clan, their ally. But Waal is likely hiding a relationship with Elder Libur's aide. The Seentia were known allies with the Draconem, not the Socrans. If this was a secret power play by Elder Wall and his clan, then maybe his mother was involved. And of course, there is his now sealed betrothment to Kiira. He cared for her dearly, but they were friends and still very young. Both his mother and Waal ensured him that the marriage was in title only until such time they were fully matured. He still did not understand the rush, though. Neither clan had anything to gain from an early union. Kiira, of course, just wanted to make her uncle happy. She also argued that there were few other Quetz their age anyway, so their marriage was likely to happen. *The adults know best*, she opined. Still, his feathers tingled when he thought of the chain of events that led to Akeela's demise. "Something was wrong in the state of Denmark."

A picture of Saax's father rested on his desk. He stared at the 3D image of Meetus and began to worry. For several nights he dreamt of him. He was on Seln Base and looked weary though still wearing his usual smile. He pictured him preparing to depart for home; but before his private vessel could depart, a large explosion shook Seln. He wanted to run to protect him, but his legs were gummy and useless. Screams filled his mind as his wings flailed helplessly. Each of those mornings, he woke up drenched in perspiration, shaking violently in his nest. *It's a dream* he would tell himself. *Just a figment of my overactive mind. Besides, this is likely a result of Akeela falling with her killer running loose. I'm just afraid for my own family. That's all. My dad is away from here and fine.*

He was due to train with Kiira in an hour. They secretly continued armor practice each morning. General Jaak was naturally aware and often in attendance. Akeela mentioned to Kiira that he had provided the wristlets. On occasion, the General would whisper to each of them a new technique to work on before excusing himself from the large room that served as their training facility.

Two weeks had passed since the combat demonstration and tensions remained high. A determination had not been publicly made as to who attacked Akeela, but Jaak had warned Kiira of Mota and Kwentas. They were closest to her the evening she dropped. Video footage was also conveniently aberrant during the demo. They were only briefly interrogated due to a large uproar by their clan elders. It was preposterous they argued. As there was only vague circumstantial evidence, Jaak was forced to cease his interviews with them.

Saax's mother argued every evening that Jaak was audacious and full of hot gas. He only looked for a reason to usurp the throne, she claimed. Saax continued to silently acquiesce to her ministrations. But, he never stopped to think of himself or his part in the overall scheme that was afoot. Over the past few months, he developed a deep loyalty to Kiira, not just as her friend and soon-to-be husband, but as her protector. Her life, he reasoned, should come before his. At the moment, he could not act as her formal guardian, but despite their age, he intended to relocate to her quarters once their marriage ceremony was complete. He would take residence in Akeela's quarters and protect his friend to his last breath.

He thought of Kiira again and wondered what it was like to have to give the order to evacuate Terr. It was such a tremendous decision to make and at such a tender age. He did not envy her at all but felt great empathy for her. He did wonder, however, the validity of the claims that Seentia clan made about the state of Terr.

With some time to kill before his workout, he opened up a terminal and began to read. He saw that the state of the ocean was indeed grim but not beyond repair. If it were corrected, the atmosphere would soon follow. What to do with the humans who ruined it, was another issue altogether.

His eyes poured over column after column of data. Saax applied a plotting algorithm and produced a clear solution to correct the acidification of the ocean. He thought that if he could easily have discovered this, why hadn't Seentia clan mentioned it. Surely the Quetz scientist must have come to the same conclusion? With a quick flick of a talon, he deleted all his research and left no trace behind. He would tell Kiira about it after practice, if she seemed up to it. Saax did not want to further upset her if he could avoid it.

The teenager went to his closet and selected his most humble robe, which to any of the commoners, was likely worth a half Stel rotation of wage credits. He dropped the garment on the floor and dragged it across the floor vigorously with his foot. Satisfied that it would infuriate his mother, he unceremoniously lifted it from the floor and swung it across his newly muscled shoulders before departing for the Supreme Chancellor's quarters. He knew that Kiira would approve of his ragged look.

He peered again at his father's portrait. "I want to be like you Dad. You are my inspiration."

CHAPTER 4

Mota

The ceiling lights were dimmer than usual, and the air temperature was a bit warmer than usual. Mota enjoyed the thrill of romancing a potential mate; and Kwentas was the most eligible joyride available at headquarters. Firmly built, taller than average, and with the silkiest of royal blue feathers, he was every available female's dream, and some not so available. As she flicked her wings gently from side to side and lowered her head, with her eyes still on his, Kwentas puffed out his chest and occasionally stomped his manicured talons on the ground by his gold-gilded desk, a recent gift from Lün.

Despite his frequent trysts with his elder, Kwentas understood that she was married and therefore, her wealth was not obtainable for the moment. However, the younger Mota was not only an up-and-coming political newcomer; she was uniquely attractive, something that other more senior birds had already caught onto. Regardless, it was only a matter of time before she too came rapping at his door. He looked across the obsidian desk at his guest and purred his desire to spend some intimate time with her. Maybe as soon as their duties were complete for the day. But, both Mota and Kwentas were always on the clock. He with Lün, and she with Libur and Waal. She was also spending time with Fugax. The thought of them together nearly caused him to regurgitate his afternoon repast.

"So, Fugax has been speaking quite a bit of you lately. Anything serious between the two of you?" He asked casually, not wanting to give Fugax any unnecessary credit.

"Oh, jealous are we?"

"Well, he is being lauded as a hero for saving Kiln. Lün mentioned that he might even be awarded the Medal of Valor."

At the sound of Kiln's name Mota's eyes flared up. "It shocks me that such a powerful bird as General Jaak would appoint a lower caste bird as his aide, especially considering his family's rather unfortunate past. Pathetic. It didn't surprise me that he nearly lost his life a few weeks ago. Probably forgot to test his wristlet before the event."

"He's okay, but I wouldn't give him the time of day outside of work. What about Fugax, though? Are you dating him? He seems to think so, anyway."

Mota was fearful of giving away her true intentions. She wanted a tryst with Kwentas, but she was not sure she could trust him; and her objective was to one day sit as Supreme Chancellor. No male was worth giving that up for, especially a dolt like him.

"Fugax is sweet and very considerate. But we haven't made any arrangements as of yet," she said as her eyes began to wink heavily.

Without needing another cue, the handsome bird rose from his perch and approached the beguiling Mota. With two powerful wings, he lifted the delicate aide onto her feet and pressed her to his muscular chest. Their beaks nestled together as rivulets of sweat threatened to pour wet their bodies.

A door appeared at the far wall of Kwentas' office. Standing by was an appalled Lün. "What is the meaning of this?" she demanded as she strode into the room.

"Working hard, or hardly working Kwentas? And, you Dr. Mota? Shouldn't you be nestled up to Elder Waal somewhere? I hear you're doing well warming his nest most nights!"

The elder's eyes blazed with fire at the outrage of a romantic tryst taking place in her spaces. Mota ignored her look and politely excused herself without addressing the comments. She figured the old bird was just jealous of her more youthful and firm body. The door closed behind her as her short tail dallied along as she strutted out into the hallway. For a second, she could still hear the guttural growl from the old bag. As for Kwentas, there would be time for him later in the evening. But first, she needed to attend to Fugax. His star was rising and she wanted to ensure she was there to catch it. He was perfect. He was kind and attentive, as well as putty in her hand. With a little help from Libur, maybe Waal would name him as his successor. A little nudging of her own, of course, would make sure that happened. Besides, Waal indeed liked his nest being warmed.

Half a Seln cycle had passed since the assassination attempt on Akeela, and she was still not allowed access to the medical ward she was staying in. This is despite her warming up to Libur. The old vulture was too busy tending to his duties to pay any attention to her. Unfortunately, the warrior bird was still in a coma. How could she remedy that when she could not see her, she did not know?

Tired of drama, she decided to walk to the Intelligence Center. She had not visited them in three weeks, and reports of human activity had come to a crawl. Maybe the sentries simply needed some invigorating. As soon as Mota entered the confined room, two Seentia workers popped to attention ignoring the drinking vessels in their hands, spilling recycled water all over the floor. "Imbeciles," she thought out loud.

"Dr. Mota, Ma'am. How can we help you?" the male bird stammered through bits of cornmeal coming out of his mouth.

"Relax you moron. Go get your supervisor. I want to know why reports have only trickled in as of late."

"Yes, Ma'am. Right away!" The frumpy sentry nearly fell as he raced across the room to retrieve his supervisor, who at the moment was sleeping steadily in her private office. In less than ten seconds, though, she ran out, disheveled, to meet her clan leader's aide and her new boss.

"Yes, Dr. Mota. Sorry for the delay. All has gone dark with the bi-peds. There are still some ramblings about the explosion of their aircraft, but not much else, aside from the intercepted message I forwarded to you earlier this week."

Mota's left foot struck out like a lightning bolt and tenaciously latched onto the supervisor's right leg. "What intercepted message? I have not received any such thing!"

Fire flew out of Mota's eyes as her foot managed to tighten itself further. Her victim pleaded with expressions of pain and forgiveness.

"I'm so sorry Doctor. It was supposed to be sent to you two days ago."

"That is my fault," one of the obtuse males stated. "I thought I hit 'send'. It's sitting right here."

"Bring it up now!"

Mota slowly released her razor grip on the supervisor, relishing every delayed second of pain she inflicted on the ragged bird. "I expect more of you as a female. Maybe I was wrong. Fix yourself and your pathetic sentries. Or, else!"

"Yes Ma'am. First thing."

"Now, brief me on the message."

The chill air did little to ease the sweat pouring from the trio of buffoons as they looked up at Dr. Mota, careful not to make direct eye contact with her. The female chattered away explaining who the characters were and her assessment of the message.

"I believe they could ultimately discover our home base. For now, it is likely that they think one of their human adversaries has taken up residence here, but of course, that will not last long."

Mota ended her seething as she took in the information. "It means we could be going to war soon with the bi-peds," she let slip. "Outstanding work. I am sorry for being so upset earlier. Despite the importance of the message, it works to our advantage."

The three operators looked in awe as she apologized to them, a thing they were not accustomed to since she was first appointed as Elder Libur's aide.

"Just remember. Not a word of this to anyone. You'll speak of this to me and only me. No matter what," she emphasized. "And, when it's over, you will be richly rewarded. Count on it," she spoke through a large grin.

CHAPTER 5

Kiira

Akeela lay perched on a deep incline. Her red-feathered chest rose and fell rhythmically without assistance. After more than a Seln cycle, the powerful and attractive officer had not woken up. Kiira's uncle had been remiss to tell her that maybe it was time to assist her passage into other-Terr; but she heard him speaking to the physicians on the other side of the wall, Jaak ever-present in their conversations. Privately, Jaak cautioned her about keeping up hopes. He also told her that he was doing everything he could to help Akeela.

As her guardian and mentor was stable in her coma and did not require any mechanical assistance, she did not see why Akeela could not be moved into her own royal spaces and have a medical team stay with her there. In this way, she could remain close to her at all times, and should Spirit Terr decide to take her, she would be there to hold her hand. It also seemed safer for her.

She remained by Akeela's side for an hour before rising to attend to the duties she was elected to fulfill. The senior doctor was still talking to Waal, and Jaak was still listening in and on occasion, making a comment about Akeela's care that he knew would infuriate his colleague. Kiira spoke with a clear voice.

"Doctor. Do you see any reason why Lt. Colonel Akeela cannot be transferred to my quarters if you provide a medical team to care for her?"

Jaak remained rigidly footed as Waal mumbled some words before his turn. "My dear, that is not good for Akeela. She should stay here where she is safest. Consider…"

"Dear Uncle, I mean no disrespect, but I believe that I asked the physician for his opinion," she interjected.

Jaak mustered all his control over his facial features to keep from smiling and laughing. His granddaughter was coming of age. Waal, on the other hand, was stupefied. His niece quieted him and in front of a subordinate and his most detested colleague no less.

Through tremulous eyes, the doctor addressed his Supreme Chancellor. "Well, Your Excellency, my only concern would be that should she digress she will not be in here in the hospital for us to properly attend to," he stammered.

"With all due respect Doctor, her condition has not changed in more than half a Seln cycle. Besides, if she passes on, I would rather she is close to me and not in a medical ward. And, I am aware of the risks."

"Well then," he continued, glad he was addressing his leader and not her uncle. "I will make the arrangements to have her transferred along with a permanent medical team."

"I will interview all of your team prior to their arrival. Anyone who will be that close to the Supreme Chancellor must go through me first."

Waal nearly growled at the increased influence the General was seemingly amassing. "Very well. I will also see to it that the space is properly cleared for the Lt. Colonel."

"No, Elder Waal. That falls under my purview as well." Jaak stared matter-of-factly at the statesman.

"Elders, please… General. I am ready to return to my hall. And, Uncle? Please attend to any questions that the doctor may have as he prepares to transfer over Akeela to me.

With a quick flash of her common robe, Kiira turned to leave the facility but waited for the General to finish his duties. She still did not trust him but instead recalled Akeela's faith in him to ease her mind. Political foe or not, she believed that honor, loyalty, and code were firm tenets in her ad hoc guardian. She also had no choice but to endure him. Yet, thus far he seemed anything but her enemy. So why did she continue to feel uneasy as if some string pulled at her?

"General?" Kiira kept her eyes trained at the far end of the hall they traversed. "Were you ever married? I have always known you to be alone." Kiira asked her question with pure sincerity, something not lost on Jaak.

"Indeed, many rotations ago, I was. Her name was Rob'n and she would have loved you. The two of you have very similar spirits." The General's voice grew dim as he spoke.

"I'm sorry. I did not mean to upset you."

"Oh, not in the least. I simply look forward to seeing her again someday. She was very special to me, and was filled with love and compassion for all life," he said through a generous smile.

"I beg your pardon, but what happened to her?

Again, Kiira's words were filled with love, and Jaak caught himself wanting to break down. He lost his wife, and then his son. He could not even acknowledge Kiira as his own blood. The thought that he might even lose her to an assassination had not left his mind. He had to wonder what he was willing to sacrifice in order to prevent that; and the answer was always 'everything.' If he could remove her from office, then maybe she would not be seen as a threat. She would never forgive him, as she would face a likely exile. But she would be alive.

"My nest mate passed away from an illness. She was always weak. I was even warned from nesting with her for that reason. But although her body was frail, her intelligence was as fierce as the talons on my feet."

The pair stood by the door to Kiira's quarters. Jaak paused momentarily to inspect the area before allowing Kiira inside. "One day, I will have to show you her holo-image."

Kiira looked up to her escort. "Then we must make the time to do so. She does sound like an amazing Quetz."

CHAPTER 6

Commander, Space Port Operations

Dark side of Seln

Progress report number two to the Clan

Construction presses forward as no further tachyon probing has been detected. Water extraction and purification continue unabated. Energy to matter converters operating well within specifications. The first tithe of ship construction is complete. Despite our successes, morale was ebbing. However, thanks to the Distinguished Lord Meetus, First Nest Mate of Elder Lün of Clan Stora, negative ideations have been curbed. His presence is spirit-sent. Only one individual seems to not accept her position here on Seln, Dr. Pulchri. Even with regular visits by Lord Meetus and myself, she continues to self-isolate outside of working hours, spending much of her time mumbling to herself. Her former lover has not had much success at reaching her either. A communication link to headquarters medical facilities has been established, but she disregards the appointments, claiming she is too busy and healthy regardless. I do formally request interference by her clan elder to compel her to speak with medical professionals. In the interim, her quarters are monitored around the chronometer.

This message sent via prime secure on tachyon wave beta-two.

Long live the Clan.

CHAPTER 7

Pulchri

Seln dust managed to make its way into her quarters, settling on the spartan furniture and smooth polymer floor. Everywhere she stepped, it was beneath her. Due to its dry and particulate nature, it made the floor as slick as grease. Adding insult to injury, her perch felt like it was made of burrs, jabbing and poking her no matter how she accommodated herself. The ceiling, though was emanating a strawberry glow, unlike the pure white lighting back in the mountain. Due to the amount of energy required by the auto-mols, camp lights were dimmer due to the use of more energy-efficient frequencies. The red light also made detection of their camp virtually impossible by any potential human probes.

The bony fingers of her aging hands ached from finishing up the job of manually manipulating all the necessary circuits on the replacement board. At least the job was done. All that was necessary was to receive the order to execute her mission. She thought of her pleasant husband momentarily, before images of her virile lover crashed into her mind. It was time to emerge from the room and rejoin the minute society. Maybe the base commander will finally get off of her back about speaking to medical. She also wouldn't mind getting her feathers fluffed after dinner. It had been too long and her disease was debilitating her body more every day. *Enjoy it while you can*, she mused.

Tired of sitting on her cramped perch, she stretched out her legs until her knees popped. After a few kicks of her legs and flaps of her wings, she was mobile again. A black robe rested against her office chair. Black was the color designated for the entire Seln team and was chosen to show solidarity of the multi-clan group stationed on Seln's dark side. After wrapping the robe across her sagging shoulders, she stepped out of the room and into the dimly lit main hall. There, a grumpy resident stood, shocked that the old scientist had emerged from her quarters.

"Good day," she smirked as she walked past him. "Odd place to hang about, isn't it?"

"Uh," was all that he was able to murmur as a rivulet of drool escaped his beak.

"See you at dinner," she called out as she reached the bend in the small hallway, never turning around to look back at him again.

The dining room was full, with only a few open seats available. Spotting a chair by the base commander, she asked if she could join his table. Like the appointed sentry, his beak hung open, bits of synth meat and veggies visible in his mouth.

"Well, Sir. By the contents in your gullet, I guess dinner is spit-roasted bovine and root vegetables," she said coyly.

"Dr. Pulchri. You are very welcome to join my mess. And, I must say. I am quite relieved that you have joined the living once again."

A few of the bases' more senior officers looked at her, stunned, as they were certain that they were days away from sedating her so that she could be sent on a fast track back to Terr. Fortunately for them all, she left her isolation just in time. Pulchri examined the short menu that was presented to her on a crystal tablet by a volunteer steward. Satisfied with her meager selection, she flitted her eyes about, discretely scanning the room. Behind the commander and two tables down, was her part-time lover, Vir who has locked his gaze right at her. There was a subtle hint of passion in his blue eyes. *Dessert would be served after all*, she thought. She understood that the community was likely aware of her tryst. But keeping the charade up gave her a lot of excitement.

She casually returned her eyes to the commander who was speaking about the status of the ship and the other necessities that would get them space-bound in a few Stel rotations. Thoughts of her orders filled her head as Meetus entered the room. *Odd*, she wondered. *Why would Meetus' wife order her husband to Seln Base at this time? No matter. Business was business.*

CHAPTER 8

Jaak

Jaak studied Kiln carefully, noting his eyes and posture. Several weeks had passed since the assassination attempt and Kiln's unplanned drop from the ceiling. He methodically tapped his desk as the officer gave his report.

"Thank you. You seem perturbed as of late. Is Fugax's recent fame rubbing your feathers the wrong way?"

Kiln dropped his head slightly. "No General. I am happy for Fugax. It's just that I am hiding the embarrassment of being saved by him. How much longer must I endure the jokes and snickering from the lower castes, not to mention my supposed friends?"

"It will pass, my young apprentice. Just go along with it, and for Terr's sake, don't let them think it bothers you. That will only egg them on further," Jaak continued.

Jaak seemed disturbed for a moment but quickly collected himself. Fugax was happily on leave from Waal's service to attend to and protect Kiira, while he caught up on clan duties. Being so close to Kiira for a full Seln cycle taught him about the unpredictability of birds. She was so young yet so very capable. If she should survive an assassination attempt, her leadership over the next several deca-rotations could be pivotal in the Quetz's survival. *What an amazing creature*, he mused.

He addressed a concerned-looking Kiln. "You have already sworn your allegiance to me. Now I need you to swear one more oath. You must carry a secret until such time that you must reveal it. Swear it, or denounce me." Jaak's eyes radiated with seriousness.

"My Lord and Elder. I swear," Kiln intoned as he took a hardened knee on the bare ground.

Jaak collected his thoughts as he stood up and looked down

at the Major. Kiln was a deeply loyal creature that he could trust even if he hadn't spared his family from working in the mines. The young officer remained patient as he subdued himself to his commanding general.

"Thank you, Major Kiln. What I am about to reveal to you is known only by me. This information is very dangerous; yet, I am compelled to inform you of it, in case something happens to me."

"Sir, I will die protecting you. Do not worry about that. Please spare yourself from whatever it is that is haunting you," Kiln pled.

"Thank you, but with the attempt on Akeela's life, I don't think anyone is safe here. Now, please listen."

Jaak took a deep breath and placed his left wing atop of Kiln's head. His left knee bent as he lowered himself to the ground and filled Kiln in with the secret.

Kiln politely interjected. "But if what you say is true, how do we better protect the Supreme Chancellor?" Kiln asked.

"To begin with, we will forego our plans to take the throne. Removing her from power may not protect her, regardless. Besides, I don't even believe we would have the support. My gut tells me that our allies do not have our back. Times have changed and so we must adapt. The Chancellor must be allowed to rule with you and I by her side. We will also need to sway Elder Lün's son to our side. That should be easy enough. He's clearly in love with Kiira."

Kiln secretly let out a sigh of relief. He always saw the magic in Kiira's eyes, even when he was a teenager and she a youngling. Deep inside his heart, his true allegiance was to her, always to her. And, now he knew her greatest weakness and felt his heart throb with the desire to protect her.

Jaak himself felt comfort in his decision to abort his previous plan and to give his clan's full support to whatever decision his leader made.

"I need to go relieve Fugax. I've had enough time with my other duties. See to it that you continue with a review of all sensors. And for Terr's sake, go eat something. You look famished."

"Yes, General. Absolutely," he replied.

Jaak rose up from the floor and adjusted his purple robe. The two military officers walked out of the room, with Jaak headed to Kiira's quarters and Kiln to the dining hall. Each for their own reasons felt it necessary to sacrifice their lives for Kiira should it be required. But first, they needed to discover who killed Eensul and who tried to kill Akeela. Urgency was growing.

CHAPTER 9

Waal

Thanks to that infernal bird's meddling, Waal could no longer beat upon his aide. Fugax was now a blood-sworn, devoted to protect Kiira, which meant he was beyond his reproach. And, because of his recent and continued combat training, Fugax's defensive skills were well beyond his own. Adding insult to injury, Waal's servant now stood before him preventing him access to Kiira's quarters while she napped. Such insolent behavior deserved punishment he could no longer mete out. Waal remained seated in the fancy waiting area surrounded by military zealots just outside of the Supreme Chancellor's inner chamber, his face and body perfectly composed as his heart burned with fire. A door appeared and the barbaric Jaak entered as his lemmings rose to acknowledge his presence, something they did not do for Waal.

"Aah, General. So glad you are finally back. Maybe you could explain to me why I am not allowed in to see my own niece."

Jaak turned to face the perched elder. "Waal, we have gone over this. While your aide is acting as guardian to the Supreme Chancellor and to Lt. Colonel Akeela, he takes orders from only me and Your Chancellor. Besides, I am about to relieve him of his duties, so if you happen to require his services," Jaak said as he raised his right eyebrow. He continued. "He is yours until he is required back."

Waal rose from his perch and sneered. "That rabble is being replaced as we speak. I will be sending him down a caste."

"Ooh," Jaak said. "I am so happy to hear you say that. I am making arrangements to have him join my ranks. A bit unprecedented, true; but, he is more than welcome to join my clan as an officer. As it turns out, he is a more than capable Quetz and would compliment my staff very nicely. And, as he would no longer answer to you, he could become guardian to the Supreme Chancellor until Lt. Colonel Akeela awakens."

The steam inside of Waal left at once, stunning him. His talons were being clipped at every turn. It reminded him of playing second to his sister. A moment later he retorted.

"I guess I'm truly the lucky one. Fugax is air-headed he forgets to lace his rag of a cloak. Besides, he was never more than a latrine cleaner. Oh, and I will see to it that my niece chooses her own guard."

"With your influence, no doubt?" Jaak a foot taller than his colleague looked down at him without emotion.

"Naturally. Now, I demand to see my ward. If you fail to allow me admittance, I will see to it that the other elders hold you accountable for the Lt. Colonel's tragic state. It was your responsibility after all to ensure safety for us all, and you failed. We could have you imprisoned in no time at all."

"Highly unlikely considering I am appointed by the chancellorship. I was never elected."

Knowing the discussion was fruitless, Waal attempted to barrel past the general but the three sentries enclosed upon him immediately.

"Don't worry, Elder Waal. I will see to it that you see your niece. Shortly."

After Waal begrudgingly retook his seat, Jaak entered the inner quarters. It was nearly a quarter of an hour before he was granted admittance to see his niece. Inside, Kiira was gracefully perched opposite of Jaak and Fugax, with an open seat remaining for him.

"Uncle, please forgive me. I was napping earlier and did not want to be disturbed. Fugax was simply obeying my orders."

"Let bygones be bygones, my dear. I only wanted to ensure your safety of course," Waal chirped.

Fugax looked to his supreme chancellor and after receiving a small nod, rose up and left the room without acknowledging his elder, something Waal vowed to correct through some covert machination. Kiira looked up at her uncle through heavy eyes.

"Tell me Uncle. How have you been?"

Abhorring the fact Jaak was in the room, Waal deflected. "My dear, I am only concerned for you and Akeela. I pray every night to Spirit Terr to either fully restore her or guide her to the after Terr. My heart breaks for her.

"Thank you Uncle," she replied. "If only we knew who would want to hurt her? She has done nothing but protect me throughout my life. What has she done to deserve any of this?"

"She protected you," Jaak nearly said. But, he remained quiet, opting to listen to the politician, hoping to glean a clue.

"I understand, but we should consider giving her peace. After all, why should she be forced to suffer?"

"My guardian is in a coma, yes. But, so as long as she breathes on her own, that is how she will remain. My decision on that matter is final."

Silence pervaded the room for a minute before Kiira broke it for them. "Uncle, will you join General Jaak and I for dinner tonight? It has been a while since you have dined with me. Not since…"

"My dear. I will see what I can do, but I did promise Elder Lün I would visit with her tonight."

"Uncle, I am not in the mood to hear anything about a marriage plan. That will remain on hold for a good while."

Jaak smiled. Whatever plans that foul feather had, they were being stifled.

"Oh no my dear. We only mean to discuss Seln progress. Her husband is there reporting back to her daily."

Sensing an opportunity to do actual planning with Lün without her son's presence, he continued. "But, if you would like to see your friend, I can ask for Saax to dine with you. Would that be acceptable?"

Jaak secretly passed his approval through a coded toe tap, to Kiira. When it came to security, she now relied on him heavily.

"It would be nice to see my friend again. Yes. Please make the arrangements for me."

"Of course, of course, my darling. Let your uncle handle everything. But, now that I have seen you are well," Waal said, despite Kiira having seemingly aged a full two Stel rotations in a matter of weeks. "I must depart. I have much business to take care of for you."

Jaak cringed at the words Waal uttered, knowing full well that whatever Waal did, always served him instead. But, it was not his place to say such. Kiira may be young, but she was their leader.

CHAPTER 10

Saax

As much as he missed his father, Saax's thoughts increasingly focused on his friend. Akeela's attack seemed unprovoked and as much worry as he had for his clandestine instructor, he cared more for how Kiira was feeling for the Quetz she was so closely bonded to. Whether on his back asleep, perched on the floor, or eating, his mind never left her.

He was surprised by his mother's order to dine with Kiira at Elder Waal's suggestion. Neither his mother nor Waal knew that he and Kiira trained everyday but the idea of spending time with her in an open social setting came as a relief. General Jaak would be there as well, though. But he liked the General. Despite his family's dislike of anyone of the Draconems, Jaak was a patient yet demanding instructor, with a great breadth of wisdom and a sense of humor. Saax also sensed a sorrow in the old warrior bird as he got to know him. Kiira was more reluctant to trust him but did so slowly. Saax on many occasions also happened to catch Jaak's eyes peering over towards Akeela. Yes, she was his subordinate officer, but Saax could not help but feel there was something more.

Lün instructed her son to wear his best robe, a sequined garment of fine gold material with flecks of blue that matched his eyes. Saax thought it over and opted to don an everyday covering made of simple synth-leather, dyed gold that once belonged to his father. With a few minutes to kill, he carefully sat down on his fastidiously made convex bed, a chore one of the many servants attended to every day. With a quick warble, he activated an EM tuner and then chirped a tone commanding the AI to select human music. A list of several stations showed up on a holo-projector. Naturally, he did not know what the symbols meant or what type of music he would hear. He did, however, recall which symbols his father had introduced him to three Stel rotations ago on one of his rare visits. He chirped again and the frequency was set. An unfamiliar voice echoed in his moderately sized room. The name James Carr appeared on his holo-projector before it dissipated. The song was "Forgetting You."

The lyrics, "How can I forget you, when you fill my heart with so much joy," echoed around his room.

Saax caught himself swaying to the music's rhythm and felt as if he had consumed a bit of casaba wine. Another chirp and the lighting changed into a myriad of dancing colors throughout the space. The crescendo hit and Saax caught several beads of water falling from his celeste eyes, wetting his royal blue facial feathers. His mother would have been mortified, but his father would have embraced that bit of human-like evolution. He thought of Kiira again. She was his friend, but he loved her more and more every day, just like in the human song he rocked to. But, he would never be away from her. Not his Kiira to whom he intended to devote his life to beyond that of a piece of paper. He was determined to make sure that whatever scheme his mother and Waal concocted, failed.

As quickly as the music from the radio station started, it abruptly ended, as a message arrived stating it was time to depart for the Supreme Chancellor's private quarters for supper with the Chancellor herself, Kiira-Ave and clan elder, General Jaak Razor Claw acting as escort. The lights in his room returned to a normal ambient glow as he walked out into the foyer. Lün, who flitted about dramatically growling orders at her aide, for the sake of her present custodians, anxious for every detail to be perfect prior to Waal's arrival, spotted her son's attire. Her beak dropped open as her eyes flashed largely in surprise, but was unable to utter a single word. By the time she pulled herself together, it was too late; Major Kiln had whisked her son away in a flurry of blue feathers.

Upon entering the Supreme Chancellor's quarters, Kiln announced their guest and escorted him to General Jaak, who was seeing to Akeela's care.

"My dear boy. How are you this evening? Not too sore I take it," he quietly whispered in Saax's right ear.

"Just a bit General, but the pain is more a comfort than a bother." Saax smiled openly as he peered at the mighty bird.

"Very good. You will make a fine warrior, should the need ever arise. Mark my words."

The two males looked about uncomfortably for a second or two before Saax spoke up. "And how is Lt. Colonel Akeela doing today? Any changes?"

Jaak lowered his head slightly, pondering how to respond. "As of yet, she is not getting better, but nor is she declining. She remains stable. We all pray for the best."

"Indeed Sir. I keep her in my nightly prayers as well," Saax stated.

A small chirp on Jaak's wristlet informed him that Kiira was ready to entertain her guest. With a quick flick of his wing, Major Kiln darted to stand beside Kiira's doorway. As the wall dematerialized, Kiira stood waiting. Kiln bowed and then slowly offered his right wing. Kiira looked seriously at him before accepting. After two steps, she busted out laughing. "Why must we follow such archaic procedures General?" Kiira asked, as she now walked without further care for decorum.

"Your Excellency, I am just a humble warrior ill-equipped to answer such questions on formal etiquette. I accept you as you, so please feel free to ignore Major Kiln's wing."

Kiira thought for a moment as she espied Saax. "Nah, I actually like that part. You're a chill feather in my book Major," she said through a few giggles.

Saax nearly snorted at hearing his friend, who despite her station acted the child. It also meant that she was growing accustomed to the General and his staff. As they made their way into the dining hall, Saax noticed that Kiira shot an eye towards the room where her guardian rested. He knew that she spent as much time as possible with her and was still hurting. So much had been taken from her in such a short period of time. His heart reached out for her.

Reaching the formal dining room, each of the birds stood by their seat as they waited for Kiira to take her seat, except for Major Kiln who stood a few feet away, prepared to depart as soon as they sat. He planned on waiting in the adjourning room until asked to escort Saax back to his quarters. But Kiira, had other plans.

"Major. Would you kindly join us? It would be my sincerest pleasure if you supped with us as my second guest." A large smile had formed across Kiira's face as she addressed him. Saax, did not know the General's aide very well, but had felt at ease with him whenever their paths crossed.

Kiln attempted to reply. "I, uh, uh well, I…"

"The Major," Jaak said through a genuine laugh of his own. "Merrily accepts."

The room broke out into cackles as the quartet finally found their seats, Kiira at the head of the table, Jaak to her left, Saax to her right, and Kiln to Jaak's right as his aide. Jubilant servants poured from the kitchen area carrying trays of glacier water, casaba wine, diluted with fresh juice and sparkling water, and rendered fowl fat to dip warm amaranth bread in. For over two hours, the quartet ate and recounted many tales from their past. Saax shared many fond memories with his father who was currently on Seln base. Kiira, recounted the rare moments she spent with both her mother and Akeela at the same time. Jaak only uttered a few thoughts about his wife; while Kiln spoke of his family's struggles and the immense gratitude he had for his elder. Saax peered over at Kiira who looked at Kiln with great compassion.

A few minutes later, and Kiira signaled to Jaak that she was ready to retire. The General promptly signaled Kiln who quickly rose from his seat and attended to Kiira.

"Thanks for coming over Saax. See you tomorrow morning liver lips," Kiira said.

"Not if I see you first monkey breath."

Jaak and Kiln looked at one another as if surprised by the behavior of the youth. Grinning, they each shook their heads.

"Major. Continue to attend to Her Excellency. I will escort young Saax back home."

CHAPTER 11

Mota

Splashes of pastel pinks, blues, and violet colors transformed the once plain room that served as the elder aide's personal quarters within Libur's great space. Delicate silk throws, comfortable pillows, as well as an exquisite bedding perch and obsidian desk furnished the area. Despite her royal bloodline, Mota's family had lost much of their wealth in the Great War centuries earlier, forcing them to scramble for position once again. Dr. Mota, however, having reached the next stage of reclaiming her family's birthright, felt it necessary to lavish herself with finery so that her seniors would further recognize her station. In her gut, she knew it would happen. She needed only to ensure it.

With a click from a polished copper talon, her matching metallic robe noiselessly fell to the floor, slinking down across her back, pooling around her delicate feet. She raised her left wing to activate her EM scrambler, a new prototype her clan was developing. After a quick warble, she was invisible across the entire EM spectrum. And, every sound she made was also masked. The real benefit of this new prototype, though, was that it allowed her to activate any door and pass through it without detection.

The young and ambitious scientist slunk out of her quarters and into the main mountainous passageway. Other Quetz milled about, some of them holding private conversations when they thought they were alone. Mota, careful to physically stay away from them, snickered at her newfound freedom. *I'm in a playground of her own making,* she mused as her muscles twitched with excitement.

After a few minutes of walking stealthily, she arrived at her destination, the ornery and brutish General Jaak's set of personal rooms. She knew that the General and his popper aide were currently with Kiira, giving her full access to his spaces. She gingerly stepped about, momentarily forgetting that she could neither be seen nor heard. Remembering this, she eased up and moved about casually.

Various archaic weapons adorned the walls of the cave room. She thought it would be just like Jaak to squander his given title and prestige with barbaric implements of war. He was not brought up like the regular royalty, so she wasn't really shocked by it. His desk, however, was something even she envied. It likely cost a fortune that this buffoon saved up his entire life for. Once Jaak was ousted from their home, Mons Luz, she would file a form to make claim to the ornate object. His worn and meager desk perch, however, she would do without.

She was looking for any type of evidence she could use to revoke his position, and if she was lucky, imprison him. But, she could not access his personal computer node without a record of its activation. She would never be discovered, but it would sound many alarms. She decided to move on. On his desk, a crystalline pad lay dark. She could not access that either. In truth, she did not know what she would learn. She was looking for a "red herring," as the bi-peds called it. But at least she was getting a good field test of the new wristlet, and so far it was working as she designed it. The extra hours she spent studying engineering on her own were paying dividends.

Mota looked around a bit longer, anxious to get back home so she could prepare for bed and was nearly by the door, when it appeared on its own. Jaak entered as she quickly moved out of his way. Her heart rate spiked, forcing her to calm herself down. *What is he doing here?* she wondered. *He was supposed to be guarding the brat.* She looked at the old bird as he sat down by the desk she deemed to be good for him. Excited, she quickly positioned herself behind him, giving him a moderate berth should he decide to lean back.

The holo-screen lit up. Her violet eyes stared at the screen, disappointed at the mundane communiqués he was reading. *Patience*, she thought to herself. After ten minutes of nothing, an image caught her attention that sent her mind in a tailspin. Before her, were several video sensor feeds. Jaak poured over them with the efficiency of a master at security. She could not keep up with him, but before he left the sensor feed, she did notice something. It was feed of the hidden corner outside the chancellorship's quarters. That flea-ridden bird must have seen her testing out its ability to hide her from the other sensors. Her blood boiled. She was also infuriated that the General had access to all of the compound's sensors without her knowledge.

She thought she had seen enough when Jaak opened up the plans for his coup. Again, her heart raced, sending shivers of excitement down her back and all the way to her toes. *That bastard. He planned to overthrow the Supreme Chancellor himself!* She quickly snapped a static image of the screen with a tap on her wristlet, which she held at eye level just before he deleted the plans. The General, however, had more to show her. He had detailed accounts of how each of the elders planned to set him up. *So, he knows. And, he is smarter than I realized.* She took static images of that evidence as well, freely laughing out loud as she did so, no longer worried of being heard.

Satisfied, Jaak stood up and headed back out the door with Mota following him, curious if he would lead her elsewhere. He did. Jaak walked back to Kiira's spaces and spoke with a weary but happy Kiln.

"The evidence is destroyed. The coup is officially over," Jaak uttered quietly to the Major. "Now go get some rest, my friend. And, I'm glad that the Supreme Chancellor invited you to dine tonight. You earned it," Jaak continued with a wink of his eye.

Nothing had ever angered Mota more than what she just heard. She was in no way anxious to dine with the child leader, but she and her family fought hard to regain their former glory. Yet, before her, a bird of peasantry accomplished what she had not. Jaak disappeared into the interior spaces, and Kiln was gone. Certain that she had what was needed to bury Jaak, she made her way back to her room. She thought of telling Libur and Waal, but doing so would not serve her completely. Surely, she would see satisfaction with Kiln and more importantly Jaak at a tribunal. She understood that to achieve her goal, she alone needed to be the master and keeper of the new intelligence. One way or the other, it would help her towards her goal. And she could take over the hidden sensors the Draconem set up for herself. Knowledge of her soon-to-be power made her feel alive in a way she never felt before. The Chancellorship was now in her own grasp.

CHAPTER 12

Kiira

She circled her opponent with glaring eyes. Saax had resoundingly beaten her time after time this morning. Jaak showed no sympathy for her and instead growled at her to use her mind and not her emotions. She wondered if Jaak had trained Akeela in the same manner.

"Think Kiira. Your opponent is stronger and faster, but you know his skill set and his mind. Use that to defeat him!" Jaak barked.

Kiira saw a few bits of loose stone beneath Saax's dominant leg. She recalled a story Akeela told her about a match she had against a superior fighter. Kiira moved to her left, knowing Saax would read her feign and instead meet her on his own left side, when she shifted and attacked with her right. As she had anticipated, his left supporting leg slipped sending him to the ground. She quickly pounced onto his chest and made a cutting motion with her right hand across his throat.

"You got lucky that I slipped and fell," he cried with joy. "It's about time you got a lucky one."

Before Kiira could retort, Jaak spoke up. "No, Saax. That was not luck. Her Excellency spotted your left leg standing on the loose gravel. She played you."

"Yes, I did hippo brain." Kiira stood up and assisted Saax to his feet.

"You never cease to amaze me," he said through a partial smile. He rubbed his back for a second before resuming his fighting stance.

"That is enough for today," Jaak said.

"But we still have half an hour," Kiira protested.

"Yes, but I would like for the two of you to listen about fight theory for the remainder of the time. Sparring has its clear benefits, but you must also learn about why certain techniques work in certain situations and don't in others through question and answer. It will pay off more than you think. Strategy requires more than muscle memory."

CHAPTER 13

CLASSIFICATION: TS (AUS ONLY)

University of Perth, Perth, Australia.
Internal note from the senior tachyon researcher to the Dean of the Physics Department

All preparations are made for our final attempt. After a series of physical tests on all circuitry and software, we have determined that all systems are operating well within parameters. To ensure that optimal detection capability is met, all equipment was moved to a remote facility deep in the outback. Security has been arranged with the Royal Australian Army, with only soldiers with a clearance allowed on site for guard duty. The test date is set for the evening of Tuesday, March 01, 2022.

To further encourage morale with my team, it would be my pleasure to invite you to accept the final seat for this test. Should we be successful, your presence would be appreciated as we celebrate. All signs signal towards a positive detection. So, should you accept this invitation to witness history being made, simply reach out to my executive assistant so that your travel arrangements can be prepared.

CLASSIFICATION: TS (AUS ONLY)

CHAPTER 14

Jaak

The mountain lay dormant. Only a handful of sentries remained awake to monitor sensor outputs. Jaak lay perched snugly in his bed with only one eye closed. The open eye stared straight at the ceiling, anticipating any change in the lighting. Every hour he rotated which eye to see from, and every hour he wished he could seal them both. In the last month, Jaak went from daring politico to a weary relic. He recounted an old human adage. "Human." The word resonated within him. There was no rest for the weary, and his bones ached at every turn. *Our Chancellor is correct to want to leave. The hairless apes are poor stewards of Terr and she is beyond repair.* Images of Rob'n danced in his mind as he spoke to her memory.

His mind suffered from exhaustion, as too many recent conflicts weighed upon him. But he needed to protect Kiira at all costs. *There is no rest for the weary*, he recounted again. *Not if I am going to save her*, he added. Rob'n answered him.

"You still have more fight in you Jaak. Don't give up now. Your shoulders do carry a heavy load, but in time, you will set it aside as I once did. As your son, once did as well."

"You were and always will be my strength, my darling wife. Oh, how my heart aches without you to keep it warm."

The image of Rob'n chuckled lightly. "No one lives forever Jaak, and eventually, we will reunite. Take comfort in that."

"That I do, my love," Jaak replied.

Spiritual lights flowed from the ceiling down to his tired-looking face as fanciful images of him dancing with Rob'n filled his mind. He recalled how they flew together over the Ural Mountains, swam in the depths of the oceans, and sang to one another every night. *There is no rest for the weary*, echoed again.

"Will we dance again under a starlit sky?" he asked.

"Every night," she answered.

"You can touch my wings with your beak," she added.

"Only if you kiss my eyes," he responded.

For hours, he recalled the poems and dirges he recited to her as they courted, and how she smiled gently at his unpolished tone but loved it all the same. He proposed marriage after a lazy dinner on top of this very mountain so many rotations ago as the full moon lit up their faces with a vibrant and gray light, their hopes reaching Seln. Despite her acceptance of all his advances and promises to love him throughout eternity, fear overtook his young form. To calm himself, he consumed a bit too much casaba wine. Rob'n who did not care for it, understood and remained quiet.

"I am so afraid," he said to her.

"Afraid of what my love?" she whispered.

"I fear that Terr will come crashing down on me, squeezing the very life out of my withering bones."

"You are not fragile Jaak," Rob'n replied softly. "You are the most powerful Quetz I have ever met, and graced with a heart of pure gold."

Jaak's wings shook almost uncontrollably even after consuming two vials of the potent drink. With every ounce of courage that was left, he raised tremulous eyes to meet hers.

"I never fully understood the sanctity of life. I am a warrior. We fight and sometimes die. It was the way of my world."

"Was?" she softly asked.

"You see, I had nothing to lose. I lost my parents, was raised by my uncle, and now he too is gone. So, I was reckless quite a bit, challenging myself to several daring feats. I had nothing to lose," he stressed.

Jaak gulped. "And then I met you," he stuttered.

"And what of me, Jaak?"

"You taught me that love is worth protecting. I love you with all that I am, and will always love you even after every breath has left my body. I did not think that someone as coarse as me could ever love someone as magnificent as you."

Jaak's voice warbled. "I love you so much and cannot stand to think of living if you are not my wife and nest mate."

Jaak lowered himself onto his knees and bowed his head to the ground. "Inside and out, across all space and time, you are the most beautiful creature that has ever lived. Would you please join wings with me? I am begging you, to please be my wife?"

Rob'n was compelled by the genuine compassion that flowed from her courter. She slowly slipped both of her wings beneath him, and caressing his head lifted it up so that he could face her. Jaak, mortified of what she would say, was compelled to look away.

"You are the one and only love of my life, Jaak. You could have asked me the day we met, and I would have accepted your proposal, as I do now. I will marry you, and of course always love you."

On the opposite side of the room where Jaak rested, Akeela opened an eye briefly and then resumed her sleep. Jaak did not notice, nor did any of the advanced machines monitoring her.

Two hours later, Kiira and Saax entered the large private hall and walked up to a still soundly asleep General. They giggled causing the warrior to snap awake instantly. He fought to clear his eyes with numb wings, but his ears caught the voices that lightly snickered.

"We did not want to wake you General," Kiira said. "For a change, you were resting peacefully."

"We thought you deserved it," Saax added.

Jaak promptly stood up and apologized to His Chancellor. "My sincerest apologies. I don't know what happened."

"You just needed rest," Kiira said before excusing herself and Saax as they walked to the dining room for breakfast.

CHAPTER 15

Pulchri

A few feathers were scattered across the meagerly padded nest. Pulchri looked blankly up at the ceiling exhausted and out of breath from the second love session she had in two weeks. Her lover stood next to the nest, adjusting his robe and smoothing out his tail feathers. She did not care that he needed to rush off. He claimed to need to prepare a report, but she knew better. She overheard some of the other younger birds talking about a beak rave. One of them had managed to make a bilge wine down in the engineering spaces using scrap casaba melons. It could probably strip paint, but the youth never thought twice about getting intoxicated. She remained on the bedding as the young scientist departed after a quick peck from his beak.

Most other widowed birds would have felt at least a twinge of jealousy, and perhaps she did. But, there was no need for it, as long as he was willing to spare her a few minutes once a week. Besides, all preparations were made to execute the plan. Once she received the encoded message via a seldom-used engineering comms line, she would give the command to start the chain reaction. Not a single soul present at Seln base would have more than a few seconds to understand the repercussions. She thought of Meetus. It would be unfortunate if he remained, as he was always very thoughtful and kind to her. Truthfully, she did not understand why he was still there, considering who sponsored her clandestine work. No matter, the entirety of her race faced extinction at the hands of humans. Like her, he would find the peace the rest of her race would be denied. It was a kindness.

Rested after her evening workout, Pulchri sat up bored and decided to read a bit at her desk. There was an old human book she continually put off from reading. It was a collection of related stories written by an exceptional writer. His name was Chaucer; and the book was *The Canterbury Tales.* She stood up and walked over to her desk. There on the surface was a crystal tablet. She picked it up and activated the device. An easy glowing light instantly illuminated her face. She warbled quickly and the entirety of Clan Stora's collection of literature appeared before her. Another quick tone and the human contents were presented as categories. There was horror and science fiction, which seemed nonsensical. *How could science be fiction?* There was also romance, which mildly caught her attention, as human sexual relations were rather similar to that of her own race. Classical! Authors were sorted in order of the human alphabet. After another perusing another listing, she found what she was looking for. She scanned through the book quickly finding little interest until she happened up on a story called, "The Wife of Bath's Tale."

She took her time reading it, instead of doing the quick scan that the Quetz used to pour through documents quickly. Every word seemed to bounce off the sheet, drawing her deeply into the longest story of the book. Thirty minutes later and she was done. She found Chaucer to be a bit queer in his necessity to defend the morality of a woman juxtaposed to the blatant obscenity of men. While the Quetz noted that the human concept of equality between their sexes was shifting, it was still far from equal. She thought proudly of her two marriages and the joy that each brought her. She supposed that the Quetz were simply more evolved and had they continued to guide humans, maybe their females would not have endured so much maltreatment.

Satisfied, she deactivated the device and paced about the small room. The nest she was just making love on was disheveled, with synth garments tossed about. A black robe was beside the bed. She casually tossed it to the floor an hour and a half earlier as she rubbed beaks with her male friend. On the other side of the room, scraps of tachyon-capable circuits and wires littered the floor. There were bits of food by them as she ate and worked at the same time, mixed with small amounts of moon dust. A shrill note caught her attention at her desk. Her holo-monitor flickered twice and then went silent. It was a signaling mechanism that she devised to discreetly let her know of any incoming messages.

After ensuring the door was secured, the scientist approached the plain desk and activated the screen. Her fingers clicked a code on the holo-surface after the screen appeared. A simple message flashed before her eyes. Dry red feathers shivered across her back as beady eyes scanned the screen in anticipation. More than two weeks had passed since she acknowledged completion of her work without any confirmation from her contact as having received her encoded transmission.

Her bones were aching again, and she needed to rest. The carnal adventure had taken its toll after all. Her cancer was treatable to a limit she had already surpassed. The medication's ability to fight the deteriorating disease was rapidly losing its efficacy. Soon, she would be dead and would have to suffer through not being able to walk a few meters to relieve herself. She needed to expire sooner rather than later. She prayed the communique was what she was desperately waiting for.

The words on her screen were simple enough. They read: "Execute forty-eight-hour countdown." She breathed a sigh of relief.

CHAPTER 16

Waal

Sounds of woodwinds thrummed the ears of the two Quetz. Bi-peds called it jazz, Waal had mentioned to Mota, in passing. Her eyes met his, as she remained silent, constantly gauging her mentor and would be executor of her future rise to power. Waal spoke casually, well aware Mota was toying with the idea of passing him some tidbit of information. *If it were important, she would eventually confide in him*, Waal thought to himself. So, he concentrated on the erratic nature of the melodies that filled the room instead.

Mota wondered if she could trust Waal with this level of information. Despite his willingness to guide her towards ascension to the role of clan elder, she understood that it served his own purposes first, that being the expulsion of Jaak from the Quetz. The other two clan elders supported him in this matter. This, she knew as well. In her mind, there was one true power and that was information; and the individual that controlled it, could wield it. Mota had the technology to gather intel without being detected; and she just learned that Jaak aborted a plan to seize the throne. *But, what would Waal do with the information? Would he question the means by which she collected it?* It was too risky a venture. She would simply sneak into his spaces and deposit the data anonymously. That would put him in a defensive posture as much as it would be offensive.

Waal met Mota's eyes finally, tired of the cat and mouse game and spoke. "So, rumor has it, you and I are fooling around. How comical?"

"Comical? It was our intent. It allows you to see Lün without drawing attention and me to sleep with her clandestine lover. It seems like serious business to me," Mota stated matter-of-factly.

"Aah, and what does the traitor Fugax think of those rumors?" Waal let slip as he raised his eyes to peer at the smooth and glowing ceiling, with a glass of human grape wine from the part of the European continent known as France.

"You promised to never bring up his name," she scathed. "And, he does not ask. He sees you as too old to do anything. He thinks that you are nothing more than an old mentor."

"His mentor? I almost forgot. So, you are clearly holding something back from me. Care to share?" he asked.

The attractive and brilliant Mota anticipated he would question her look and was prepared to answer him forthright, with a faux tone of being caught unaware.

"Oh, I was only. I am sorry for that Waal. I was only attempting to determine if you would be willing to hear my good news. I wasn't sure, so thought of delaying. It is good news, though."

"Oh? So, you completed your part of the deal, then? That would be great news. But, let me guess. It's just good solid progress again?" the elder questioned, his eyes turning red with every sip from the titanium dioxide vessel loosely in his left hand.

"He was in a mood after all," she mused. "In fact, Waal, I'm done," she said calmly and with the look of a bird that just won a game of avian chess. She reached a wing into her shimmery robe and produced two gold devices.

A delicate talon reached across the smoked-quartz table and retracted back towards him, making an audible screech. The devices seemed innocuous enough. Waal just needed to figure out how to get them to Kiira without arousing suspicion.

"And how do they work?" he asked indifferently.

"Just pair them with a crystal tablet and you will be able to track their position and then deactivate them with a simple command."

"Well I guess you do deserve to move up in the world after

all." Waal's stomach grumbled, prompting him to look down on the table for a leftover morsel he had prepared for the evening with Mota.

"I don't understand how this will help us unseat the General," Mota queried.

"Simple, my dear. Once my niece and Saax have a mishap, the other clan elders will then have an excuse to unseat him."

Mota eased at not having to hear Waal mention his niece's name or title, but acted cautiously with regards to the plan only Waal, Lün, and Libur allegedly knew of. She, then, would be the scapegoat.

"What kind of mishap are you talking about Waal? I wouldn't want anything to happen to your niece and certainly not Saax. Lün would see to it that I'm boiled alive if she discovered I modified the wristlet that hurt her son," Mota said sincerely.

"No real harm will come to either. They will only be exposed momentarily. Just long enough to give us reason to go after Jaak's credibility. Besides, no one knows of the plan. Each of us elders has a role to play that none of the others is fully aware of. Lün is responsible for exposing our presence to the bi-peds, you represent Libur, and I see to anything regarding my niece," Waal continued.

Mota was concerned. She was the only bird in on the plan that was not an elder; and now she knew the general roles everyone played. She figured she was expendable and a liability. Fortunately, she quietly usurped control of Seentia's Intelligence Center. She had her own tricks to play as well; and with her new advanced cloaking device, she had an edge in evading a possible attempt on her life when this was all over. Without skipping a beat, Mota made a move.

"I was thinking that with Fugax's recent popularity, maybe I should propose to him. It could help me secure favor as the new elder for my clan once Libur passes on. What do you think?" she asked coyly.

"Are you mad? You can't stand him. And what would you do about Kwentas?" Waal seemed disturbed by the idea.

But, Mota pressed forward. "Don't be mad at me Waal. It's simply a political tactic. You, above all else, realize that. And, maybe there could be something between us. His star is rising after all," she said flirtingly.

CHAPTER 17

Saax

Three days. That was the number Meetus gave his son when asked how much longer before he returned home. Disappointed eyes stared blankly at the cool wall opposite him. He had hoped his father would have returned a week ago, but he guessed three more days was not so bad. He just wanted to speak to him about his feelings for Kiira. She was his friend and yes, their marriage was already arranged. But, he still felt awkward about being open with her with regards to how he felt when he was around her. Thinking of her made him smile though. Having dinner with her, goofing around, and even martial training alongside his friend was exciting. It also eased the soreness of not having his father.

Exhausted from sitting and doing nothing, Saax walked out of the room and into the main hall of his family home. His mother stood by the door next to Libur. Before he could pick up any of the conversation, the Seentia elder departed. Lün turned to face her son, a well-placed grin already in place.

"Aah, I see you have finally woken from your nap. Well enough. Supper will be ready in one half of an hour. In the meantime, follow me into the library. We need to talk about the wedding."

Saax's mother turned and walked over to the large room filled with the expanse of human literature.

The room's lighting was turned low just the way Libur preferred it. As a guest, his wish was accommodated. Saax shrugged his shoulders and looked to the floor as his mother took a large luxurious seat.

"Why was Libur here? His clan is not exactly our ally," Saax uttered as he peered at his mother.

"He was here to discuss the wedding arrangements, Saax, which is why I need to speak with you."

"What about?" he interrupted.

"Elder Waal was here earlier, and we both agreed that the wedding should take place as soon as possible. Tomorrow even," she claimed.

"Mother, that is preposterous. What is going on? Kiira and I are not your political pawns!"

Lün's eyes flared at her son's insolence. "Do not raise your voice at me boy!" she thundered.

Saax shot up from his seat and strode over to where his mother sat. "The marriage is off," he sneered. "I will not exchange vows with my best and only friend in order to appease some political tactic you and her uncle schemed up."

Saax walked away as Lün continued. "I am doing this for you! You ungrateful hatchling! You are just like your father, feckless and lacking in vision. Go then! Go sulk in your quarters," she spat venomously.

"My father? Where is he, by the way?" he asked by his room's entrance.

"You know where he is. Don't play games with me child," she chided.

"Yes. He is on Seln base doing nothing but wasting away on your orders," he shot back.

Lün strode across the room to hit her son across the face with her wing, but with a single step Saax closed the distance between them, nullifying her demeaning strike. Saax pulled her into his wings. Calmly, he looked down into her eyes. "I love you Mother. I just choose to no longer be your pawn."

The matriarch stood there stunned and limp in his arms. She figured that this could happen, though. Saax was too much like his father, despite her trying to keep them apart. Regardless, plans changed. She would have to convince her son to marry Kiira quickly. The how was what she needed to figure out.

After a few minutes of sulking, she shook her feathers and slowly walked to Saax's room. She signaled her presence. Not hearing a response, she waited a few seconds before entering.

"Saax," she pleaded. "I am sorry for not considering your feelings. I should have asked you about marrying Kiira and not forced it upon you. If you would like to reconsider, then we should sit with Waal and Kiira to talk about this. I was only thinking of you and believe it or not, Kiira as well. Marrying her would increase her standing and could offer her the extra protection her clan desperately needs. But, I want to respect your wishes as well," she said.

Saax looked up from his nesting bed, his eyes red. "Thank you Mother. I appreciate that," he muttered.

"And, I promise to no longer send your father out on diplomatic missions. You miss him, as you should. I am sorry, too, for what I said about you and your dad," she pleaded.

"That hurt," he finished.

Satisfied, Lün rose and asked Saax to follow her to supper. She said she would ensure that they ate without interruption and would follow their meal with a nice stroll to the planetarium. They walked and talked that evening, and recalled Saax's first steps and squawks, and how they used to play the hiding game when he was young.

Saax felt a great weight lifted off of his shoulders as he stepped back into his room exhausted from the trial of emotions he underwent. Lün, too, felt relieved as her ambitions were still alive. Tenuous, but not dead.

CHAPTER 18

Quetz Headquarters, Seentia Intelligence Center

Subj: Intercepted U. S. Navy classified message to the Secretary of the Navy

Status: Guarded. For Dr. Mota only.

Secretary,

Project Trochilidae is ready for mission execution. All mechanical and electrical systems tested satisfactorily. Our chosen pilot, call sign "Chanks," has completed all training preparations and has been fully debriefed.

All military personnel who will provide security are cleared and debriefed. Hand-picked state troopers will aid in perimeter security only. Air support personnel have also been debriefed; and will escort all manned aircraft away from the area and shoot down any non-DOD UAVs.

All personnel, military, DOD civilian, and police have signed NDAs.

We are standing by to penetrate the shield around Mount Rainier, upon your orders.

Very Respectfully,

Admiral K. G. Korn

CHAPTER 19

Kiira

Kiira may have been the Supreme Chancellor, but her eyes betrayed her innocence momentarily, as she looked squarely at Jaak, her eyelids quivering. She spoke privately with Waal a few minutes earlier, who seemed to be covering the fact he was upset about Saax calling off the marriage. Kiira, who was not opposed to helping her best friend secure his future, albeit by her side, was also relieved. She was not ready for that, even if it was only paper. She dreamed of someday falling in love and making a handsome bird her nest mate and husband. If that happened to be Saax, then wonderful; but she was not exactly willing to let go of all of her options. Besides, Saax did remind her of a bald rhinoceros.

"General, please tell me about her," Kiira pled.

"About Akeela?" he asked.

"No, your wife.

You mentioned her in your sleep that morning. I'm a little curious what she was like. How she looked. If she was smart. Loving?"

Kiira's demeanor was so sincere that the aging warrior easily capitulated. He had not openly spoken of Rob'n since his son's passing. As a child, Kaylor barraged Jaak with questions about his mother. His innocence could not be denied, so his father told him all that he knew of her, which was quite a bit every day that he was asked. Jaak lost all that remained of his wife. As his secret ally, Eensul, took in his granddaughter for her protection after Kaylor died. Maybe the day he could tell her about it all was coming. But, he feared the circumstances that would lead to it.

"Well, Supreme Chancellor," Jaak began.

"It's just Kiira," she interrupted. "Please. It's just the two of us, so please honor me by using my name and not my title."

"Of course," Jaak replied as his heart continued to warm. "Her name is Rob'n Tara. She was the most gentle soul imaginable; and a sharp intellectual," he added.

"Every time I wanted to thunder on about the state of our politics, she eased my spirit and then, more often than not, corrected me. It was infuriating at times, but she was always right. In fact, it was more her influence than my uncle's that helped me achieve my current rank and position. If it were not for her health, you may be sitting here speaking to her about me," he said smiling.

Kiira sat with her head resting on her hands. She felt drawn towards the bird she knew little of, other than hearing Jaak speak aloud about her while he slept. She felt it important to learn about her, for Jaak's sake mostly, as he clearly missed her.

"How did you meet, though? Wasn't she from one of the other continents?" she added curiously.

"Indeed. I met her in the Carpathian Mountains. She seemed to thrive there more so than here. Cleaner air, perhaps."

"Why didn't you just stay over there, though, if it was better for her?" Kiira implored.

"She insisted on following me so that my career would continue to advance. She always put me first and would not take no for an answer. And, Kiira, she always got her way." Jaak smiled again at that last bit.

"Yeah, I'm the same way too. I don't really want to marry Saax. Not now, anyway. We're still too young. But, if it would have helped him, then I would gladly make that sacrifice. He is my friend and I care for him."

Jaak smiled. "Indeed. Lt. Colonel Akeela mentioned how you were obstinate yet kind. You remind me of my wife."

"You really miss her, don't you? Because, I miss my mother

so much. It's like she's not really gone. Just on a trip to the other continents." Kiira felt closer to Jaak as of late, not only because he protected her, but because they both were hurting for loved ones.

"Words cannot describe, but yes. I know you miss your mother too. As for Akeela, do not lose hope. Although she is still in a coma, she does not require any mechanical or drug assistance. She's just in a deep sleep. Time will only tell, but I think she may just pull through. And your idea to relocate here was brilliant. You are making an astute leader, Kiira; and I am very honored to serve you."

The two birds sat and conversed for hours, first in her office and later over supper. Kiira took notice of how Jaak relished every last bite of a commoner's meal. Had she been able to read his mind, she would know that he did not really care for corn gruel. But, much of her lower caste subsisted on it, due to its high nutrient density. Only the upper caste could afford synth meats and vegetables. It was not an issue of technology, but rather a self-imposed rule of law established by the clan elders millennia ago. It was something she aimed to rectify. Jaak, disliked it as he was once forced to live off of it as well. Still, he ate without complaint and did so ravenously.

Kiira stopped eating and solemnly addressed Jaak. "I don't trust my uncle. I'm not sure why, but I don't," Kiira said cautiously, staring at Jaak's eyes as he paused his eating.

He was not sure how to respond but settled on the old adage: "Trust no one, Kiira."

Her eyes narrowed as she prodded the General further. "But, you know something, don't you?"

"I know a great many things but do not pass them on in order to protect you," he said.

"I don't need protection because I'm young. I can fight," she avowed.

"Indeed you can, but your mother's tragedy could be yours if you are not careful. We have not seen trying times such as these in a very long time. Besides, I did the same for your mother."

"What? But weren't you two political enemies? You even openly fought to overthrow her in the name of reclaiming Terr from the humans." Her voice rose alongside her passion.

"No Kiira. That is only what she and I wanted everyone to believe."

"What? What do you mean?" she queried.

"Well, you have to believe me that only for the time being, it is in your best interests that you do not know. Akeela knew and look where she is at," he hammered home.

"I simply do not like being kept in the dark."

"Agreed. Nor should you remain when the time is right. Believe me, I will tell you all in the near future. As for your uncle, do not trust him. Trust yourself and only yourself."

CHAPTER 20

Commander, Space Port Operations

Dark side of Seln

Progress report number one to the Clan

Construction of the ship continues per our schedule. Water collection efforts are also per our schedule.

Our issue with Dr. Pulchri has seemingly resolved itself. She has increased her time with the crew with high spirits and shows no signs of her previous reclusive behavior. Although we are pleased to see her doing so well, based on the recommendation of my medical staff, I strongly urge you to release her from this mission and allow her to return to Terr as soon as possible. The Distinguished Meetus is gracious enough to allow her passage on his private vessel when he departs early the next day. Unless you disagree, I will ensure that she is on board.

There is one other concern that we are currently investigating. We have detected some anomalous auto-mol behavior. Our technicians have reported strange concentrations of the autonomous devices in the vicinity of the ship moving in a large circle. As of today, they are not near critical speed, but should the concentration increase, then there could be cause for greater concern. I have assigned Dr. Pulchri to investigate. It is her area of expertise, and the work could keep her occupied as we prepare to send her back home. Should the situation worsen, I will contact you as soon as possible.

This message sent via prime secure on tachyon wave beta-two.

Long live the Clan.

CHAPTER 21

Mota

The blank walls of the small room were living murals. Prior to Kwentas arriving for their nightly ritual, Mota activated the internal holo-projectors embedded into the wall. Instantly, she was surrounded by the beaches of Terr, so real to her visual senses, she could almost smell the salt in the water and hear the gulls in the sky, things she did not care for. She signaled her personal computer to release scents of lavender and azaleas along with the sounds of the ocean breaking.

After the lavender hit her nostrils and released the endorphins she required to relax, she found that she no longer pined over Kwentas, though she was still bitter, as he could not make love to her that night. Instead, he briefly spoke to her about plans for their future. He left because he would never disappoint Lün; and she would not allow him to be gone for too long anyway. Lün always needed something. Mota knew what that something was, but remained quiet. Soon enough, she would be in a position to take all that she deserved. Everything. But, for the time being, she pinched her eyes closed and tussled about in her nest unable to get comfortable. No matter how she positioned herself, something felt off. First, her neck and then her back. Later, it was her legs that were falling asleep. Her wings ensued.

A vial of natural sleeping agents rested on a nightstand. Her eyes looked at it momentarily before deciding against it. She was lonely in a way that no male seemed to satisfy. No matter who she chose to nestle with, she always felt unsatisfied. The males were strong and passionate, but their ardor was only skin deep. She required more. More love, more vigor, more fire. A particular bird caught her attention about ten Stel rotations ago. She was too young then to act on impulse. The ramifications of physical intimacy at so young an age could have hurt her political aspirations. No longer. It was time she mates with the bird of her choosing. Soon, she would seize the title of clan elder and no longer leave her feelings to mellow in the shadows. She would be open about herself and damn anyone who dared scoff at her. Tonight, she hoped she could at least get a head start. If her chosen would have her that was.

She strutted to her compact bathing station and set her steam bath temperature to a moderate-high. Instantly, she was enveloped in hot-scented vapors. Seconds later, and the tension in her muscles melted away. Fully cleaned and feeling only a little sleepy, she stepped out into her room, leaving the steam to run. Her nest, she noted, was filthy. *It's filthy by her standard anyway*, she thought.

She gave a quick warble and moments later, her attendant flew into the room. A blur of bright red plumage rushed into the room sleepy, but prepared to serve her mistress. She was a mature unmolested female whose sole purpose in life was to minister to senior clan members with their every whim. Mota, however, had been attracted to her since her teenage years; but never caught the attendant's busy eyes, until she was assigned to her upon appointment as elder aide.

The scared servant kept her eyes downcast, afraid of any wrath her superior may have for her. A firm but quiet voice forced the mature bird to look up.

"My nesting sheets are filthy. Change them at once," she demanded.

Despite her age and station, the attendant was very attractive, likely due to genetics. Without hesitation, though, she flitted about the room as she ripped the sheets off and shoved them into a laundry chute hidden in the wall by the nest. Above it, she opened another secret compartment and pulled out fresh synth-silk sheets to replace them. Her blunted taloned fingers moved rapidly with expertise as she made the bed. Finished, she stood by the nest, waiting to be dismissed.

"Look at me," Mota ordered.

The attendant cautiously lifted her eyes towards Mota without expression and remained quiet. She heard from her co-workers that the new aide had a temper.

"Do you like me?" Mota asked with sincerity and warmth.

Mota's appearance was gentle, something the mature bird did not anticipate. Tremulously, she responded.

"Of course, Mistress."

"Tium, isn't it?"

"Yes Mistress," Tium answered.

"Tium, do you find me attractive?" Mota asked.

"Yes, of course," she answered, as her body shook.

"Please don't be afraid of me. I am asking for honesty."

"You are very attractive Dr. Mota," she whimpered.

"But are YOU attracted to me?" Mota persisted.

Tium was always drawn to the elder aide, but being well beneath that station, kept her distance as much as possible to avoid suspicion.

"Be truthful now," Mota warned.

"I am Mistress," Tium said. "Please do not punish me," she pleaded.

"You mistake my intentions. Given my history, I don't blame you." Mota met Tium's eyes. "I am asking, not ordering you to stay with me tonight. But only if it pleases you."

Tium was dumbfounded. She wanted to allow herself the honor of fantasizing of the beautiful Dr. Mota, but was fearful of even that. Now, she was given the opportunity to do much more.

Timidly she answered. "But I am no one and not worthy to even meet your gaze."

"Nonsense. I have always been attracted to you, and as

individuals, shouldn't we decide who we can love?" Mota pressed.

"Yes, Mistress." Tium began to slowly relax. "I would love to spend the night with you," she said with growing confidence.

"A steam bath is waiting for you. I will patiently remain here. Oh, you may use my name privately. But, in truth, it excites me that you call me mistress. Maybe I should call you the same."

Before Tium turned away to walk to the bathing room, Mota slowly unfastened a robe she had slipped on shortly after her own bath. It slipped off her shoulders, revealing a sleek and sensuous body of pristine ruby feathers. Tium barely controlled her excitement as she walked away, disrobing in the process. The blood in Mota's body boiled as she waited in trepidation for her new lover to return. The scenery on the walls changed giving a live view of the cosmos. She lay down slowly on the nesting bed. It finally felt comfortable. *Sleep will find me after all… but not yet*, Mota thought wistfully.

CHAPTER 22

Kiira

The female bird Kiira, thought of as sister and guardian, slept deeply. She had not awakened in a Seln cycle now. As much as the young supreme chancellor wanted to break down and cry every moment of her day, her responsibilities prevented it. She did, however, take comfort in Jaak's words. Aside from being asleep, Akeela was otherwise well. That bit of information was also a very well-kept secret. Jaak ensured this by attaching security pins on each of the medical staff. Anything they said or even motioned would be reported back to him. Even Saax and Waal were unaware of Akeela's bio-stats. The monitors attached to the warrior displayed false information. Only he, the physicians and nurses, and Kiira knew the truth.

Kiira took a small portable seat and moved beside the sleeping warrior. She chose to spend her free hour before supper rubbing Akeela's wings and legs, to help aid circulation. *This will help when she wakes up*, she thought. Kiira thought of her sister's age. She was old enough to be her mother. But, Kiira's thoughts shifted to the attacker. Whoever did this to her needed to pay.

The more she thought about it, the more she understood that Akeela could die if the attacker or an accomplice really wanted it to happen. Moreso, someone or some group wanted Kiira out of office. Prior to the attack, she would have attributed it all to Jaak. Now, she was certain that it was not the case, as Jaak was also fond of her Akeela. And, as she was now learning, she was his informant. That did not bode well for Kiira, but he was overall responsible for her safety. With her mother dead, likely by the same hands, he had a responsibility. Still, she was reluctant to fully trust him. Jaak seemed to be honest with her, but there was something he was holding back too. She felt that, when they spoke about his deceased wife. Yet, his words and manner were sincere. Kiira also felt the unrelenting love Jaak had for Rob'n. It was undeniable. *So why do I feel that he is deceiving me somehow?*

She continued to massage Akeela gently from head to taloned toe, hitting each muscle group until a chime sounded, announcing her dinner was ready. She looked for Jaak and saw him sitting at a small portable desk reviewing documents, wondering if he was ready to eat. He did not seem to be, when he looked up briefly to meet her gaze. Just then, Akeela mumbled. It was a singular syllable; but her eyes were cracked open. Kiira quickly turned and yelled for Jaak, who instantly dashed towards them. As soon as he reached them, Akeela resumed her slumber.

"I will call for her doctor. He had just left for his dinner. Standby," he said.

As Jaak spoke to the physician via a secure channel, Kiira shed two tears from each eye, as she laughed with happiness and a renewed hope.

"He will be here in one minute. How is she?" Jaak asked.

"She's back asleep," she cried. "But she saw me. She saw me Jaak," she said jubilantly.

"And, all you did was sit there and massage her?" he prodded slowly.

"Yes. Jaak, I need her to wake up. I really need her. She is all the family that I have left."

"Yes, of course Kiira," he replied. "I understand completely. But, don't forget to talk to her as well. She can hear you and your voice may be all the encouragement that she needs for a full recovery."

Kiira knew that he was being sincere; but she did not care if he was an enemy or an ally at the moment, so as long as she could get Akeela back. A minute later, the doctor entered the main hall out of breath and rushed towards his patient. He looked at the monitor, clicked a pattern of holo-buttons on the screen, and then examined Akeela. She looked to be sleeping just as she was before. No change there, which was good. The monitor now displayed the correct bio information. Brain function, normal. Heart function, normal. Lungs and all of her organs were normal.

"She is certainly only in a deep sleep," the doctor said. "And, is no longer in a coma. However, she will still need time for her body to fully recover. Thus, she may remain in a sleep state for a bit longer. Terr will only tell. In the interim, Your Excellency, you should continue to spend as much time by her side as your schedule permits. Your continued presence may be partially responsible for her survival."

"What do you mean?" Jaak asked.

"Just that Her Excellency's presence could be reaching Lt. Colonel Akeela's mind. She hears her and senses her presence. It very well may be giving her a reason to live."

The elder physician politely excused himself and continued on with a physical examination with various devices, always noting one thing or the other. Satisfied, he continued his conversation with the Supreme Chancellor and the General.

"Everything is perfect. I will instruct my team to modify her care to match her current turnaround. I will also tell them to speak to her as if she is their friend. Kind words may continue to help her. If there isn't anything else, I will leave the three of you and head off to address my team. They should be back here in less than ten minutes."

Jaak and Kiira both thanked him and said they would be waiting for the arrival of the evening crew.

"One last thing," the doctor added. "I would advise you to have your meals in her presence. The smell of food and your chatter may further stimulate her."

Satisfied, he walked out of the room after being dismissed, leaving Kiira and Jaak alone with Akeela. Jaak continued to caution Kiira and told her not to expect a quick recovery. "Should she wake up fully, she will be very tired. We will have to rehabilitate her," he said.

"Yes, of course," Kiira answered.

"Should I have our dinner brought out then?"

"Yes, please. And Jaak?"

"Yes?"

"Thank you for everything."

The aging General smiled largely for the first time in many years. He dismissed himself and left to speak with the kitchen staff. Shortly after, a few birds bustled about preparing a mobile table and moved it by Akeela, unaware as to why. Kiira, Jaak, and the doctor all agreed that the recent good news should be kept secret. The staff likely assumed that maybe the Supreme Chancellor's guardian was turning for the worse, and the Chancellor was spending as much time as possible with her because of it.

CHAPTER 23

Waal

Two gold wristlets rested in the palm of Waal's plump hand, as he seemed to weigh their technological worth by their heft. He had just finished testing them. Each time he depressed the button on his screen, the field shut off. He was also able to monitor their position. He thought of how he would switch Kiira's and Saax's wristlets without detection, and recalled that his niece and her beau had the bad habit of ripping them off after every discrete flight. He just needed a reason to be there after they returned from one. Then it occurred to him. She and Saax were no longer getting married. He could say that he was there to speak to them both and congratulate them on their recent display of maturity and their decision to wait on their nuptials. After distracting Jaak over a tidbit over Akeela, he would switch them. Fortunately, his niece was in mid-flight which would hopefully give him the opportunity that he needed.

He stuffed the devices in the pocket of his robe and strode out of his quarters. It was time to punish his niece and Lün's stupid son. Jaak would take the blame and he would unanimously be elected to be the Supreme Chancellor, with Lün at his side. Her part of the plan was due to take effect, and with her recent shunning of Saax, they would rule without worry. Mota was working on framing the General which would seal their victory.

Just then, a memory of his sister resurfaced. In it, she was self-righteous and condescending towards him. Many years ago, as children, she approached him. Waal had expressed his feelings about raising children to his parents. He did not want any, he said. Too much of an effort. His parents, argued about the importance of continuing on the Quetz race as well as their particular bloodline. Eensul, naturally, backed them, often jeering Waal, unabated. After the dinnertime discussion, she had followed him to his personal quarters, still pestering him.

"You are such an oaf Waal," she nagged.

"Leave me alone suck up," he retorted. "You don't plan on having kids either, or have you forgotten?" he started to heat up.

"No Waal. I said that I would prefer to help out a family by adopting a child in need. I would prefer that to birthing my own child. There is a difference," she clarified for him.

It occurred to Waal that his niece did not have much of a resemblance to his sister. He assumed she carried the traits of her father. But who was her father? Eensul purported it to be a soldier she had temporarily fallen in love with. Yet, the secret figure never materialized nor did she ever mention his name. Her excuse was that he was from a lower caste and that she did not want to embarrass the family.

No. Kiira could not be her biological daughter. But whose child was she? That he could not figure out. But, he did have Kaylor assassinated. Could Akeela have been with a child? She was a career soldier destined to be more than a personal guard, even for such a powerful elder. Kaylor dies and then she is made a personal guard to my sister's child shortly after. But, that would require Jaak's involvement, he mused. *Kiira must be his granddaughter. And her death is even more important to me now. She is not blood!* He paced about his room with renewed vigor as he continued to plot, still boiling over at his previous lack of insight. If Kiira was indeed Akeela's child and not his sister's, then he could convince Lün that she was not needed. Saax's desire to not marry was no longer of consequence.

For a moment, Waal pondered his blindness over the last several years. He paced the room back and forth walking across its length, avoiding furniture. The room darkened and the beautiful vista displayed on the interior walls faded into emptiness.

"Sister," he thought. "Your arrogance blinded you."

"You were always the fool, Brother," the voice in his head retorted. "Never able to see the world from beyond your own beak."

Waal pinched his face as he folded his wings in front of him.

Eensul, the perpetual tail kisser, dared one too many times to placate him. After their parents passed, she even tried to play the role of mother with him. She was barely three rotations older than he was.

"Who do you think you are?" he roared at the figment of his sibling. "You were nothing more than flea-bitten squab. How dare you patronize me!"

But, the voice implored. "Little Brother. Are you that much of a megalomaniac? Don't you see that all I ever wanted was to help you? I always loved you, even after you killed me."

"You couldn't have known that, Sister," he spat. "It was a perfect murder. I was even able to shift suspicion towards Jaak, albeit temporarily."

"Leave him alone, Waal. He never did anything to harm you. You know that. Let go Brother before it's too late." The voice was softer in tone as it pleaded with him.

"The Draconem were never our allies. And yet, you conspired with them to protect a hatchling. The hatchling of the female that humiliated me!"

"She never humiliated you little one. You killed her husband simply because you were jealous. If you felt any shame, it was due to your own ego. You are horrible, Waal."

"Leave me alone!" he thundered.

"As for Kiira, she is my daughter. I may have adopted her, but she is my daughter and your niece," his sister's voice proclaimed.

"No!" he roared. "She is the granddaughter of our enemy!" Spittle flew from his beak as he yelled into the vacant room. "You conspired with our foes!"

"Jaak was always a friend to me, Waal. As for you, though. Are you not conspiring with the Seentia clan? Are they not your enemy's ally?"

"I am doing what is necessary to protect our race," he said defensively.

Waal resumed his pacing as he flexed his wings out, his heart beating wildly in his chest. After several erratic gesticulations, he tucked in his wings and took a deep breath.

"No one trusts Jaak. Soon, he will be removed from office and imprisoned for life." Waal mumbled as he eyed his desk perch.

"And, no one trusts him because you led the other clans to believe that he killed me," the voice responded.

"Well, in a way he did. I always assumed you two had some sort of relationship. Why else would you have appointed him as the next ruler of the Draconem? He was not next in line. I always assumed it was more romantic in nature. But, now I know the truth," he said venomously.

"Listen to reason, little Brother."

"STOP CALLING ME THAT!" he screamed.

"What, little?"

"Why aren't you dead? DIE, DIE, DIE, you wretched old bat!"

The door chime rang. Waal found himself panting and halfway up to the ceiling, his light-blue wings furiously beating. He lowered himself down to the floor and caught his breath. He accepted his visitor. It was Mota.

"My dear, come in come in. I was finishing up some calisthenics. We older birds must remain active if we are to stay healthy," he said through a large grin. "How can I help you today?" he asked.

Mota nonchalantly pressed him about details for the next elder council.

"Such triviality. Why would you come all the way over here to bother me about that? You could have simply messaged me," Waal stated matter-of-factly.

"Well, I think it's important that we keep up friendly relations, don't you think?" she asked as she shook her lower torso, meaning to catch his attention.

Waal looked at her suspiciously. Could she have heard him ranting? He didn't think so.

"Oh well, in that case my darling, we will meet tonight to discuss the latest Seln report. We aim to discuss the issue with the auto-mols. Have Libur ready to explain the anomaly," Waal said ignoring her come-on.

Mota gladly accepted the rebuff and agreed to speak to Libur about the auto-mol issue. Once in the hallway, she looked down at the wristlet and felt the power it gave her. She just learned that Waal was not only responsible for killing his sister. He was outright psychotic, speaking to Eensul as if she was in the same room. And, Kiira was not his niece. She was Jaak's granddaughter? Or, at least that's what he is speculating.

CHAPTER 24

Kiira

The walls of the Sala Eld reflected live images of Seln Base. The proto-ship was centered on the main wall. A skeletal picture showed the elders the status of her build. To its right, the compound that housed the scientists and engineers seemed small in comparison. To the ship's left, documents of auto-mol progress, water reclamation, and methane consumption flickered. Kiira entered the room and glided to her seat. Comfortable, she addressed the room about her concerns.

She looked about the room eyeing each of the representatives before landing on Libur, who sat composed in his copper seat.

"Please explain the issue of the auto-mols and any updates," Kiira ordered.

Libur seemed almost unwilling to address his supreme chancellor but capitulated as if waking from a slumber.

"Well, uh Your Highness," he began. "We don't know what caused it, but the concentration is increasing steadily. According to the leading scientist, the ramifications are negligible without a catalyst," he finished with a casual flick of his wrist.

"Do you mean the same scientist that Seln Commander reported as being unstable?" she pursued.

"Well, but she is doing rather well as of late. It could be nothing more than a bio-chemical shift due to her advancing age," was his reply.

"Elder Libur. Would you have me believe that Dr. Pulchri is undergoing menopause at her advanced age? That is preposterous," she pressed with a raised voice no one in the room was accustomed to hearing from her.

Libur was taken aback at her tone and defensively mentioned

that Pulchri was ordered to return to Terr onboard Meetus' personal shuttle, to which Lün responded.

"Yes, Supreme Chancellor. I already spoke with my husband and confirmed that he will return with Dr. Pulchri, this time tomorrow," she said.

"Thank you Elder Lün, but that does not remediate the issue. We have an aberration in auto-mol behavior that is dangerously close to catastrophic. And, our expert opinion is coming from a scientist whose own behavior can best be described as erratic," Kiira pressed with increasing frustration.

"Elder Libur. You will see to it yourself and depart for Seln Base as soon as this meeting is adjourned," Kiira ordered.

"Uh, Supreme Chancellor," Waal interrupted tactfully. "That seems premature, don't you think?" he asked.

Lün's blue eyes drifted to Libur indifferently. They were only allies to remove Jaak from office, but historically, the two elders and their respective clans were on opposite sides. She figured he was unaware of her plans and thought of the auto-mol issue at face value. It was a distraction. Jaak on the other hand, studied Waal carefully, as his foe acted to defend Libur, who was until recently Jaak's supposed ally.

"Elder Waal. Uncle. To me, this matter is as serious as the reason it started, the demise of Terr. It is my belief that this anomaly was created in an attempt to sabotage my order to depart this planet. My decision is made, and Elder Libur will depart for Seln shortly," she said firmly to her uncle. "Is that understood Elder Libur?"

Libur acquiesced without complaint. He saw no reason why he should not go and decided that the trip would be a nice escape from his wife. Jaak, on the other hand, began to shake indiscernibly. Something disturbing was afoot.

For the rest of the hour and midway into the second, the elders discussed administrative minutiae. None of the elders asked for an update on Akeela, which eased Jaak. He did not feel like answering their questions. Satisfied that all topics were covered, Kiira asked for an adjournment vote. After all members agreed, they departed, Kiira leaving first, with Jaak by her side, and Waal sulking behind them.

The live holo-images of Seln Base, displayed on the wall of the Sala Eld, remained activated for an hour after the council meeting ended. A bright streak lit up the holo-screen. Seconds later, a gaudy but small ship emerged in front of the compound and then softly landed on the roof, before disappearing into the large Seln building.

CHAPTER 25

Saax

Due to the recent activity at Seln Base, General Jaak had strongly urged Kiira and Saax to not go out and fly. He argued that the risk was too great. Saax, agreed, as he did not want anything to happen to his friend, who he surmised was the true target of the recent turmoil, here and abroad. Still, his wings ached for adventure. Kiira had banned all nonessential flights shortly after ascending to the throne; but her life depended on her ability to defend herself and evade if necessary. As such, their outings had been kept a secret. But, as he learned from his father, information, no matter how well-guarded, will always be discovered in some way or another.

Everyday was increasingly more difficult. His father was due to arrive in less than twelve hours, and his sound advice would be helpful. Saax always cared for Kiira. She was his best friend. But, after demanding that the wedding be called off, he found that he was in love with her. He was no longer confident that not marrying her was the right thing to do. *What if she meets someone else*, he thought quietly. He saw her most mornings, though. It was their shared ritual to train and fight one another with and without shield armor. Yet, she was now invading his every waking moment. If he did not rub noses with her, he thought he would die.

He thought of his father and wished the twelve hours were twelve minutes. But things were as they were, so he settled on some light meditation instead. He breathed in slowly as he sat on his office chair and tried to relax. One deep breath in. Kiira's face pops up laughing. Another breath and she is smiling. Yet another, and she is blinking her eyes at him, enticing him to peck her. He cleared his mind and tried again, but her image would not relent. He was in trouble.

Dissatisfied, Saax stood up and walked over to the family library. The human capacity to tell stories continued to amaze him, even after all of the years that he walked past the multitude of literature. *How could such barbarians produce such refined and emotional written works?* He opted not to use the crystal pad to search for something to read and instead used his own keen eyesight to read the names on each of the rectangular volumes. For nearly fifteen minutes, he scanned the room until finally settling on a thin leather-bound book. Knocking into a weathered volume with the tip of his right wing, the hundred-year-old printing of Daedalus and Icarus landed into his hand.

He read about the plight of the imprisoned humans and how the older of the two studied the flight of birds and fashioned wings from their molted feathers. Saax found the tale odd, as he understood that man's eventual flight could never have occurred in the manner depicted. It would require a significant amount more of engineering for them to finally taste the skies and a lot less avian plumage. Still, the story captured his imagination. The two humans flew as if they were related to his kind. But, the younger did not heed the warnings of the elder and as a result perished at sea.

He wondered if Kiira would enjoy the tale as much as he did, and planned to recount it to her in the morning. He carefully replaced the satin bookmark in its original place and returned the book. Dinner would be ready soon and he had not bathed in several days. He needed to be on his best behavior, his mother warned. Elder Waal was going to be joining them for dinner. Why that bird managed to make his way into their home nearly every night, as of late, he did not know. His father certainly would not have approved, not that he had much say. So, he walked back to his quarters and stepped into a mild steam bath.

After he was done, he pulled a gold robe his mother had pre-selected for him. It had not been pressed. He thought of calling a servant to press it for him but thought otherwise. It would be a nice experiment to do the labor himself. After carefully attending to the delicate fabric with a steam wand, he donned the garment and entered the dining room. Waal was already there, speaking to his mother about the state of the Quetz.

"My boy," he called out. "Please join us," Waal politely asked.

"Thank you, Elder Waal," Saax replied. The words felt like acid in his gullet.

"So, how are you feeling now that the stress of a wedding is gone?" Waal asked through his veneered teeth.

"The wedding never stressed me Elder Waal. But, I am happy that my father returns home tomorrow. I hope that some semblance of normalcy will return along with him."

Waal scowled slightly at the words, as Meetus did not openly care for him. Lün interrupted with a more diplomatic topic.

"I see that you are wearing the robe I picked up for you. It looks very elegant on you. Don't you think so Waal?" she added, hoping a compliment from her friend would break some of the clear and unexpected chilly tone her son was using on her guest.

"Oh, yes. Very becoming," he noted.

"Yes, thank you Mother. I pressed it myself just now. What an invigorating experience," Saax said with some pride.

Upset at her son's behavior and Waal's clear disapproval, Lün again attempted to calm the situation. She clapped her wings and several servants rushed into the room, carrying trays of food. Waal, as their guest, took his seat first, followed by Lün and then Saax who allowed himself to plop down instead of gracefully lowering himself. Waal also aimed to easing tension and quickly brought up his niece.

"My niece speaks of you quite often Saax. The two of you have quite a friendship. Much like your mother and I did when we were your age."

"I was not aware you spent time with the Chancellor, Elder Waal. I figured with the General being there as much as he is as of late, you would steer clear away," Saax spat.

"Young man!" Lün exclaimed. "You will ask for forgiveness at once! Elder Waal is not only our guest, he is your senior and a clan elder."

"Yes, Mother," he said more politely. "Please forgive me, Elder Waal. I have been upset as of late, and my father is not here to offer me council."

Waal wanted to take the bait and thought of offering the young male some council, but saw it as a trap and decided to let it go. After all was settled, they tore into fresh venison. Lün had offered to treat Waal again to such a refined and costly meal, so as long as he promised to not cancel again. Naturally, he promised with his wings crossed behind his back. Luckily, the three Quetz sat and filled their stomachs with fine food that Saax knew Kiira would not approve of. But he had his own political games to play, and getting under Waal's feathers served him well, he thought.

CHAPTER 26

Human Report. Archives.

Some humans are noting the chemical changes of Terr, or Earth as they refer to her. Limited but widespread activity is spreading in an aim to reduce the emission of carbon into the atmosphere, reduce cement production, and minimize deforestation. However, despite their well-intentioned efforts, their governments have done little to support them or turn around the impact their race is having on the planet.

It has been noted that certain nations have gathered together and united, have declared through various accords, that they would reduce their climatic impacts. These statements, however, are empty, as they have done nothing practical to reverse the steadily climbing trend of carbon output and the subsequent greenhouse effects. Their words, in fact, are nothing more than political machinations. The elite of their race seek to further subjugate their lower castes through highly restrictive carbon reduction measures while increasing their own. These actions will bear no fruit. It is our belief that humanity will not subvert the effects of their lifestyles until it is too late.

Further, their desire to harness clean and sustainable nuclear fusion power is also without merit. Organizations such as OPEC and the large oil magnates that run it, will not cease to increase their profits at the expense of their very lives. This self-destructive behavior is psychotic. As such, only two options are available to save ourselves: flee Terr or destroy all of humanity.

Long live the Clan!

CHAPTER 27

Jaak

The fledgling warrior stood proudly next to his instructor, Major Kiln, as General Jaak surveyed him closely, noting the crisp look of the purple robe that covered the young bird's shoulders. In a matter of just over a Seln cycle, Fugax mastered the art of self-defense and offense. Jaak felt pride for the has-been elder-aide. He felt a faint chill in the air when he informed Waal that indeed, Fugax planned to relinquish not only his role as elder-aide, but also his fealty to the Socrans. The aging General did not sugarcoat anything when approaching the Socran elder. He simply stated what was going to happen. Naturally, Waal played it off as more of a benefit to himself. *He is useless*, Waal argued.

But, Fugax had proven himself repeatedly to his trainer and to the head of the Draconem. Thanks to the abuse he suffered at his elder's hand, he felt a deep sense of loyalty to those who embraced him. He fought and trained harder than anyone else, Jaak had ever known; and, despite his slightly diminutive stature, he was fierce and cunning. Day after day of physical and emotional torment by Waal, Fugax grew numb to physical duress and found himself able to endure large amounts of pain and discomfort. All of this, he channeled into his training, which coupled with an unrivaled work ethic, also thanks to Waal, he excelled and had even bested Kiln on several occasions.

Jaak retreated a few meters away. He cleared his throat and addressed the initiate. "Do you Fugax of the Socran clan hereby renounce all loyalties to the Socran?" Jaak asked.

"I do," he avowed with a resonant voice.

"Do you then pledge your allegiance to the Draconem clan?"

"I do," he answered.

"Never in my days have I witnessed such faith and dedication by a single bird to achieve what few can. You have mastered our defensive arts and excelled at tactical strategies. Moreover, you have already sworn by blood oath to place the life of your Supreme Chancellor well above your own."

Jaak paused momentarily as he eyed the Supreme Chancellor and Dr. Mota who acted as observers, Kiira as it was her duty, and Mota because of her supposed deepening relationship with Fugax. Jaak continued without the dance of pomp and circumstance.

"I hereby announce you Captain Fugax, head of my personal guard and leader of Dracons!" he roared.

Kiira and Mota acted jubilantly and cheered on the young officer. After nudging of wings with the General and then Kiln, Fugax made his way to Kiira and knelt before her, thanking the chancellor for her support, as it was her clan he departed. Jaak joined him as Kiln scurried off to attend to matters, after asking for his dismissal from Kiira.

The main hall of the Draconem clan was utilized for the ceremony in order to give Akeela peace as she continued in her discreet recovery. Jaak and Kiira did not want anyone to know that she had awoken temporarily. Currently, the walls displayed moving images of ancient Quetz warriors in training, marching, and even flying, urging Jaak to recall the day he too transferred over to the Draconem. He was born into the Seentia clan; but, after his parents passed, he moved in with his uncle Colonel Ferum. Like Fugax, he trained night and day in order to earn his officer rank.

After some idle chatter, the group of Quetz leaders approached an array of delicacies, a rare treat for the hard-beaked Kiira, that covered a large thin table. In front of them were synth proteins such as quail, winter hare, elk, salmon, conch meat, and emu. Various exotic fruits and vegetables were also present. Jaak spotted steamed purple carrots, a favorite of his, which he rapidly stabbed at with his talon. Kiira and Fugax swallowed several delicate quail eggs. Mota, however, played coy and pecked only lightly.

Jaak allowed himself a brief moment of repose and lightly

sipped some casaba wine. It seemed that all could return to normal. He just gained an ally with Fugax, Akeela seemed that she might recover, and the other elders seemed stumped. The assassination attempt, he thought, was not something they were all in on. Besides, he felt that they were out for him, and now that he showed his allegiance to Kiira, there was no need to attack him. Or so, he believed.

After the festivities ended, Jaak escorted Kiira back to her quarters, while Fugax and Mota departed together to their own private time. He was not sure about his new captain dating Libur's aide, though. His feathers still shivered whenever he was in the same room as her. But, Fugax had been dating her for several weeks now and seemed in control of his emotions. The new position further emboldened him, he thought. Regardless, he would keep a keen eye on her and her interactions. Sensor logs indicated that she often spent time with Waal, but it was only for short spurts and did not amount to the two having an intimate relationship. She did, however, manage to disappear on occasion. He passed it off as her spending time in her lavatory or possibly napping. He figured it was nothing to worry about.

CHAPTER 28

Kiira

Saax stared at Kiira solemnly as she giggled at him. After a few seconds, he broke down and joined in her merriness. Saax argued against flying today, despite his strong desire to do so. Kiira, on the other hand, needed the escape from her duties and worry over Akeela. They each wore their wristlets and activated them as they stood on the precipice of the mountain, on the side that faced away from human civilization.

"Ready dodo brain?" Saax asked.

"You know it, monkey butt," she replied.

They were invisible and in their armor, ready for some needed fun. Once again, they could feel the air shoot past their feathers as they free-fell from the cliff. Seconds later and they were arcing back up towards the sky.

"Play that bi-ped music," Saax said to Kiira.

"You mean humans, and what music?"

"Sorry. The one where the humans fly in those metal contraptions shooting at each other," Saax said.

"Aah, I think you mean 'Danger Zone!' I like that one too," Kiira pointed out.

A quick chirp and music filled their armor, resonating across their bodies, filling their ears as they revved up their speed. In their joy as they listened to the hip beats and riffs, they conducted various aerial maneuvers, such as loops and sudden stops in mid-air, before continuing along. Halfway into the tune, they were in Timber Creek, Montana, the scenery below them nothing more than a blur of colors. They eventually slowed down to only a few meters per second, in contrast to the music's tempo, to note the beauty of the terrain around them. A few hares scattered about the ground. A doe and her fawn rested lazily on a small patch of grass, occasionally sniffing at the sky. Even the insects seemed at peace. No matter how far out they looked, there were no signs of civilization. They were in a veritable Garden of Eden. Kiira closed the distance between her Saax, when their wristlets instantly failed. They were visible and without protective armor hovering over a narrow river between two rock formations.

"Land, land we're visible!" Saax shouted.

"Into that copse of trees!" Kiira commanded in response.

Their wings outspread, the pair glided down and alit on the moist soil to the left of the gentle river and felt mud making its way between their taloned feet, a new feeling they did not register. They moved quickly as their eyes surveyed the area looking for humans. *They could not be spotted*, they thought in unison. Certain that they were alone, both Kiira and Saax chirped various commands at their wristlets. No response from either. The devices were nothing but dumb gold. Kiira looked at her friend, and saw that he too was filled with terror.

"What are we going to do?" she asked.

"What our race has always done. Survive."

"Saax, we are out here alone without any form of communication or protection. We are sitting ducks." Her eyes trembled in their sockets. There would be uproar, primarily from the lower castes, when word spread that the Supreme Chancellor and the son of Elder Lün snuck out for a joy flight, and lost their cloaking ability.

"I just endangered the entirety of our race," Kiira said with downcast eyes.

"We," Saax replied. "I am here with you and partly to blame."

"Yes, but as Chancellor…"

"Kiira. Let's just figure out how we are going to get home,"

Saax pleaded.

Kiira took in a deep breath and steeled herself to the soft ground she felt oozing between her toes. “Agreed. Well, we have water. Unfiltered. But, it’s there. We can also hide here in the woods during the day. Fly only at night. But what about food?”

“Are you seriously hungry?”

“No you fool. But we will be soon,” Kiira admonished.

“I think I will wait for food and water once we are back,” Saax snickered.

“And when will that be, you loon?” Kiira looked straight at him. Don’t forget how fast we were travelling. By my estimation, we are about a five-day flight from home, if we travel by night only, which we will have to adhere to,” she stated matter-of-factly.

Saax nodded his ascent, but asked, “five days, really? Our best bet is that Jaak was tracking us. Of course, we did sneak out. He may have put too much trust in us.”

“In me, the stupendous Supreme Chancellor,” she said as a bitter tear escaped her right eye.

Saax studied it in unabashed rapture. “What is that?” he asked stupefied.

“It’s called a tear,” she said bitterly. “Humans do it as a sign of profound emotion. Happiness or sadness.”

“Amazing. Does it happen often?”

“No. This is only the third time for me.”

Saax edged himself closer and wrapped a blue wing around her soft-feathered shoulders. Kiira instinctively leaned her head on his wing. “We are in serious trouble”, she thought aloud. The sun was still approaching its peak inclination. This meant that they had a long day ahead of them. And, a warm day. Despite the chill in the air, the two birds were accustomed to the much cooler temperatures inside of Rainier.

"Hey Kiira, do you know how to get home? It just occurred to me that we don't know which way to go."

"Well, we did fly east. So, if just go in the direction the sun sets, we can maybe get close.

Saax looked down at his failed wristlet with narrowed eyes. He thought of possibly fixing it. From a young age, he demonstrated a high level of engineering skills, as he tinkered with various gadgets along with his father. The image of his father rushed at him. *He should be home soon, and maybe he will go out looking for us; but too bad no one knows our location.* He needed to fix their wristlets. But, he did not have a toolset.

"I could maybe inspect our wristlets to see what's wrong, but I don't have a tool set."

"Do you think you could actually fix them, though?" Kiira looked slightly optimistic.

"I don't know," he said. "Depends on the issue. If it's fried, then no. Either way, I don't have any tools."

"Like this," Kiira asked smiling as she extended a soft hand towards him, holding a small rectangular box.

"What the what" Saax asked astounded.

"Akeela always made me keep one. Besides, I am pretty good with electronics as well. Between…"

"the two of us," he added. "We might at least…"

"get the comms going," she finished.

"Well then. Maybe we should stay here, then. Last known position and all… We could subsist on raw fish and all the water we can drink."

"Yeah. Let's pray to Terr we don't get dysentery," she complained with a laugh.

"And not throw up raw fish."

Kiira stuck out her tongue and shook her head. "I think humans call it suu-shee."

"They can call it what they will. I'm swallowing whole and not chomping down on it."

"Stop being such a baby, Saax. Besides, if we hurry up troubleshooting the devices, we may not have to drink or eat. Hop to it, Peter Rabbit!"

"You got it fuzzy bunny."

Behind the two friends, a small glass bulb nestled in a small plastic box, flashed red repeatedly. Above it, a black lens took still images of them every six seconds and transmitted them back to a local ranger station, just two miles away. The intent of the camera was to capture the behavior of the local fauna and any potential poachers. Two miles away, a young thin Ranger woke up from a nap, his soiled boots propped up on his desk. A slim brown hand quickly shook him by the shoulders startling him, nearly sending him crashing backwards to the wooden floor.

"Wake up doofus. You're not supposed to be sleeping on the job," a beautiful brown woman said with a gorgeous sounding accent as she giggled.

"So says my girlfriend who is always half an hour late for work," the blond man replied as he yawned deeply.

"Do you want me to look good or not," she exclaimed as she turned his chair to face him as she sat on top of him.

"You always look good, baby. And, that's a fact!" he sheepishly smiled with brilliant white teeth peeking out like small mint Chiclets. He moved to kiss her when she shouted across his left ear, her left hand pointing at the flat screen monitor.

"What is that?"

CHAPTER 29

Pulchri

Seln Commander asked her to investigate the auto-mol behavior. She looked across at him, as calm as a molten feather, not even remotely upset that just three hours ago, he informed her that she would be sent back to Terr on Meetus' shuttle. But the trip was delayed, he told her, until after she can assess the situation and rectify it.

"Do you know what is causing it?" he asked.

"Indeed," she said bluntly.

"Well, can you explain what is going on, please?" he continued with rising frustration at her nonchalant tone.

"No."

"Whatever your issue is, please put it to the side until after this is resolved. There are many lives at stake, including on Terr that depend on you," he pleaded.

"The situation may seem dire, but without a catalyst, it is perfectly harmless."

"I know that!" he yelled.

"It's a specific catalyst," she said past a sneer.

"Which catalyst then? I am growing weary of you Pulchri!"

Two other officers alongside Elder Libur and Meetus watched patiently, as they sat across the table from Pulchri. Meetus reasoned that she might be behind the dangerous levels and speeds of auto-mols circling about in some underground chamber the micro-molecules created. But he could not figure out her motive. Libur incorrectly passed off her behavior as a symptom of her age.

“This catalyst,” she replied as she pulled out a small silver tube from underneath her robe.

“What does it do?” the commander looked at her nervously, afraid to approach to agitate her.

“It makes things go boom,” she said as she depressed the touch-sensitive surface that acted as a button. One second later, everything and everyone was gone.

Data flooded the instruments of the Perth team. They cheered and danced wildly as their screens produced plot after plot of evidence of a massive tachyon signature. And, it came from the dark side of the moon. Cases of Australia’s finest beer were consumed and a few babies were conceived. There was cause for celebration.

Part 3

CHAPTER 1

Jaak

The former General loomed about his recently vacated quarters. Only a simple nest remained for him to sleep on. The disappearance of the Supreme Chancellor and the complete destruction of Seln base somehow fell solely on his shoulders. Three elders voted unanimously, in the Chancellor's absence, to strip him of his rank and restrict him to quarters awaiting punishment, after a new Quetz leader was chosen.

The evidence against him was of his own doing. His machines were infiltrated and his former plans for a coup discovered. But, he could not understand how he was to blame for the disappearance of the two young birds. He did not sanction the flight and did not have the authority to disapprove it. He certainly had no idea about Seln. Yet, evidence showed up on his machine showing otherwise.

Kiln and Fugax showed up regularly to attend to him. They, too, knew something was amiss and had their own theories about what they had recently witnessed. But, there was nothing they could do. Once a new Supreme Chancellor was elected, Jaak would be imprisoned in the deep recesses of the mountain. The dark and frigid prison had not been used in millennia, not since the days of war alongside humans. It remained a place to bury what needed to be forgotten.

His two aides remained loyal, as he shriveled up. He ordered them each to remain vigilant and to not give up on Kiira and Saax. He looked at each of them and said, "Do not believe anything any of the elders tell you, especially Lün. The black cloak she wears to mourn her son and husband is nothing more than a charade. I saw it in her eyes."

They each nodded. They did what they could to help run the Draconem clan. The ancient colonel, who acted on Jaak's stead, was not allowed in the elder council meetings, where Jaak was judged and found guilty; but he did not complain and remained quiet, opting to sleep all day. The two young officers supposed there was a plan to negate their clan and the colonel was either complicit or just too old to be effective. Kiln was aware that Jaak was in the process of preparing Akeela to be his colonel while he, Kiln, would take her position. So, likely, the old officer was just ill-prepared to assume the responsibility of leadership.

Jaak's officers, though, filled him in on whatever paltry intelligence they could gather as his worries steadily increased. Two full days had passed and there was no sign of the younglings. Kiln informed him that their hidden network was exposed, and there was not much he could do. Fugax, he said, was having better luck. Due to his relationship with Dr. Mota, he was able to gather a few tidbits. Jaak had the feeling Mota played both sides of her wings, but still did not trust her. He did not know what that untrustworthy creature was doing as her loyalties seemed to shift often. Jaak also didn't care for Fugax dating her. But he had confidence that his young captain was not stupid and no longer easily swayed by feminine wiles.

The exterior chime sounded and before he could grant access, Mota strode in proudly. Kiln and Fugax moved to the side to give her clear access to the deposed General.

"You couldn't give me the courtesy to grant you entrance?" Jaak asked without emotion.

"Not right now. No. I have something you need to hear and don't have a second to waste," she said quickly. "So please listen up. We found them. Don't ask me how. But we found them; and they're alive."

"That's wonderful," Fugax chimed.

"No, it's not. I overheard Waal speaking to Libur via secure comm to Seln just before the explosion. The wristlets failed, according to a brief signal transmission from the Supreme Chancellor and Saax. They cannot get them to fully reactivate, though. Just send non-audio signals. I then overheard Waal and Libur squabble over a poorly executed plan and the aftermath of it."

"What do you mean?" Jaak pressured.

"They signaled the Supreme Chancellor and Lün's son to hold their position until they prepare a soldier to fly out there with working wristlets."

"And…," Jaak said impatiently, his vigor rapidly increasing.

"And, they are not sending anyone. There is a human 'ranger' station in the vicinity of their location. There are also a number of video-capturing devices in the area. Chances are, they have already been detected by humans."

Kiln spoke up unafraid of Mota's opinion of him. "Abandon them, why?"

Mota looked at Kiln for the first time without looking down her beak. "If they are captured and/or killed, then they can wage war against the humans."

"I thought they disagreed with my rather rash idea," Jaak added.

"Not in the least General. Apparently, they just wanted you out of the picture first," she replied.

Fugax folded his wings as he began to move his feet back and forth, contemplating an idea. "I can go out to them. I just need their location and a pair of fresh wristlets. I'm beginning to think the elders planned this from the beginning," Fugax said as he flicked his feathered tail about.

"I can get the EM devices, but getting out of here will be difficult. Everything is on lockdown for obvious reasons. I can modify the wristlets that will allow you to bypass all of our security but it will take a few days."

"They don't have a few days, though Mota," Kiln piped in.

"Yes, they do," Jaak said. You forget that Akeela had been

training the Supreme Chancellor as well as Saax. They will be safe for the time being. However, I'm concerned about the human presence. We can deal with our presence being known. Losing our leader to them, I cannot."

"And what has Lün to say of this?" Fugax looked exasperated at the thought of a mother not sending an army, let alone herself to save her son.

"She is not mourning," answered Mota.

"Not even for her husband?" asked Kiln.

"She planned that," replied Mota.

"Something is foul in the state of Quetz. Our leader is missing along with the bird to whom she was betrothed; and her plan on Seln base is obliterated. Someone please call Shakespeare to write up this tragedy," Jaak bellowed.

The gravity of the situation increased with those words. The four Quetz examined the possibilities of the situation, with Mota revealing only what she felt would benefit her. She did not explain that she had already developed the wristlet and meant to delay releasing it to them to ease any potential suspicions. She also claimed it was an idea one of her colleagues had privately briefed to Libur a few weeks ago.

"Now that we have a plan, let's make sure we execute it flawlessly," Jaak said as he looked about the room ensuring they all understood their roles.

CHAPTER 2

Saax and Kiira

The two young friends looked at each other as their despair grew. Two days had passed, and thus far, no one had showed up to escort them back home. Both had tried to repair the wristlets, even cannibalizing from one to make the other serviceable.

He knew that he could not give up hope, not with his father likely storming around the mountain demanding action. *But, why then, were they still here?* Kiira was resting. As she did the fishing deep into the evening, he stood the majority of the day's watch, keeping his eyes open for any movement from the humans. He thought they were isolated, but imagined people were good at showing up when you least expected them to.

Saax turned his head as he attempted to swat away a common fly and noticed something neither he nor Kiira had noticed previously. It was a small flashing red light. How they did not spot it at night, he could not explain. Kiira was out fishing and he was likely sleeping. But, he should have caught it. Cautiously, he approached knowing full well that it was not natural. Just above it, was a small black piece of glass. It was a technology he had learned about in his education, a material developed by heating silica. The Quetz had long since abandoned it due to its fragile yet dangerous nature, opting for the more advanced crystalline materials they employed to this day.

He turned and saw that Kiira was still sleeping deeply. Retraining his eyes on the device he got a closer look at it. It was concave and something he recognized. It was a viewing device. He quickly shot his beak into the glass lens smashing it into bits. He moved his body quickly, furtively looking from tree to tree, checking to see if there were similar-looking devices. He scoured the woods in the immediate vicinity, ensuring to remain within the canopy of the forest. Satisfied, he walked back to Kiira, who snored softly.

"Wake, up," he said. "Kiira, we need to leave."

The isolated Supreme Chancellor was in a dream. In it, she saw Akeela, suffering under her uncle's talon. She twisted and turned as Waal dug a well-honed talon across her chest, drawing blood that stained her ruby feathers to almost black. *This is just a dream,* she thought. *Nothing to worry about.*

A shuffling of leaves and cracking of sticks startled her out of it. But Saax's unusually loud voice got her up. She lay on the cool and moist ground, with her head propped up on the root of one of the many trees that were providing them with shelter. Weary but startled eyes stared up at her disheveled friend. He panted heavily through an open beak and bored holes into her head with his wide eyes. Nervous, she sat up quickly and addressed him.

"You're scaring me, Saax. What's wrong?"

"I discovered an optical sensing device. It's only a few meters away."

"What?"

"There was a flashing red light. A few leaves were blocking it; but somehow I spotted it when I was patrolling our little area," he said as he fought to control his wings from twitching.

"We need to destroy it immediately!"

"Already did; and I surveyed the immediate vicinity. All clear from what I can see. The real problem is there is a transmission device attached to the optical lens. Someone is likely watching us and could be headed our way."

Kiira remained firmly seated, thinking about the catastrophe she was responsible for, and how her entire race was likely exposed to humanity. *And, they will exterminate us before we can leave Terr for another world. What have we done?*

"We need to continue trying to fix the wristlets," she said.

"I cannot take it any further," he replied.

"Try Saax! We are done if you don't!" Kiira spoke through dry sobs but a still determined outlook steeled her resolve.

"Kiira. No one has answered us since yesterday morning. I think maybe they just can't pick up our signal or something."

"But they have our position. I just don't know why they aren't here yet. Maybe they were discovered already, thanks to us."

"No Kiira. We still have the shield wall. They can't detect us there. If only my dad," Saax started to say.

"Enough with your dad, Saax. He can't help us. No one can apparently."

"I'm sorry. I shouldn't keep bringing him. It's just that I miss him, and he would never let us down."

"I'm sorry about what I said about your dad. I'm sure he is terrific. But, I think maybe my uncle was right. Jaak is our enemy and was fooling us all along. He is the army! Maybe he took control of the Quetz now that I am out of his feathers. I feel so stupid!" she roared loudly.

"Take control Kiira!" Saax reprimanded.

"Sorry," she replied softly. "I guess we should start our trip back. We can step out in the open tonight and do some celestial triangulation then spend the rest of tomorrow resting. Then tomorrow night, we depart and stick to the river as long as possible so we can always have something to drink."

"There's a full moon tomorrow night," Saax said. "I hope it doesn't brighten the sky too much."

CHAPTER 3

Mota

The same three guards at the Supreme Chancellor's waiting room stared at Mota but acted fearful of her now that Waal was acting as interim chancellor and had given her unrestricted access. Above them on the walls, the same three functioning relic weapons hung decoratively. Mota blatantly looked at them before returning the guards' stare. *Real power was in wisdom and intelligence, not physical strength*, she thought to herself.

She proceeded to walk past the guards with a large smile. Inside the main chamber, Waal was standing by a still sleeping Akeela, looking down at her with disgust clearly present on his face. Mota approached him.

"How is she?"

"Exceedingly difficult to kill apparently. Isn't it customary for an elder to speak first in a conversation, by the way?" Waal asked rhetorically asked.

"Do my tail feathers no longer excite you, Interim Supreme Chancellor? Or, maybe you have forgotten how you got here?"

Waal raised an eyebrow and then spun on his left heel to face her, his robe sailing along. The enigmatic elder she once knew was gone and was replaced with something she knew him to always be. A tyrant.

"As you wish, Supreme Chancellor. We all know that it is only a formality now. I pledged my allegiance to you."

Satisfied with her response, he spoke more calmly. "Mota, play your cards right and I will name you as Libur's replacement. Probably sooner rather than later, I would prefer. We will see."

"Thank you Your Excellency. It would be an honor."

"Of course, my dear, there will have to be sacrifices," Waal continued.

"What type?" she asked suspiciously.

"Nothing much. Just that you stop seeing Kwentas. Unless you want my future bride to throw you in a cell with Jaak, I would highly recommend it. Of course, who am I to stop you?"

Fortunately, Mota was already done with Kwentas, though she had not yet informed him that their relationship was over and that he had been replaced.

Both birds were looking away from Akeela, unaware that the monitor feeds were synthetic. Only the doctor and his select staff still knew the truth, and they were secretly loyal to Jaak. Akeela barely opened an eye and stared at them intently, listening all the while. She could make out Waal by the look of the back of the head, but she couldn't make out the female. She attempted to move a foot and could not, so settled for intelligence gathering. She had just woken up but already knew that Jaak was imprisoned. The revelation was shocking, though, she was aware of the General's suspicions.

"I am not seeing Kwentas anymore. He bored me. Besides, Fugax is the true catch," she argued pertly.

"Aah, yes. My old aide. He will be disposed of when the time is right."

"What? Waal, his popularity is increasing rapidly, especially after he accepted his position as Captain of the Guard. You risk rebellion if you kill him."

"His popularity is exactly why he will be terminated. He remains loyal to Jaak and with his new status, could become a leader amongst the Draconems. Besides, you will be the one to kill him. If you still want your seat, that is," Waal said as he sniffled. "Besides, I seem to recall that you abhorred him. Unless, of course, you have fallen for that sniveling twit."

"Really? I would never. I am only looking out for you," she said. Mota was truthful in part. She was not in love with Fugax.

She had a true lover now. But, killing her new ally was bad for her future. She could care less about Waal, whose pompousness only continued to inflate.

The conversation ended with Mota leaving the room concerned for her own well-being. She understood that Waal wanted her to assassinate Fugax so that she would be the one to take the fall and then be summarily executed. Besides, even Fugax began to see her more as a friend. His popularity bolstered his confidence and allowed him to see females with a more discerning eye. She needed him as an ally, though, and decided to protect him as much as she could.

CHAPTER 4

Kiira

The time had come to depart. The sun was nearly set, and the moon was a large orb floating in a silent sky. Saax fidgeted briefly as his taloned hand continued to play with the one remaining functioning wristlet. Kiira insisted he wear it, but he refused stating that *he lived to serve his Supreme Chancellor. Her life was more important than his.* Frustrated at his recent sense of loyalty to the office, she relented and snapped the device just below her left hand.

Full dark was less than five minutes away, but it could not come sooner. She shook her feathers about as if trying to remove dirt that clung to her pores. She looked left and right afraid some childhood monster would peak around a tree. Saax sat there impatiently but still, ready to get the trip back home underway. A twig snapped in the distance catching Kiira's attention. Saax said it was likely an animal again. A few deer had already approached them. Like the other forest creatures, they were curious and no longer felt threatened by them.

Something snapped again, this time much closer, and it was followed by a ruffling of leaves. The two large birds stood up this time, instinctively taking a defensive posture.

"I don't know what that was," Saax whispered. "But, I don't think we should find out."

"Agreed. Let's go. Now!" she commanded.

Saax gripped a small human-made leather bag they found and filled it with berries earlier, along with the remnants of the cannibalized wristlet. They left the canopy of trees and entered the open land by the river. With powerful thrusts of their legs, they hopped into the air and spread their wings.

Voices roared from seemingly nowhere and before they knew it, humans in green multi-pattered clothing sprang out into the open behind them. A few wore bits of branches attached to their clothing and sulked close to the ground. The rest stormed at them. Kiira looked back briefly and saw that they held oddly shaped black devices, similar to the tachyon scimitars of their past, and that they were trained at them.

"Fly," she roared!

But, it was too late. Multiple pops echoed the darkening night. Slowly, they gained altitude, with Kiira at the lead. But, one of those loud cracks was more of a thud.

"Go, go, go, Kiira!" Saax yelled.

She looked over her shoulder and saw shock on her best friend's face. Then he was nothing more than a large violet mass tumbling through the murky air and landing awkwardly on the ground with a sickening thud. She wanted to go back to him, but there was nothing she could do to save him. If she were able to make it home, she could at least tell his parents what befell him. Maybe they could rescue him. But she had to think of her race. They had to come first. Tears poured from reddened eyes as she dove into another copse of trees before popping back out and then back in again. She kept this up until she no longer could hear the bi-peds.

Terror continued to wrack her mind. Akeela's words of wisdom soon resurfaced and she practiced her breathing until full calm was restored. Kiira realized that bi-peds, too, could fly, with the aid of machines that was and that the loud woomp, woomp, woomp was just that. So, she made the decision to fly just above the treetops and dive for cover every time she heard loud aerial noises. After three hours, the trailing bi-ped machines relented.

The chill air rushed past Kiira's feathers in a way she was not accustomed to, kissing her skin and lifting each feather up. It was an invigorating feeling that she couldn't relish. She looked to her left, praying Saax would be there. He wasn't. *He never would be by her side again*, she thought. Tears burned her face, flattening her red feathers to her face. The moon was already setting, its sinister face mocking her. She had less than hour of flight before she would not be able to see any longer. Ahead of her was a dark dense forest she could rest in. She hoped humans would not secretly spy on her as well. Either way, it was only a rest stop. As soon as night arrived, she would take flight again.

A few seconds later and she firmly planted on the ground, her cramping wings thankful for the repose. There was no doubt in her mind that she would make it back home, some way or another. And when she did, she aimed to recover Saax's body. She would not allow those disgusting hairless apes to desecrate her friend.

Kiira lost herself to her thoughts as she fought to sleep, when a chirp on her wristlet caught her attention. A second then third chirp ensued. She listened carefully, ready to battle when she heard a familiar voice address her.

A blue light soon emanated from its body and there before her, was Fugax with a large look of relief on his face.

"Your Excellency. Thank Spirit Terr you are fine. But, where is Saax?" he asked showing genuine concern for her friend.

"Gone. Killed by the bi-peds," she growled through a clenched beak. "My best friend and future husband is dead."

CHAPTER 5

Waal

A freshly groomed, blue-feathered wing gracefully moved across Akeela's face. In his younger days, this female humiliated him by denying his request of courtship, opting instead to marry Jaak's son, Kaylor. That flea-bitten animal was taken care of. Soon, he would finish his revenge by killing Akeela as she slept.

"The lot of you were not smart enough to outwit me. It took me a long while, but I did learn your secret," he whispered into Akeela's ear. "Too bad. I would have allowed her to live as chancellor for a bit longer. And, to think, all I needed to do was nullify you, which was quite easy," he snorted. "I used the same auto-mol toxin that I used to kill my sister, Eensul. So easy. Of course, I did not plant it on you as I did her. One of my lemmings did that for me, the irony being that your insistence on being by Kiira's side at all times, made it possible. Lucky for you, I need to take care of Jaak first. Consider this small reprieve a gift," Waal finished.

Satisfied, he walked back to his desk in the chancellor's private quarters. He loathed Kiira when she sat at the desk, but now it was his. The fate of all Quetz rested on his finger alone. A chime sounded. It was his new aide, another young red feather. She gracefully closed the distance between them and graciously waited to be addressed.

"What is it?" he asked without any real care.

"Your Excellency. I came to report that your niece's wristlet is no longer sending a signal. Dr. Mota believes that locating her is no longer viable and that she is lost to us forever," she finished.

"Oh, you bring such troubling news to my poor old heart. And, what will I do for comfort. Please come to me. I need to be consoled."

The young and attractive female bird stood by him and

wrapped her delicately feathered wings about him, his face buried deep inside her bosom, where he smiled and pretended to sob. She held him for a bit longer and released him after he gently lifted his head.

"Thank you my dear. Is there anything else?" he asked.

"Only that your supper is ready. I had the chefs prepare your favorite. Roasted venison and wild pig with all the dipping sauces you love. All freshly caught and not synth."

"You are so wonderful. You will spoil me rotten if allowed. And, I allow. I do hope that you will dine with me. I don't think I could eat alone after all this trauma has befallen me," he pleaded.

"Naturally, Your Excellency. It is my duty to satisfy any of your desires."

Minutes later, the pair sat and discussed their personal lives, mostly Waal's as he gorged himself on a meal worthy of his stature. As they finished up their dinner, a servant entered the large dining hall.

"Elder Lün is here to see you, Supreme Chancellor Waal," the melancholy bird stated. "Shall I see her in or have her wait?"

Waal had planned on escorting his new friend to his private quarters but he needed Lün's help in officially securing his seat. "Let her in, please," he said with a smile, though he was afraid she came with negative tidings. Either way, he would take the time to digest his meal and then lay with his female aide. He excused his aide and bade her to wait for him in his private office. Lün entered looking distraught.

After ensuring they were alone, she spoke. "Jaak is missing along with his aide, Major Kiln. Your old aide, Captain Fugax is also gone. All sensing logs show no evidence of their departure, and yet they are no longer here," she warbled.

"If there is no evidence then they are likely hiding somewhere in the lower mountain levels. There is nowhere for them to have gone," he replied impatiently.

"I have risked far more than you Waal. I sacrificed my husband and son so that we could rule our people together. This is a serious issue that we are facing. Don't you dare take it lightly," she spoke through a raised and stressed voice.

"You never meant to sacrifice your son until he turned on you. As for Meetus, you never loved him, so stop the melodrama," he returned.

"What of Akeela? When will you terminate her life? Soon?"

"There is no rush. She is still in a coma, and her monitors show that she will never recover. Besides, she makes for an interesting talking piece, don't you think?"

Lün sneered at the thought of a living decoration. Even she was disgusted by it. She was beginning to second-guess her alliance. *Maybe Waal was not to be trusted after all. Maybe he never intended to rule with her.* With nothing left to say she left Waal to his dessert and returned to her own spaces, where she felt safe. She would remain there as much as possible until everything settled.

Waal belched loudly. Happy, he stood up and walked to his office where his aide was resting on a large divan, her eyes halfway closed. He grinned again and moved towards her, his feet moving like a proper soldier, in anticipation of the evening.

CHAPTER 6

Kiira

"We don't have time to waste. I will explain everything momentarily, but we need to get airborne." Fugax motioned with his left wing and handed Kiira a new wristlet. "Put this on, please, Your Excellency. Time is wasting."

Kiira did as she was asked, her face downtrodden. She wasn't ready to marry, but she thought maybe she should have. *He will never experience love*, she imagined. And, she did love him very much. He was her 'monkey-butt.' She wanted to laugh at the thought, but found herself incapable. Captain Fugax broke her out of her daydream.

"Your Excellency, we must depart. Please," he pleaded gently.

Snapped out of her stupor but still exhausted, she refocused her mind. Fortunately, wherever they were going, they would get there quickly thanks to the new wristlet. The pair walked out into open land, just as she and Saax did earlier in the evening and activated their wristlets. In a few seconds, they were flying towards the darker part of the sky, without music, and without Saax. They were also not going home, Fugax informed her without explanation.

After two minutes in the air, a mountain hollowed out by lava was below them. Kiira recognized it as Mount Saint Helens. Fugax led the way, and soon, they were inside a smoothly carved-out tunnel. Rubble on the ground told her it was recently excavated. They deactivated their wristlet devices and walked through the orb lit hall, where at the end sat Major Kiln and General Jaak.

"General…Major. Why are you here? Why am I here?" she asked contentiously.

"Kiira, Your Excellency. There has been a coup. Your uncle and Lün conspired together in an effort to oust you. We are not sure how, but someone, switched your wristlets out. But, where is Saax?"

"Deceased," replied Fugax. "Her Excellency reported that he was shot down from the air by humans as they were departing for Rainier."

"Bi-peds," she returned. "And they will pay for it," Kiira spat.

"Yes, of course. But, first we need to deal with our own. My army has been nullified. My First Officer, Colonel Claw, is too old and his mental capacities gone. Akeela was meant to replace him prior to the assassination attempt."

"How is she?" Kiira demanded.

"We don't know truly," Jaak answered.

Kiira paced about the small room before slowly sitting on the ground, her eyes heavy. "Why weren't we rescued? Can you answer that, because bi-peds know of our existence again, now that they have the technology to wipe us out if we are not careful. I can only hope that we can further stimulate the auto-mols on Seln so that we can leave soon."

Jaak responded. "Kiira," he murmured. "From what we learned from Mota, you were intentionally abandoned so that you will be caught leading us to a war between our two races. A war our current leadership intends to win via a new super-virus tailored just for humanity."

"I am inclined to believe they deserve it," she countered.

"As for Seln. Well, maybe you should take a seat first."

"No. I will remain standing. Continue," she ordered.

Jaak took a deep breath as he looked straight into youthful eyes that bore far too much weight for their age. "Seln station has been destroyed, taking our ship with it. All souls were lost, including Saax's father."

Kiira lowered her head down onto her chest and closed her eyes, no longer sure what world she was living in. Jaak sat beside her and placed a weathered wing around her shoulder, giving her comfort.

"There is much that we need to accomplish," Jaak said. "But first we need to rest. All of us."

"First tell me about Seln station. What happened?" Kiira did not bother to look up as she asked.

"A senior scientist name Pulchri. We think she is behind it anyway. There were reports of her behavior descending into solitude and then returning to normal, just before all was lost.

"I remember her. I saw her once when my mother and I visited Libur's office. She seemed kind. Why would she do this to us?" Kiira asked.

"Likely, because Lün put her up to it. After her nest-mate passed a few rotations ago, she became somewhat lonely. She could have been easily manipulated," Jaak concluded as the quartet closed their eyes.

CHAPTER 7

Carol

The Bloomingdale's business suit, exceedingly costly patent leather shoes, and Louis Vuitton purse were replaced with a pair of Kuhl pants and shirt, hiking boots, and a canvas backpack. Carol's cameraman wore jeans, a tee shirt, and cheap sneakers, his everyday outfit. The old man who ran the gas station just outside Mount Rainier National Park told them about an old dirt road leading to the mountain that was abandoned thirty years ago after the interstate was built.

"It'll be rough going as the road is not paved and all, but the canopy would hide them from them choppers," he garbled. "Getcha to within three miles of the mountain. Take some hiking gear though," he concluded before returning his attention to a dusty flat-panel TV sitting on the wall to his right. The Huskies were ahead in their game against UCLA.

Carol paid him fifty dollars for a hand-drawn map and directions to the old route, as well as his silence. Dave, her cameraman, had shaken his head afraid that what she was getting him into was outside the network's knowledge and very illegal. People being erased by the military is illegal.

Fortunately for Carol, her spin classes gave her the required pep for the arduous hike. Dave and his hefty gut did not fair as well. Of course, on top of his own food and water, he carried the heavy camera equipment. As it turned out, the three-mile trek to the mountain was closer to five and the path was all but gone after the first two. The uneven ground was mostly granite with patches of loose gravel and dirt throughout making walking a heavy chore. Dave panted lightly and wanted to stop; but Carol kept pushing ahead, with the sight of her toned rear, as his only motivation to keep up.

Overhead, they heard the whoop whoop whoop of a large helicopter. They were getting closer to the base, Dave thought. He called out to Carol and asked her to stop for a minute. He needed a break. He was six foot four and heavy set. She was only five foot two and trim. Carol stopped and looked at him, sorry that she brought him along. If not for the hi-res camera Dave operated, she would have come out alone. A Go-Pro and her cell phone would have sufficed. But, she may want to air live if need be. She relented only after seeing all the extra weight he was carrying for her and settled herself on a large flat rock a few feet up ahead.

"Smoke 'em if you got 'em," she called out.

Dave made a face and plopped down next to her. He was not a smoker. More of an IPA kinda guy.

Dave broke out a couple of hearty ham and cheese sandwiches and a large bag of generic salt and vinegar chips he crammed into his backpack along with a few bottles of extra-sweetened tea, also generic. Carol who nibbled on a peanut butter Cliff bar and sipped from her large bottle of Smart water, wondered how he managed to stay alive. She sat quietly resting her body as her mind calculated the amount of time needed to complete the rest of the journey. She could sacrifice a good fifteen more minutes and still be okay. So as long as tubby didn't slow her down any further, that was. If he did, though, she would start the climb without him. Fortunately for Dave, all they needed was to get above the tree line so they could get a solid view of the military exercise.

The exercise was classified, of course; but Carol was also an old sorority sister of a certain field-ranking officer and was able to get the information she needed after filling her with a few alligator-tail shots. Her friend told her only that there was an exercise at the mountain and that it was related to the story she was covering. If she could manage to get above the tree line on the Eastern side, she would be in for a treat. *But don't get caught please. And, we never spoke*, she finished past a large belch.

The face of her Apple watch read 0915. *Time to go*, she thought. She put her phone down on the rock as she turned to look at Dave and saw that he was lying down on his back, his feet dangling over the side and his face smeared with grease. He was a slob. Loyal, but still a slob. Carol could not help but feel bad for him. Despite the flab around his waist, he was actually very nice and fun to be around. She even toyed with the idea of dating him. She had gone out with high-powered lawyers, doctors, even a mayor and found all of them to be pricks, always concerned about their appearance and their jobs. She was just a mindless trophy. But, after several years of men who wanted to keep her down, she gave up and decided to no longer date. Her life's work was too important to give up for a McMansion with a biggie-side of kids. She was not the mothering type, which did not bode well with her previous men of choice. Dave, on the other hand, sacrificed his own dating life, limited as it was, to support her.

Her partner in crime was beginning to snore and his face was cherubic and innocent. It was a shame to wake him. Her left hand reached out and gently rubbed his belly.

"Wake up sunshine," she cooed.

"Wha?" The stout man opened his bleary blue eyes to see the almond-skinned beauty that was staring down at him.

"Come on. It's time to go."

"How long was I out?"

"A little over ten minutes, stud. You know, you're cute when you sleep," she added gleefully.

"Uh, really?" Dave saw Carol as an exotic beauty. Her mother was Mexican-American and her father British giving her sharp European features with a warm tone. She was a stunning brunette with hazel eyes whose beauty excited him everyday, even when she pulled his leash and led him on crazy adventures like she did early this morning.

"We have a long day ahead of us. So we need to get a move on." She paused and looked at his gentle eyes. Satisfied, she continued. "But, when we are done, I will make you the most fabulous dinner you've ever had. And, I will even pick up some of that micro-beer you like. The dog one. Sound like a plan?"

There was no complaint. A minute later and they were back on the trail, Dave following immediately behind the woman of his dreams. After an hour, they reached their destination. They could still hear the helicopters circling the area, like vultures on the hunt for carcasses. But the main event was yet to commence. Carol's sister told her it would take place exactly at noon. It was only ten-thirty. Feeling a bit tired herself; she motioned for Dave to join her back under the cover of the trees. When he took a seat beside her, she turned her body and leaned over. She kissed his cheek, and when he turned in amazement, she kissed his mouth as she moved an arm around him. Her kiss was returned with such honesty and passion that she instantly made up her mind.

CHAPTER 8

Jaak

Kiira rested. It was not the deep sleep she was accustomed to from just over a Stel rotation ago, but she still slept. Jaak toyed with the idea of telling her the truth about his paper coup, that he laid to rest. But, the time was not right. She just lost Saax, their presence had just been exposed to humanity, and there was another coup she would need to face. *It would be too much, too soon*, he reasoned.

As Kiira's old wristlet was damaged and no longer functioning, Fugax tossed it into a pit of exposed magma just to make sure it would not inadvertently emit a signal. The new devices that Mota handed to them, however, were not traceable and held greater capabilities, chief among them, their ability to avoid detection. What this tech allowed them do sent shivers all along his fading feathers. Jaak did not trust Mota, but they all needed her. He only prayed that whatever she was up to, it was not a setup. If it was, then it was all over.

Fugax stirred and slowly opened his eyes. Kiln followed. The military trio huddled together and softly began preparations for Kiira's re-entry into headquarters. Once in, they would need to assemble the entire population and present her as their still-alive Supreme Chancellor. Lün and Waal would need to be tried for treason and murder. *But flea-bitten dogs bite back*, they argued. *They all better be prepared for an ambush*, they agreed. If they were caught with their hands in the air, they would be disintegrated. No evidence left. Also, Draconem guards were likely already replaced with those loyal to Waal and Lün.

The trio continued developing a plan as Kiira continued to rest. Her flight was taxing and she needed to be alert enough to defend herself. But, once awake, she would be fully briefed just prior to their departure.

They would not delay their entrance too long. That would give their adversaries too much time to prepare for them. And, they were preparing for them. *By now*, Jaak figured, *that his adversaries knew of his trio's disappearance. They will assuredly know that we are planning something.* He hoped that Mota would not betray him. She was the one who fed Fugax Kiira's location in Montana. If the other elders knew that they recovered her, then there was no telling how they would react.

"It's simple," Kiln began. "We will make our way into the Supreme Chancellor's quarters, secure the scimitars, and then make a live announcement to the general population."

"You are assuming they have not already taken the weapons," Jaak retorted.

"We can activate our armor prior to switching off the EM scramblers on our wristlets," Fugax countered.

"Yes," Jaak said. "But our armor can only absorb glancing shots from a scimitar. Direct shots and slashes are too powerful for them to deflect. Even glancing shots can be lethal depending on where it lands."

"Major Kiln should sneak into the Draconem clan and rally our warriors," Kiira added.

The three males turned at once to see a fully awake Kiira. She yawned deeply before speaking again. "General. You and I will enter my quarters and ensure Akeela's safety first. Then we can face Waal. Fugax. You seek out Dr. Mota. Have her record everything that takes place. This will give us the evidence we'll need to defend ourselves should a tribunal take place."

Jaak looked at his young ward proudly. "But we are not entirely sure we can trust Mota. Sorry, Fugax. I know you have feelings for her, but this is the Chancellor's life we are dealing with."

Fugax remained quiet and nodded that he understood. Kiira, though, understood where the General was coming from and offered a solution.

"General, I understand why you are concerned." She turned

to Fugax who was looking at her raptly. "Fugax. Tell Mota that due to her loyalty, I will appoint her as Libur's successor. She will rule Seentia clan."

"That should get her attention," Kiln offered. "But what about Lün?" he continued. She is no less a threat."

"She will be dealt with along with Waal," Jaak answered. "For now, let us concentrate on surviving our little plan."

"Agreed. When do we start?" Kiira asked.

"One hour prior to midday," Jaak promptly replied.

"That's in less than three hours," Fugax said with an eyebrow raised as a smile formed across his beak.

"Indeed," Jaak said. "The sooner, the better. But, first, we need to rehearse until we are all perfectly in sync."

CHAPTER 9

Mota

Around the corner of the hallway, Mota spotted her hidden nook. She wanted to sneak out one of the scimitars from the chancellor's waiting room. Waal just replaced the three oafs with his air-headed aide. Despite their repulsive look, they were trained security personnel. This idiot was busy buffing her azure-painted talons. He was just appointed as interim chancellor and already he was acting the buffoon. Mota was already reneging her secret alliance with him. And now she was certain it was all a mistake. Maybe she needed to reconsider her position. Hopefully, it would not hurt her chances of achieving her ultimate goal.

The three scimitars hung on the wall unobserved by the foolish aide. Mota approached the weapon furthest away from the young red feather and took it, placing it under her right wing and out of detection. With grace and aplomb, she walked out of the door, Waal's aide none the wiser. Mota then casually strode down the empty hall and placed the dangerous weapon in her hidden nook, after attaching an EM scrambler to it, allowing it to remain out of sight. After she was done, she stealthily returned to her intelligence center.

Still under the protection of the wristlet, she looked at the large visual display in front of her. Two goons studied the screen, noting the increasing bi-ped presence. One of them took notes and prepared a simple report he would likely pass on to his supervisor, the female Mota had put in charge. She waited as they did their job and signaled for their supervisor to join them. When the supervisor popped out of her humble office, the brief commenced. A bi-ped military operation was underway, in accordance with the intercepted reports they received. *Bi-ped hovercrafts are circling the mountain unceasingly*, they told her. *Their radio communications state that their new flying device will commence penetration of the shield barrier in just one hour.*

Mota listened to their conversation and noted that despite

their putrid appearance, they worked diligently and followed her exact rules without error. *Perhaps she could keep them around a bit longer.* The supervisor took in their report and walked back to her office where she prepared to signal her. Mota calmly walked out into the hallway and deactivated the wristlet after noting the hallway was empty. She then received the communication from the other side of the wall. "I'll be right there," she chirped.

A few seconds later, she formally entered the space and accepted the report she had already overheard. A war was about to begin that even Waal was not prepared for. Libur was responsible for intelligence gathering, so the blame would fall on his memory for the unexpected intrusion and relegated to the history books.

After her briefing, she congratulated the team on a job well done, much to the team's amazement, and then left for her own quarters in order to privately communicate with Fugax, if need be. *He should be arriving soon*, she thought, *along with Jaak, Kiln and the two missing teens.* She just settled into a chair when a chirp announced someone at the door. It was Kwentas. She started to ignore him, but he relentlessly pursued her, spouting poor poetry and promises of love. Begrudgingly, she allowed him entrance. He wanted to more than talk, of course, but she did not have the time, nor the inclination.

"What do you want Kwentas?" she asked. "I'm busy right now."

"Mota, please. You keep ignoring me. Are you trying to tell me that you prefer that sniveling twerp Fugax over me?"

"Kwentas. You are not going to gain my favor by talking about him that way. Besides, you still give yourself to Lün every night; and I don't like to share."

"That's no different than you and Waal," he clamored.

The false rumors of their affair had annoyed her from the beginning but were necessary, as they offered her protection from the other elders and their families. But the lies weighed heavy on her.

"Kwentas, this will no longer happen. You and I are over. Please leave," she said sternly.

"I think you are forgetting that Fugax is now a fugitive," he remarked snidely.

Red eyes flared back at Kwentas. "Get out of my spaces, and if you ever approach me again outside of business dealings, you will find yourself with your little wing clipped!" she thundered.

Kwentas instantly regretted his comment. It came out of frustration, as her lack of desire for him threw him into a loop. He was not accustomed to rejection, and his ego was severely bruised. His friends noticed how Mota no longer cozied up to him in the common dining hall and began to mock him. Naturally, he aimed to correct the issue.

"Mota, I'm sorry. Please forgive me," he pled.

"You are forgiven as soon as you leave my hallway. I have work to do and you are in the way. But, you should know and never forget that you and I will never ever share a nest again. That is over. From here on out, we will only maintain a business relationship."

Dejected, Kwentas left the room with his beak hanging down to his chest. Mota took a deep breath to calm herself from the affront she just endured. Just as she resettled herself, Waal summoned her.

CHAPTER 10

Waal

The interim chancellor moved his rear along the throne as he kicked his legs up and down with glee. The Sala Eld never looked so enchanting to him. For years, he dreamt of this very moment. His sister's rise to power was a nuisance, but his determination paid off. He selected images of the Saturnal sky to emanate throughout the empty hall as selections of his favorite music gently wafted down to fill the room. *Oh Sister, how you have failed. You stole my birthright, but I took it back. You stole it again through deception with that little imp; but again, I bested you.* Waal wore the robe of a Supreme Chancellor, white but with silver-colored accents to represent his house. It was a bit presumptuous; but his ascension was nothing more than a formality now. In two days, Lün would officially cast the only vote to elect him to the seat he currently occupied.

Not a single warning chime sounded when the main entrance door appeared, along with his bride-to-be. For the first time since their childhood, Lün appeared weary to him. He motioned her over with a strained look of caring.

"Come dear. What is troubling you? You are not still upset over our children, are you? They are easily replaceable."

"What do you know of children Waal? Saax was my son. I may have been a bit rash in allowing you to desert him amongst the 'humans.' " The last word came out with acid.

"There is no need to be sour with me. I practically raised my niece," he said feigning injury. "Besides, the two of them would have imprisoned us were they to learn what happened to Seln base, especially your son. With his father gone, he may have even turned a more vicious claw on you.

"Waal, I appreciate your sacrifice, but Saax was of my flesh. You will never know the difference," she retorted defeatedly.

"Oh my dear, but I can. You see, I already made the

arrangements to clone your son and my niece. They will be raised as our children, none the wiser, and can be molded the way we see fit, without interference from your husband or my sister."

"And who did you make this arrangement with? Libur? He's dead!"

"Patience," Waal said with a gruffer voice. I tasked Mota with the particular duty."

"Mota?" Lün asked indignantly. You truly are a fool!"

"Nonsense! If she expects to receive my blessing as Libur's successor, she will do as she's told!" he snapped.

"Yes, and what happens after she ascends?"

"Exactly what will happen to all who oppose us."

"Too much blood shed Waal. Too much."

The leader of the Stora clan turned her back to her future husband, giving him a view of her tail feathers. He took the insult in stride.

"But, I don't want Saax cloned. Have Mota desist there. Do what you will with your niece."

"Surely you must want another son, this time more obedient?"

"No, Waal. I want no such thing. This is all a mess, and I erred in participating in this coup. My tail feathers tell me it was a mistake that will fold in on itself."

"For your sake, I hope you don't go back on your word. Our wedding is nearly here. Do not humiliate me, Lün."

"Or what? You'll assassinate me next, like you did Akeela? Has she even died yet, or did you foul that up as well?"

"She is in a coma and will not recover. The monitors speak

the truth of this. Besides, I will finish her off as soon as I take the throne," he sneered.

"One last thing. Jaak will return soon. How do you plan on keeping him out?"

Waal looked at Lün matter-of-factly. "I already changed the shield frequency. In order to pass through, he would have to move at a slug's pace without armor. And then, it will be open season by the new guards."

Lün recalled from her more pleasant and youthful conversations with Meetus that an underground tunnel existed that led from the forest to the dungeon layer of the mountain. She was about to correct him on the matter before deciding to remain quiet.

"You are an astute bird, aren't you," she quipped before turning on her heel and leaving Waal to himself once again. *What a fool*, she thought to herself.

CHAPTER 11

Kiira

"Tell me, General. How exactly do you plan on getting in?" Kiira was glad they had the new and still secretive EM scrambling technology. But she failed to understand how that would help them get past the shields. Basic physics told her that EM scrambling was ineffective when passing through another EM field. They would be spotted and the element of surprise gone.

"Your Excellency. On the East side of the mountain, there is a secret entrance into the mountain hidden under the canopy of vegetation. It was sealed many hundreds of rotations ago. Once inside, we can move about freely and casually make our way to the interior of the mountain."

Kiira looked about the interior of the volcano. She spotted Kiln and Fugax stretching their leg muscles in preparation for battle. But, Jaak sensed her apprehension and gently pushed her.

"What is it? Something is bothering you and it's not the entrance?"

"I feel guilty. You are out here risking your life for me and all the while, I was not sure if I could trust you. My uncle repeatedly warned me about you; and when our wristlets failed a few days ago, I assumed it was your doing."

Jaak grinned warmly as he looked down at Kiira. For years he played the role of her family's nemesis; and now here he was as her most devout ally. He hoped to tell her the truth if they survived.

"Trust no one, Kiira Ave," Jaak said gently.

"That's what Akeela always told me. I miss her."

"And, maybe she will rejoin the living. Keep the faith."

Kiln and Fugax rejoined the pair. They finished locating the precise position to the hidden entrance by accessing the Draconem archives using a backdoor to their network. Kiln displayed a 3D map on a portable holo-projector and highlighted the tree-covered area. The two field-grade officers then briefed a simple but effective plan to Jaak and Kiira, highlighting the access and exit points inside the mountain. Each role was specifically laid out. Jaak and Kiira would make their way into her quarters with Jaak in the lead. If the room was clear, they would turn off their wristlets and announce her safe return to Rainier and the treachery she and Saax had endured. Kiln would summon the Draconem warriors and place them on patrols with orders to apprehend the remaining two elders. Fugax would need to locate Mota and keep her by his side as they trekked back to the Supreme Chancellor's quarters. As they were not entirely sure of her allegiance, she needed to be kept close.

"What is our backup plan?" Kiira asked.

"There is no plan B. It is all or nothing. Let us pray that there will be no further loss of life," Jaak stated gravely.

"Indeed," the others said in unison.

Kiira sat quietly as did the others, each rehearsing for themselves what they needed to do. Kiira, however, focused on Seln. Her plan to save the Quetz was destroyed. They would start again with stricter controls, but with bi-peds having discovered them, the plan could be moot. They would likely be fighting for their lives in the near term. Sadly, Meetus would not have that opportunity. If Saax were alive, he would be devastated. She missed him more than anyone right now. He made her happy in ways no one else could. And, how could they? They were more than friends. They were spirit mates in Terr.

Images of Terr's beauty filled her mind, pine trees, rivers, blue skies, animals of all ilk, exploding with energy and tranquility. At one point in time, she had a similar feeling about the technological delights of people. Now, those images were grotesque and unnatural. The thought of the incandescent and neon suns that bi-peds created and their subsequent pollution soured her stomach. The irresponsibility of mankind! They ravaged forests ruining endless ecosystems and habitats, spat chemicals and carbon into the sky to choke out life, and desecrated the oceans, committing unspeakable horrors there. But, if the Quetz left Terr, they dishonored their home and God. Jaak was right from the beginning. It was time for war. It was time for genocide.

Still, the thought of taking life shook her. She even avoided fresh meat, preferring to consume her vegetable-based foods as much as possible. Even at Fugax's ceremony, she tried to maintain her diet. *Not only was it better for the environment, it was better for her body. Killing was wrong and if she were capable of it, what other evil was she capable of committing, too*? she pondered.

Jaak shook her gently. She had nodded off. "It's time, Your Excellency. We must move."

She stood up and gave her feathers a good shake, knocking dust and large debris from her body. The two young officers disappeared before her eyes, their wristlets now active.

"Ready, Kiira?" Jaak asked.

"Yes," she replied.

Seconds later and they too were invisible to the naked eye. After activating her visor, the other three warriors came into view, along with their clamoring voices and squawks. In unison, the quartet kicked up and flew straight into the late-morning open sky.

CHAPTER 12

Naval Air Station Whidbey Island

The base commander was behind the wheel of a white government sedan and maneuvered it to the northern side of the base with Admiral Korn riding in the passenger seat. They quickly approached a singular tan aluminum building that stood in contrast against the open cement field. Because of the secrecy of the mission, Captain Pam "Echo" Jensen issued a base holiday for that Friday and hand-selected the personnel that stood guard duty, leaving the base deserted. With no one allowed into the interior of the station, she sped past every stop sign and stoplight well above the speed limit.

The two senior officers spoke about their kids and families, intentionally avoiding any work-related conversions, as they made their way to their destination. Echo pulled the plain white vehicle to the side of the building where the shade was highest and put it in park before killing the engine. Two men, both navy commanders in olive-drab flight suits, rushed to meet them and promptly escorted them inside of the gray building after rendering their formalities, where a command center had been established ad hoc. At the center of the room a black floor-to-ceiling curtain wrapped around into a circle, concealing the new weapon that was about to be field-tested.

"Commander Johnston. Are we ready?" Echo inquired.

"Yes, Ma'am. The curtain is only for extra precaution but our pilot is ready to board. He's currently in our little ready room resting," the short thin man replied, his pencil mustache wiggling along with the motion of his tan skin as he spoke.

"Very well. Admiral Korn intends to speak to him first."

Admiral Korn walked with Commander Johnston to the ready room as Echo and the other senior officer moved towards the curtained area. Together, they pulled the curtain back and revealed the new marvel of aviation. The metallic aerial machine shimmered like a pool of quicksilver, catching light from a limitless number of directions and revealing what looked like robotic feathers. Echo who was the first black woman Naval fighter pilot, dreamed of taking it up for a spin. Her brown eyes took a closer look at the multi-faceted surface and found their reflection staring back at her. She pulled away and saw hundreds of images of a curious woman in a poly-wool khaki short-sleeved shirt and pants. It was like looking into the compound eye of an insect up close.

Still amazed, she looked down at her gold aviator wings and imagined what Chanks was feeling. She heard a coughing sound and turned to see the other commander, who politely spoke and told her he was headed over to make sure the simple command console was ready, per the Admiral's instructions.

"I'll go help you set up in a moment, Shooter," she responded with a long New Orleans accent.

"Yes, Ma'am. It just has three large consoles along with secure comms, though. We just finished testing the set up again for a third time earlier this morning. All systems tested sat."

"Wonderful. And, no one else is here, correct?"

"Yes, Ma'am. Just the four of us."

Commander "Slipper" Johnston rejoined them and the trio strode briskly towards the console located in a back room, where two large officer chairs rested on a raised platform and two smaller, simpler chairs sat before a customized aluminum desk that supported an encrypted comms console and two headsets. The three large monitors were suspended over their heads and about six feet away.

"Slipper will handle the monitoring of all support air traffic, while I speak directly to Chanks on an encrypted channel."

"Outstanding. Thank you for all of your hard work Shooter."

A few motions later and all three large screens lit up. The monitor on the left displayed a cartoon graphic of concentric circles against a black backdrop. A few smaller green circles represented the current air support, drones and a few large helos. The middle screen, though, was just a shimmering dark grey, waiting for video input, in the form of a feed that would come from the jet fighter. The screen on the right was a zoomed-out version of the first screen, and it displayed a larger picture meant to give awareness of all air-traffic, including commercial, for the region.

The tall blonde admiral dismissed her subordinate and strode in towards the resting pilot. He was short, at only five-foot-six, a little darker and cute, with his jet-black hair cut short. He wore a faded flight suit. On his left breast, a patch with the name Commander Blas "Chanks" Garza and a pair of golden wings stared back at her.

"Hey Blas," she called out gently.

Startled, he turned rapidly and saw a familiar and beautiful face looking back at his red and bleary eyes. Instantly, he was out of his seat and standing at attention.

"Admiral. Sorry. I was just focusing my thoughts."

"Shut up you idiot and give me a hug," she said laughing.

Blas smiled and meekly walked over to his friend. The last time the two met, she was a commander and he a lieutenant. Despite the separation in rank, they formed a deep bond of friendship over their love of British lit, crossword puzzles, and French wine. She bent low and pulled him into her arms and held him tightly before letting go.

"It's been a long time Chanks. How are you and the family doing?"

"Oh, just fine, Kel," he said.

"Ready for this mission?"

"Yes, absolutely. I don't really know what I'm up against; but I'm sure that I've lived through scarier things."

"Yes, I recall you telling me about your childhood. Listen; there's been some rumblings across the intelligence communities. To tell you the truth, I don't think this shield is Chinese or Russian."

"Korean?"

"No, Chanks. The army shot down a thing a few days ago in Montana. Some sort of massive bird. The size of a Cessna…big."

"Say again?"

"Big Chanks."

"Uh, er, okay. Some sort of giant bird does sound scary but what does that have to do with the mission?" he asked confused. "Did someone take Jurassic Park too seriously and clone a giant pre-historic bird?"

"I don't know what is going on. But, Chanks, they recovered some sort of technology from the one they shot down. From what their engineers could tell, it generates some sort of field. We don't know much because the tech is well beyond our grasp. The device also seemed to be missing parts."

"Kel, did you say one of them? Does that mean that there are more out there?"

"We know there is at least one more. We also know that it flew off into the night in our direction."

"Oh, I see. This is getting scarier by the second."

"Promise me you'll be safe," she said looking through pleading brown eyes down at Chanks. "Promise me."

Five minutes later after the pilot and the admiral exchanged a few more words and a few tears, the pair walked out to the main area of the hangar, with Chanks carrying his flight helmet under his left arm. Admiral Korn stopped short of the new jet as Chanks climbed up a set of stairs and stepped into the pilot's seat. He did a quick survey and ensured all the systems lit up after flipping a common toggle switch. Satisfied, he pressed a button, and a clear bubble shut over him. The stairway was rolled away, and the curtain with it.

The hangar doors were opened simultaneously. After a second quick check, he activated the engines. A slow thrumming sound ensued. With his hand on the stick, he maneuvered the jet outside very slowly. He exchanged a few words with Shooter and moved out onto the airfield. Then the thrumming built up to an incredible roar. In an instant, he shot straight up to a hovering position fifty feet above the ground. Five seconds later, and Chanks flew away. Slowly at first, and then like lightning. Behind him, standing by herself just outside the hangar, Kel sent out a thought to him. *Be careful my friend.*

CHAPTER 13

Akeela

A single talon of her left foot wiggled. She tried again and managed to move it a bit further. She did it, but this time she was exhausted. Time was what she needed, but it was not her friend. She took several deep breaths, careful to inhale from her nostrils, hold, then exhale and hold again. After a few rounds of the calming exercise, she was able to move her entire foot. After that exercise, she did not bother with her breathing routine and decided to just rest. She kept her eyes closed and only opened them by a thin margin. Her physician, secretly aware of her recent awakening, communicated with her by touch. By gripping her thin hands with short pulses, he was able to speak to her in code. She replied in the same manner.

Waal also spent several hours a day lording over her. She overheard several of his conversations and knew of his ascension to the throne, albeit as the interim head, but only for a bit longer. He would be voted in shortly. Mostly, he quietly hovered over her, scowling or sneering down at her as if she was a worn-out piece of technology being prepared for recycling. But, on occasion he spoke to her with a soothing and calm voice, telling her how her flawed judgment all those years ago was the reason for her predicament. Waal also seemed to revel in Kiira's demise. *She was killed by humans*, he often said with the same gentle timbre.

The warrior's stomach would have turned over if there were any food in it. She was presently nourished via nutrient concentrates that were fed to her through gaseous osmosis patches. It kept her alive but her lack of mobility and calories was also thinning her muscles out. The Quetz understood early on that exercise was nearly a cure all for many of their ailments. At the moment there was nothing that could be done to properly stimulate her body. Akeela was also always hungry. As soon as things were taken care of, she planned on eating plenty of meat. *Forget the vegan approach*, she thought. *I need protein. Then revenge.*

The walls continuously projected various holo-scenes. Currently, she was surrounded by crystal clear water, with various gargantuan aquatic animals swimming past her, including blue whales and dolphins. Dolphins were her favorite of all the marine creatures. As a youngling, her parents would sneak her to areas of the world that were uninhabited by humans. Wearing a scaled down version of armor, she was allowed to enter the water. On her first trip out, a current temporarily caught hold of her. She quickly became frustrated as she fought a current trying to prevent her from returning to her mother and father, when a school of dolphins appeared and spoke to her. A translator was built into her suit, and she was able to converse with them. Like her race, they were highly evolved and intelligent. But, due to their aquatic environment, they did not create technology and manipulate their environment as the Quetz did. Nonetheless, they developed a highly evolved language and created the most beautiful poetry. She still remembered most of it.

A young dolphin volunteered to swim her back to shore and in the process, recited much of what she wrote. It was beautiful. Her name was Taleeah, as pronounced by the Quetz. Every year, Akeela returned to visit her friend. It wasn't until humans moved to that part of the world that she lost track of her, and because of the new presence, Akeela and her family could no longer visit. While she was pregnant with her own daughter, she planned to introduce her to some dolphins, so that she too could have a friendship with them.

But, she was dead. She needed to know for sure and pushed herself to regain mobility so that she could fight her way out to seek vengeance. *Damn all!* Time was moving by quickly and she knew that Waal planned on terminating her life soon. She was not sure of when, only that it was coming. Her doctor signaled to her that he was feeding her all that he could to heal her, but time was sadly still the best tincture.

Akeela continued to breathe slowly. Rested, she resumed her struggle and focused on every single muscle fiber in her body. Slowly, she felt them respond to her thoughts. After more concentration, they worked in unison. She could feel her wings and legs wanting to spring into action, as they flexed and contracted. Her strength was returning. Soon she would be able to move. With the doctor's help, she could escape with the aid of a wristlet. It would do the heavy work for her. *Soon, Soon. I am going to make Waal pay with his life.*

A presence was standing over her again. Waal, she thought. She could smell his refined perfumes. They reeked of excess.

"This evening, my dear. On this eve you will be no more. It's a pity that you likely cannot hear a word I am saying to you. Oh, I would love it if you could. Your Chancellor is dead. Yes, I know of your feelings for her. She is gone and soon you will follow her to the afterlife. If you believe in any of that. Personally, I never understood religious zealotry. There is simply no evidence to support it. I am not a scientist, but even they have nothing to show for it. Aah, yes. You pathetic worms are no better than bi-peds in that capacity."

"I dismissed your doctor by the way. His services were no longer needed. Interesting that he paid so close attention to a corpse. That is what you are, a breathing corpse. Well, I would stay longer and chat but I have people to rule. Any last requests? Oh, yes. You can't hear me."

A moment later, the plump and arrogant Waal was out of the room. She was about to die after all. But, she could not quit. It really was time to fight the battle of her life.

CHAPTER 14

Jaak

The dense forest provided ample protection from human satellites and airborne sensors for the four Quetz. They assumed that they would not encounter any humans. If they did, they could quickly activate their wristlets. However, with their cover already blown thanks to Waal's vile treachery against Kiira and Saax, it was not about exposure. It was about minimizing the exposure. Still, they chose to go without their scramblers and rejoin a nature they had spent so much time away from.

After a brisk five-minute trek through the woods, they arrived at a large rock. From what they could tell, at least one human had been there. The odors of a few remnants of food quickly wafted into their nasal passages, reeking of sodium and oil. The lot of them were repulsed by the choice of food people chose to consume. From the many intercepted electro-magnetic transmissions they received, they were aware of the pandemic of processed food. But, it was not the food that stole their attention. It was a small black rectangular object with a reflective surface. Kiln recognized it as a human communication device. They had no choice but to ignore it. Once they descended into the tunnel, it would be of no consequence. If a human followed them in, they would not be able to get past the code-encrypted gate halfway down the underground path. They would have to permanently seal the entrance, though.

Glaring down at his wristlet, Jaak warbled a few chirps. The wristlet responded by glowing. Then, the rock gently lifted itself into the air slightly and then relocated itself a few feet away. Without any further regard, they walked down an ancient stairway. After another quick warble, and the walls and ceiling quickly illuminated. Seconds later, fresh oxygen followed. The path was large enough for two of them to walk side by side, but they moved in a single file instead. Kiln led, followed by Jaak then Kiira. Fugax took the rear position.

"Jaak, why was this built?" Kiira asked.

"In case of an emergency evacuation, the Supreme Chancellor can escape Rainier safely to an undisclosed location outside of the mountain. From there, depart to another keep," he replied.

"But, I'm using it to go back in," Kiira mumbled to herself.

"Its presence was once well documented in our historical records, but most of the Quetz did not bother to read their history. Then, about three thousand years ago, Supreme Chancellor Ajax, a proud member of the Draconem clan ordered the records permanently sealed and the location of the sub-terranean corridor limited to only the heads of Draconem clan and a few other trusted individuals, though they would have lacked the necessary access codes," Jaak continued.

"But why?" Kiira pressed.

"Well." Jaak, paused. "Because in those times, political infighting was at a crescendo. Much like it is today, thanks to your uncle," Jaak answered.

"General, is that the same time that humans rode astride us in battle?" Fugax inquired, his eyes blinking.

"I hate the bi-peds," Kiira uttered venomously.

Jaak chose to ignore her comment. Her friend, and once betrothed, was just killed by them. He was shot down out of the air like a pheasant for dinner. Jaak knew that if he did not survive the attempt to restore Kiira to the throne, but if it was still successful, then she may eradicate humanity out of malice instead of necessity. And she would be without his counsel.

"Indeed Captain. We knew humans as our allies against rival Quetz factions. When the wars ended, so did our relationship with them."

"Odd how we are warring against Waal and his co-conspirators just as our presence amongst men is being made known," Kiln added.

A few steps further, and they arrived at a heavy manganese-alloy door. An archaic sensor pad was mounted beside it. Jaak had maintained the existence of the portal along with its access code a secret since taking up as his clan's elder without ever revealing them. He uttered the code without thinking twice. The door itself had not been opened since its testing shortly after installation. With loud creaks and groans as it scraped against its own hinges, the door slowly swung open, revealing the other half of the brightly lit corridor. Kiln, Kiira, and Fugax entered first as Jaak reiterated the coded tones. Nothing happened. The pad displayed a new message. *Door batteries low. Replace batteries.*

"We will have to take our chances," Jaak stated stoically. "Besides, we may end up needing to return back this way. Pray to Spirit Terr that we won't," he said with no lack of exasperation.

After a short walk, the group came to another stairwell, this one leading up to the interior of the Sala Eld. Jaak stopped shy of activating the device that would move the Supreme Chancellor's seat aside and spoke to the group.

With great formality and seriousness of tone, he said: "Let's review the plan once more. We are just beneath the Sala Eld. Your Excellency, you and I will secretly enter your quarters. If Waal is not present, we will start our announcement immediately. Kiln, you activate the warriors. You won't have time to gather armor-bearing wristlets. As such, you will need to lead from the front. Guard them, and they will fight with honor and grit. Fugax, you must find Mota and get her to us. We cannot know for sure of her involvement with Waal; but she has helped us thus far. With her by our side, she could give us what we need to imprison Waal for good."

Fugax's heart skipped a beat at hearing Jaak's words, but his loyalty was to young Kiira, to whom he swore a blood oath. As the rest focused on what they were about to do. Jaak spoke another code. Slowly, the ceiling gave way to light and open space as the quartet reactivated their wristlets, making themselves invisible once again. They entered the large room and prepared to retake the throne.

CHAPTER 15

Carol

The front left pocket of her pink hiking pants felt flat. Too flat. French manicured fingers raced across her body, patting her legs furiously, finding nothing. With a quick flick of her shoulder, a pink canvas backpack came off of her back. She tore it open and rummaged through its depths searching for the one thing she could not afford to lose, her brand-new iPhone. The shiny new device set her back close to fifteen hundred dollars, not including the Louis Vuitton leather case she picked up for several more hundred.

The words 'shit fuck' screamed in her mind, but all she managed to say was: "Dave."

"Yo," he shot back, as he sat comfortably on a soft patch of dirt.

"I can't find my phone. Can you help me?" Carol's eyes turned red as tears fought to be released onto her soft cheeks.

Her cameraman relaxed his shoulders feeling her pain. "When was the last time you used it?"

"I don't know. Just help me," she whined.

"I am helping you. So just answer the question," he said with exceeding patience.

"Damn it, Dave. I don't know. I was checking social media, back when we were having…"

"a smoke break," he finished for her.

"Damn it! Can you go get it for me?"

Dave lowered his head in anguish and asked his lord to forgive him for whatever he did to deserve the punishment he was about to endure. Carol looked at him through clearer eyes and finally noticed that his tee shirt was drenched in sweat, despite the cool forest temperatures. She thought about all that he had done for her over the last few years and the sweet little smile he carried despite the burdens she placed on him without taking him into consideration first.

"Actually. You should stay here with the camera equipment. If something were to happen while you are gone, I wouldn't know what to do."

"Are you sure?" he looked as if he saw a flying goat appear. Carol never thought twice about making him hoof it for something she dropped or unintentionally left behind.

"Yeah. Besides. You look like ass. Cute. But still like ass. If anything happens, just record it. Promise me. And, give some damn commentary."

"She thinks I'm cute." The words left his mouth before he could stop himself, but Carol was already gone.

A stunned Dave was left behind to keep an eye on the military testing as the spin-class guru put her quads and glutes to work, bouncing up and down the trail back towards the massive flat rock they rested and had their late breakfast on. Squirrels and chipmunks scattered about as she bounded down the trail, with her ponytail bouncing along to its own beat. It was only about a half mile away now. Her heart was beating steadily, and a smile had formed again as she rapidly approached their rest area. In another half hour, she would be back at the base of Rainier with not much more of sweat.

She started to feel guilty about how she had treated poor ole Dave. From the moment she met him, she looked past his beauty, inside and out. He put up with her crap on a daily basis without complaint and often thought of her. If he went to grab a donut, he was also sure to pick up a Keto version for her as well. If he grabbed a coffee, he picked up a chai tea with almond milk because that is what she drank. She never felt grateful for his kindness and surely had not returned it. In her mind, working as her cameraman was blessing enough. *What a bitch*, she thought.

She came up to the rock and saw that her phone was still on the rock, seemingly undisturbed; but the rock was not where she last saw it. Someone or thing moved it. Carol stood in shock as she looked down into a well-lit hole, with a gargantuan granite stairwell leading down into it. She remained in place unaware if she was even breathing. Her senses returned out of nowhere and she walked around to snatch her phone with sinewy fingers. A navy jet exploded on what was being investigated as either a Russian or Chinese force shield; and now a rock she was just sitting on was moved to reveal an underground tunnel. Her body's fight, flight, or freeze response kicked in. She had a choice to make. Without further hesitation, she chose to fight and started the slow descent into the massive tunnel.

She stopped at the first step to look at her phone's reception. One bar. She called Dave who picked up after two rings. But, she could not hear him. She shouted to him to return to the rock. "Forget the military! Come back to the rock now," she cried. The call dropped on its own as the singular bar was replaced with a search icon. With no time to waste, she headed down and began recording what she thought would be the greatest story to ever break in the world. What it was, she did not know, but whoever carved out the tunnel must have had giants in mind based on the height of each step.

The walls glowed internally, providing a warm light that allowed her to see clearly without harming her eyes. It was spectacular. If the Chinese or Russians did this, it must have been by magic. This was entirely someone or something else. She touched the smooth surface and felt rock, but it seemed clear. Their translucency kept her grounded. It was not radioactive. She also felt fine. And, the air itself was uplifting. Thoughts of a downtown oxygen bar surfaced in her mind.

Carol looked up, and the ceilings emanated their own soft light as well and were easily thirty feet above her head. And, the width of the tunnel was easily the same size. If not for the stairs, she would have guessed this tunnel was an underground roadway. To where, she did not know. Her phone recorded everything she saw and said. She spoke about the dimensions and the light and how she felt invigorated. *This little girl is not in*

Kansas, she mused.

CHAPTER 16

Mota

Mota left Waal's new quarters. As she walked past the sitting room, she noticed another missing scimitar. *Maybe Waal was getting nervous. Lün seemed remorseful and Jaak was still unaccounted for.* She felt the comfort of her new wristlet putting pressure on her left wrist. She no longer trusted anyone and had burned a few bridges in her conquest towards the throne to feel as if she had earned plenty of disfavors. Waal, too, was not to be trusted. As soon as he finished using her to get to his own goal, he began to treat her as expendable. She had anticipated as much but had hoped her beauty would suffice to keep her in his good graces. Apparently, he wasn't attracted to her.

She periodically looked over her shoulder and cautiously turned at every corner, her voice activation code always at the tip of her sleek blue tongue. After what felt like an eternity, she reached the safety of her clan's spaces. She warbled the command to open the door. Feeling more relaxed; she entered the large room once used by Libur to entertain guests. A senior official sat in the middle of the room speaking to a guest whose back was facing her. He stopped and looked right at her.

"Aah, Dr. Mota. Please join me and my guest. She has been waiting for you," he said. It was Ailer, Libur's brother. Due to decisions, he made early in life, he could never ascend to the position of clan elder; but he could fill in on an ad-hoc basis.

As she approached, the guest turned and revealed herself. It was Lün. She scowled internally but continued with the aplomb of a professional. As she reached the pair, Lün spoke.

"Please have a seat. We have much to discuss," Lün said politely.

"And, I have business to attend to," Ailer stated as he rose and deftly departed.

Mota took an inferior position and sat to Lün's left. She

discreetly made herself comfortable and waited to be addressed.

"It has come to my attention that you have been, ah uh, dating my aide, Kwentas. Do you have anything to say about that?" Lün scowled.

"No Lün. I could care…"

"You will properly address me as Elder Lün or Elder!" she roared back, fire sparkling in her eyes.

So she did have feelings for Kwentas, Mota thought. Killing her husband then, was more than just a political ploy to gain sympathy and remove any perceptions she was involved in the destruction of Seln base. *She wanted Kwentas for herself.* She addressed the elder again.

"Elder Lün. I was not aware of any wrongdoing by sleeping with your aide. But, uh, I am no longer seeing him. He seemed too infatuated with you. So, I moved on. He's yours if you want him."

"Impudent child. He was always mine. Know this. If you ever mate with him again, I will ensure that you are re-positioned as a maintenance worker. Do you understand?" the elder inquired through a pinched beak.

"I fully understand, Elder."

Lün quickly stood up and walked to where the door would appear. She turned her head slightly to the rear mockingly addressing the other female. "Go find your future elder and tell him that I have departed. Oh, I'm sorry if you thought Waal was appointing you as Libur's replacement. I already informed Ailer that Waal decided to appoint him as clan elder, despite his former misgivings. Goodbye, commoner."

Mota, rose and stood in shock. All of her well laid out plans were for naught. All because she allowed her hormones to rule her mind over a stupid male. But, Mota was not without her own secret plans. Only she and her new intelligence crew knew of the pending penetration of their shields. She could use that knowledge to her advantage. When chaos ensued, she would make her move and take back what the geriatric fowls had stolen from her. She was going to restore honor and respect back to her family's name.

Feeling even more determined, she walked to Seentia's intelligence center and plopped herself on a new padded seat she had installed two days prior. She looked up at the holo-projectors and saw all of the human activity. Her team rose and saluted her before returning to their duties of monitoring all of the recent activity. Mota planned on killing the three technicians in order to protect herself from any potential persecution when war broke out. But, she needed allies. And, these three birds had more than proven themselves. *When or rather if she became elder, she would create a new team of intelligence gathering operatives that answered only to her, on a blood oath*, she thought.

"Give me an update, please," she purred patiently.

"Yes Ma'am," the supervisor Na'ala promptly replied.

"The bi-ped hover crafts have been loitering most of the morning. However, our sensors just informed us of a new vessel approaching us at the speed of sound. Unlike the aircraft that crashed into our shield, this one is now slowing down."

"Very well. I intend to remain here until the breach."

The young supervisor stood by her leader, aghast that they were not treated like pond scum.

"Oh, there is one thing that caught our attention. A single human with some sort of ocular sensing device is loitering about the base of Rainier."

"Probably more of their military," Mota replied unconcerned.

"Well, that's just it. This bi-ped is not dressed the like the others. It also moves more sloppily than the rest. Should we keep an eye on him?" Na'ala cautiously inquired.

"Yes. Please keep a sensor on him at all times. Thank you, Na'ala."

CHAPTER 17

Waal

As a young bird, Waal was careful about everything he said and did. He learned quickly at the hands of his distasteful sister, that words had meaning and could be used against you. He also picked up very early on that remaining hidden was a powerful tool. By hiding himself, he stayed away from Eensul's sharp blows whenever they were alone in the same room. He also spied on her.

Right now, Waal detected a bit of anger from Mota, which was expected, and a certain distance from Lün. Jaak and his group were still unaccounted for; and the General would not go down without a fight. So, Waal selected a nice comfortable chair in the corner of the room, facing the center. He then activated his EM scrambling wristlet and went invisible to sensors at all frequency bands. He was also careful to change the devices detection frequency to an older less used one so that he could remain cloaked even from behind an active visor.

The interim chancellor sat quietly with the patience of a hunter, but not expecting anything to happen. In his mind, none of the recent events would have been necessary if had he been selected as his clan's elder. Despite his sister's seniority in age, she had proven herself to be reckless on several occasions, often challenging their parents. Although, intelligent, she did not absorb academic material as easily or as quickly as he did. So, Waal did not understand why his parents named her as heir. Yes, they argued that she was older; but had they forgotten all the trouble she created as a teenager?

Waal recalled an incident from his youth. An early teenaged Eensul had been asked to care for him as their parents travelled to Asia. She was sternly told that she was not allowed to have guests over in their absence. Eensul, of course, only reluctantly agreed. As certain as the daily rain in the mountainous area, she broke her promise; and on their first day alone, had invited her friends. During those days, the Rainier headquarters held more children. As soon as they arrived, they played music at deafening levels. Eensul also ingeniously accessed the large store of casaba wines their family kept for special guests.

Because they were young, they did not know how to drink the potent beverage and consumed too much too quickly. By the evening's end, several of them, Eensul included, were intoxicated to lethal levels. Young Waal unable to sleep because of the music went to complain one last time before alerting an elder. What he found shocked him to his core. He couldn't wake any of the teens that lay haplessly on the floor surrounded and covered with regurgitated food and drink. Immediately concerned, he called for help. Quetz medics arrived and were lucky enough to revive the lot of them.

His parents were summoned back and arrived a few hours later, feeling embarrassed and distraught over their daughter. Seentia clan's then elder explained how Waal happened upon them and promptly made the calls that saved all of the young bird's lives. He anticipated a warm hug and plenty of gratitude, but instead was met with scowls for not having stopped the bad behavior sooner.

"Your sister could have died!" they roared at the youngling. "It would have been your fault," they added.

As for Eensul, they embraced her and cooed as she lay recovering from her hangover. They were thankful for her still being alive. *All was forgotten and forgiven. Just rest*, they gently said to her. Waal was grounded to his quarters for a full Seln phase as his sister promptly resumed her lifestyle. He was punished and made to feel guilty.

Across the room, Akeela was still in her coma. He was going to execute her with a high dose of toxic auto-mols, but stalled when his feathers felt stiff. This was not the first time he hid at this corner of the room. In the last two days, it was his third time doing so. The first two proved to be nothing more than his nerves, *but nervous feelings kept you safe and alive*, he reasoned.

His thoughts shifted to Jaak, wondering what that infernal bird was planning. He deactivated the army and imposed curfew limits on them. Anyone caught disobeying, would be promptly executed. He also developed his own new militia from Socran volunteers who wanted to move up in society. Although they were not trained and armed only with stun batons, they would at least act as a first level deterrent. Still, he thought it's best to remain in the relative safety of the Supreme Chancellor's quarters and in a cloaked mode, with a functional scimitar in his hands.

His eyes grew heavy despite the early hour in the day due to his lack of sleep. Nighttime was when someone was most vulnerable. He thought of this and decided that he would sleep while cloaked. Unable to stay awake any longer, he dozed off. For twenty minutes, he dreamed about all the wonderful things his race could do on a Terr uninhabited by people. All Quetz would regard him as their savior and honor him with giant sculptures and volumes of beautiful poetry. They chanted, "Waal the Great! Waal the Benevolent! Waal the Magnificent!" His body was draped in the most luxurious of materials, newly created for him, as birds from the world over travelled to bow down and pay homage to the leader who saved them and their planet from destruction. But his fantasy was soon interrupted.

Voices were speaking freely. He opened his eyes and saw that Jaak stood in the middle of the room counseling Kiira without armor. *Kiira! The devils*, he thought. The youngling was alive. He did not know how she was located, let alone brought back into the mountain without sounding an alarm. Quietly, he stood from his seat and slowly took a few steps, before raising his scimitar. He had a choice to make. Murder Kiira and blame the General, or kill the General and then Kiira. He made a decision and took aim.

CHAPTER 18

Mount Rainier

The jet slowed down to a crawl before finally hovering in place, the wings of the plane outstretched like a hawk frozen in time before striking its prey. Based off black box data of the exploded F-35, the barrier was less than half a nautical mile away.

The microphone embedded in Chank's helmet was voice activated.

"Base command, this is Troch-1, over."

"Troch-1, this is base command, roger over."

"Base command, I am hovering within one nautical mile from the projected location of the field, over."

"Roger. How are your systems, over?"

"All systems are sat. I am ready to proceed on your order, over."

"Troch-1, proceed with caution, over."

"Affirmative. Proceeding with caution, roger, over."

"This is base command, roger, out."

The sleek metallic aircraft slowly picked up speed to just over 30 knots. One minute later, and the jet shimmered red. Then, Chank's world changed. In front of him the massive rock he knew as Mount Rainier metamorphosed. At its peak, an unknown city appeared. Entrances into the rock appeared throughout, with a few flattened areas carved out as well.

"Base command, this is Troch-1. Are you receiving my visual reads, over?"

"Affirmative. Proceed with surveillance and maintain caution, over."

"This is Toch-1, roger, over?"

"This is base command, roger, out."

Chank's mechanical bird slowly circled the tip of the mountain, capturing hi-res video and still images of the entire city's exterior. Some of the flat areas that he saw were large enough for him to hover and land on if needed, although, he prayed that he would not need to. Several enormous doors also caught the attention of unblinking eyes. They were translucent, but the reflected sunlight created a myriad of morphing colors; and even the image of his silver jet reflected awkwardly. They were also almost wide enough for him to fly through. Chank could not help but wonder that whatever it was that he was witnessing, it certainly was not man-made. There were no buildings, per se, just ornately carved portals going into the mountain. Many of the carvings that he saw seemed familiar to him.

At once his Mexican heritage kicked in. He remembered the artwork on display in Mexico, from tee shirts for sale for the average gringo tourist, to the massive murals on buildings. Aztecan pyramids, people, and animals dominated the subject matter of their art for centuries. His grandmother took him on trips to the interior of Mexico so that he could learn about his ancestry. They frequented museums and cultural fairs often speaking directly to artists and historians, both academic and amateur. Chanks found all of it fascinating; but one particular woman professor dazzled him. The professora showed him an ancient image made with charcoal black paint of a giant stork-like bird with stick legs and a long, pointed beak. He didn't know why, but the thick black lines that comprised the simple visage of this unique creature flooded his mind as he looked at the massive doors.

And there it was. His sensors screamed murder at him. There was an incoming bogey at one o'clock, at one-thousand feet, closing quickly. *Virgencita, ayúdame (Virgin Mary, help me)*, he prayed.

"Base Command, this is Troch-1. Incoming bogey, my one o'clock. It's a giant bird, over!" Chanks cried into his helmet.

"Roger, Troch-1, dis-engage now! Depart perimeter and return to base, over!" It was Admiral Korn who responded.

"Admiral!" Chanks ceased speaking as he fought the sensitive controls of the new jet. It was not his first flight, but this operational test was unlike anything he prepared for.

He recognized the massive bird at once. On a visit to the Carnegie Museum in Pittsburg, Chanks saw a full-sized replica of a Quetzalcoatlus hanging from the ceiling and another standing on the ground. The colors on what had to be a living giant flying dinosaur were different, though. This mammoth creature was solid red and covered with feathers, whereas the mockup was brown and bare-fleshed. This animal was also at least fifty-percent larger, something that was not much smaller than the dimensions of his jet fighter. What happened five seconds later, truly scared Chanks. Without warning, the flying dinosaur changed, its scarlet feathers instantly replaced with what looked scales. It was now a dragon!

What was clearly some sort of warning shot zoomed across the nose of his plane. He took immediate evasive actions, the articulated parts of the wings flaring out madly to accept the maneuvers. The creature also moved with intense speed and maneuverability he could scarcely match. Taking a hint he turned away and began to fly out as fast as possible.

"Human pilot. Do not exceed forty of your knots as you depart. It will result in a shield reaction and your vessel's destruction."

The tenor of the voice was female and spoke to him with perfect elocution in English. He did not bother to acknowledge it verbally. It was too weird. So he simply obeyed his instructions until he was clear of the area, and then shot back home at Mach-1 saying his Our Father as many times as he could manage. He trembled in his seat and barely managed to respond to the voices hollering at him through his helmet.

"Troch-1. Respond please. I say again. Troch-1, respond. This is the admiral speaking. Damn it Chanks! Answer me, please!"

"Admiral, this is Chanks, returning to base at Mach-1."

"Okay. Just relax and set the jet to autopilot. We are ready to receive you. Just breathe my friend. You are fine," Kel said softly, the sounds of her serene voice echoing in his ear.

Chank's heart raced, placing pressure on his chest. Despite wanting to rip his mask off to stop his hyper-ventilation, he kept it in place. He set the plane on autopilot and thought of his wife and son who were at home, probably grilling up a storm on their green kamado grill. It was meant to be a celebration meal in honor of his test flight, the details of which they did not know about. Instead of a nice welcoming dinner with his family, though, he would likely spend the rest of the night being debriefed by other Pentagon Officials that would magically show up right on time to detain him.

What he saw was impossible. A dinosaur that turned into a dragon? And, it spoke in clear English? His world was a lie. But, what concerned him was his superiors. He saw intelligent life that could have easily destroyed him but chose not to. The American government would only see a hostile actor, and the video he collected would be construed to show a creature that opened fire upon their vessel on their sovereign lands. Chanks saw the opposite in that regard. The city he witnessed, marvelous in its simplicity, gave a feeling that it had been there for a very long period of time. *Much longer than the U.S. has been around,* he mused.

Five minutes later and Troch-1 landed on its own. Just outside the hangar door, Captain Jensen, the two commanders and the towering admiral were anxiously awaiting him. They moved aside as Chanks maneuvered the plane into the interior of the metal building. He killed the engines, as the commanders moved about liked hurried ants to close the door.

The cockpit opened; and Chanks exited without waiting for the ladder to be maneuvered towards him. The admiral, unconcerned with protocol, rushed to meet him and threw her arms around him, squeezing the life out of her old friend.

"I thought I lost you!" she cried without a care for decorum.

CHAPTER 19

Kiln

Passageways were flooded with wide-eyed and untrained sentries holding stun batons that glowed white whenever they were waved about. Waal was nervous and was anticipating that they would return, but these birds did not seem ready to fight. If they won, it would be through attrition. If he could convince his clan to follow his orders as opposed to those from their colonel, overpowering the guards would be easy enough.

Kiln walked gingerly, careful not to bump into any of the Socrans that stood idly and confused. He was especially sure to avoid touching the batons, as contact with his EM field would give him away. After a few minutes of carefully traipsing the cavern passages, he arrived at his clan's main spaces and stepped through the invisible door his wristlet created. Several of his warriors milled about leisurely, unsure of their fate in society. His senior leader, Tech-Sergeant, Valla absently sipped at some casaba wine by a holo projector that displayed scenes of an ancient play. He approached her and deactivated his EM scrambling field.

"Major!" she blurted out as her vial of wine slipped from her hand and onto the floor. "How did you get back in?"

"That is a long and complicated story that I don't have time to relate right now," Kiln replied.

"But Elder Waal had the doors deactivated. We are trapped in here until further notice."

"Where is the colonel?" he asked.

"Sleeping, probably. His dementia has reached its peak and he is thoroughly sedated."

Good, he mused. "Listen to me carefully. General Jaak has returned with Captain Fugax and the Supreme Chancellor. He means to restore order and place the Chancellor back in power.

But, we need our clan's help. Can you muster everyone here?"

"Certainly," she replied. "But, how are we going to get out of here?"

"I can access the touch panel from the outside. But first, we need to get everyone ready. Elder Waal has flooded the corridors with Socran personnel with stun batons. They look terrified. So, if we're careful, they should simply drop their weapons and capitulate with a surprised rush."

"Understood Major. I can muster 'em up in two shakes of a feather."

The middle-aged but peppy sergeant sprang to her feet and ran off tapping on doors and calling for a muster in the main hall, as Kiln prepared his talk, thinking of an ad hoc plan to gently subdue the sentries and establish a Draconem security force to maintain order and rush the Supreme Chancellor's quarters to provide assistance if necessary. Kiira's safety was of the utmost concern. He and the General were concerned that Waal may attempt to kill her outright.

Seven minutes later and the main hall was filled to capacity with anxious warriors. Many of them grumbled with anticipation at what their banished officer was going to say. Others stood patiently awaiting orders from their Major. All of them wanted resolution and action.

"Why should we follow you Major?" a crusty old bird piped.

"You are not following me. General Jaak is here at this moment with the Supreme Chancellor. From what we understand, Elder Waal, sabotaged her wristlet along with that of Elder Lün's son. They were left to die out in the open. In fact, Saax has perished at the hands of the humans."

A loud murmur rose up in the air. But the Major ignored it and continued on. "But, to more accurately answer your question, consider this. Who locked you up like animals in a pen?"

"You make a good point," a soldier replied. "But how do we know that the General is even here? How do we know that he isn't responsible for abandoning the Chancellor and her royal friend? That's what we are being told."

"You will have to trust me like you always did before. But, I promise you this. If you don't stand with me now, then you will never be allowed to roam these halls freely."

Kiln paused momentarily as if thinking of something before he continued. "Seln base was destroyed, in case you did not hear about it… along with Second Spouse Meetus and Elder Libur."

Sounds of shock echoed in the air.

"We suspect Stora clan is behind it, specifically, Elder Lün. You have a choice to make right now," Kiln reported as he made a fist in the air and drove it down as a hammer to his side.

"You can help the Supreme Chancellor rebuild our world, because that is all that we have now, or you can stay here like prisoners. Now, you have my word that she is here. You also have my word that she will look out for our clan, instead of demolish it. Choose."

"The Supreme Chancellor!" Valla cried out.

"We will follow!" the rest of the group cried out in unison.

Three hundred warriors, red and blue, stomped their feet as Kiln secretly stepped out into the hallway. With a deft talon, he accessed the door panel and disabled the lock. The door appeared at once as he made himself visible. The whole of Draconem clan rushed the hallways screeching wildly. As anticipated, the Socran sentries dropped their batons in terror and ran to their quarters in fear. In less than five minutes, the entirety of the mountain's security measures were back under proper control. Kiln, Valla, and a young warrior made their way to the opposite side of the mountain towards the Supreme Chancellor's quarters at a double-time pace.

CHAPTER 20

Mota

A three-dimensional video of the mountain was projected into the air. Mota studied it carefully, noting the departure of the bi-ped aircraft. She sent out one of her sentries to scare it away. But, in the moments after that, the black hovering vessels she saw earlier outside of the shield slowly made their way in. Her team picked up an intercepted message from the bi-ped navy leadership to the wasp-like machine.

"Surveillance completed. Make your way beyond the shield below thirty knots. Once inside, maintain position until tacticals arrive. Permission granted for weapons release on any hostiles."

War had reached them, Mota concluded. She was forcing the Quetz's hand on the matter. Soon, they would have no choice but to eradicate the lesser species. She thought of Fugax and wondered if he had made his way back. If they didn't soon, the human presence could hinder them, now that humans were ready to kill her kind. Fugax was still a bit awkward for her tastes, but had proven himself resourceful. He had a bright future ahead of him that she could use to her own advantage.

She did miss him, although, not romantically. He was a good friend to her. And, what was friendship for but mutually helping one another. She paused her thinking when an alarm went off on another holo-screen. Waal's paltry security force dropped their weapons as Draconem personnel rushed the hallways. *So, they were back*, she thought.

Without hesitation, she barked orders at her intelligence team. "Change all video feeds in the main room! Supervisor, monitor privately in your office! Move!" she thundered.

The birds did not flinch and went to work without pause. In seconds the room displayed only internal video feeds and human news coverage. All was prepared so she could signal for Fugax to meet her there. With a quick flick, she sent word to him; and he promptly responded. He was still tip-toeing the hallways when Kiln's team started to rush out, so Fugax was about a minute away from her.

She used the time to compose herself and debrief her team. *Say nothing, report nothing in his presence*, she chided. Naturally, they obeyed her without question. Mota, however, was about to message Fugax when the blip that signified his presence on her wristlet, dropped. She tried to call him outright but was not able to connect. She tried again and failed again. Something happened to him. She rushed out of the room to go find him. She was invisible and moved about as quickly as she could. All of Waal's limp sentries were gone and replaced with stern and muscled Draconem warriors instead, who stood at attention with their backs to the wall, waiting for orders.

That didn't take long at all, she quipped. She remained invisible, though, unsure if she would be seen as one of Waal's allies. There was no sign of Fugax. She could not find him, no matter where she looked. She thought of Waal in that moment and was reminded of his sly nature. With that thought in mind, she ended her search for her friend, hoping the best for him, and made her way to Kiira's quarters instead. She hoped she would find him there.

Moments later, she entered her hidden nook. The scimitar she hid there was still waiting. She picked it up and examined it briefly. She should have studied how to use it earlier. A mistake. She turned the electronic sword over a few times and saw the activation switch. It was a fingerprint activated panel. She ran a finger over it and the blade lit up. If she hit anyone with it, they would die. That was simple enough. But, she needed to know how to fire off a tachyon burst, and there was no apparent way to do so without revealing herself. She carefully lifted the sword to the ceiling and then lowered it to eye level. As she looked down its length towards a non-existential target, the white tachyon glow changed to a crimson hue along the top of the blade. Then a holographic button appeared by the hilt. Perfect. She was ready to aid the General and Kiira, or Waal, depending on what she found. Still cloaked, she entered into the Supreme Chancellor's spaces.

Waal's aide was demurely seated by a desk, while two Draconem warriors quietly awaited orders from their General. The aide paid no heed to anything but buffing her nails, acting oblivious to the soldiers' presence. *What a moron*, Mota thought. Without another care, she entered into the main room.

CHAPTER 21

Kiira

Entering into the mountain was surprisingly easy. After stepping out into the Sala Eld, the pair passed through the portal that led from the cavernous room into her personal spaces. She and Jaak were back. The chancellor's rooms were empty, save Akeela who was resting. According to what Jaak related while they prepped inside of Mount St. Helens, she was recovering more and more every day, but still required a lot of sleep. Kiira ardently prayed to Spirit Terr that she could speak with Akeela soon. Jaak took off to conduct a perimeter sweep and just re-entered the main space striding in with purpose towards her.

"All clear Kiira. Come, let us begin your announcement to the clans that you are safe and have resumed your duties as Supreme Chancellor," he said as he tenderly placed a wing around her shoulder.

Kiira was still looking at Akeela, misty-eyed when he approached. "Yes, Jaak. Let us," she answered with growing urgency.

Kiira and Jaak positioned themselves in front of a holo-lens. Before activating it, Jaak helped her adjust her cloak about her shoulders and ensured that her feathers looked mostly groomed. If she was going to accuse her uncle of treachery and relate her account of living out in the open for several days, she could not look overly composed. The panel to activate recording was brought to life with a simple verbal command that Jaak gave. A second later, a holo-projected panel appeared in thin air. Jaak refrained from starting the live broadcast and looked at Kiira.

"Are you ready?" he calmly asked.

"Yes. I know exactly what needs to be…," Kiira uttered before being interrupted.

"Said? And, what is it you think you are going to say?"

Kiira instantly recognized the voice as her uncle's but with venom. He sounded off to her. Jaak turned immediately towards the voice, ignoring the holo-panel. Kiira followed. Waal was standing behind them in an extravagant cloak. Seeing her uncle for the first time in close to a week was a shock enough. She believed he was responsible for the faulty wristlets that left her and Saax abandoned in the American wilderness. As such, it was his fault that Saax was dead at the hands of the humans. She then wondered what other treachery he was behind. *Was he behind Akeela's murder attempt? And, what about her mother's?* What really shocked her, though, was that her own uncle, the bird who always loved her, or so she thought, was aiming a very lethal tachyon scimitar in her direction.

"What is the meaning of this?" Jaak patiently asked. "Do you really mean to murder your own niece?"

Waal sneered as a mad cry of laughter rang out. "Is she my niece? I don't know, nor do I care. My sister stood in my way of achieving leadership over the clans. Now Kiira does. So, yes."

"But if you kill her, who would allow you to continue ruling? Even your allies would turn against you," Jaak questioned as Kiira stood quietly and slowly lowered her wings in front of her chest as if to protect herself.

"Oh, no General," he said with a scathing tone. "Once I kill you, I can easily concoct a scheme placing all the blame on you. And, of course, the rest of the elders will follow my lead. Besides your only ally, Libur, is also dead thanks to Kiira's order to send him to Seln Base. Oh, and of course, the fact you plotted to overthrow Kiira."

Kiira turned slightly to look at the aging warrior whose composure remained. "You will never understand my motives, nor do I care to reveal them," Jaak uttered.

Despite the confusing news, Kiira understood that Jaak was no more a threat than Akeela. Whatever reasons he had, she knew they would surface if they could survive their current and very existential ordeal. Kiira's left foot slowly pivoted inward, placing tension on her knees.

"Why do you question my relationship to you, Uncle?" Kiira stared straight into his eyes.

"Does it really matter young one if you are my blood or not? I have been put down and kept from achieving my goals. I am the Supreme Chancellor now! It is my birthright!" he thundered with a trembling beak.

Jaak intuited that Waal meant to kill Kiira first. "You are mad Waal and overall pathetic."

"Me pathetic? Your troops have been sequestered as my Socran birds guard the hallways. The mountain is mine, you fool. You may have the brawn, but I always had the brains. You have been outwitted and outclassed General. And, here we are. I am armed with a lethal scimitar, and you hold nothing," he spat out.

"I wouldn't be too sure of your guards, Waal. Soon, my own clan members will be here. It's just a matter of time. So, no matter what you think you will achieve by killing us, you have already lost. You will never be allowed to reign over the Quetz," the General said with a level tone.

"You are delusional! I will rule. I will rule!"

As Kiira's foot continued to pivot, her wings continued to encircle her torso with her left wrist slowly nearing her face. Once it was close enough, she could whisper the command to activate her body armor and then throw herself sideways at the bird she once saw and loved as her uncle. Jaak's plan was to enrage Waal so that she could activate her armor, as his own ranting distracted him. The plan was working.

"I'm tired of this pointless discussion. Sorry Kiira, but you need to die."

Her wristlet was in range and she quickly warbled the command. Instantaneously, she was covered with her scales. She knew she could not withstand a direct hit so she snapped her body sideways just as a tachyon burst glanced past her body. Jaak responded by rushing at Waal, who was just far enough away to re-train his weapon on him. A burst fired glancing the General's left upper torso. As the shot was not directly centered on his body, he did not fall immediately, but it was lethal nonetheless. He would slowly die from particle poisoning. Jaak, however, did manage to strip away the particle sword and toss it to the far side of the large room. With Kiira's armor activated, she could easily overpower him.

Kiira gasped as she saw Jaak slump to the cold floor. Angered, she walked towards her uncle and prepared to subdue him. Death was too good for him, she thought. Instead, she would have him and any others who stood by him live out their days in the underground prison, so they could wallow until their death. As she reached out to grab him, another bird appeared out of thin air, holding a similar weapon. It was Mota. Waal grinned cruelly.

CHAPTER 22

Quetz Headquarters, Seentia Intelligence Center

Subj: Intercepted U. S. Navy classified message from the Secretary of the Navy

Status: Guarded. For Dr. Mota only.

Admiral Korn. Video footage obtained. Note: US Army personnel physically collected the same type of predatory bird captured on video by your pilot a few days ago in Montana. They seem intelligent, and based off the footage you just provided; we deem them a threat to our way of life. Per the President of the United States, via the Secretary of Defense, you are to assemble a strike force and destroy their habitation immediately. Understand that your rotary air assets are on station. Keep them there with weapons release authority until your strike force arrives to replace them. You are also authorized to arm and utilize your new secret jet. Leave nothing behind.

Secretary of thc Navy,

The Honorable, John D. Hoffine

CHAPTER 23

Carol

The long hall seemed to go on forever. To conserve her energy, Carol walked instead of ran, her phone snapping photos and sometimes recording video if something interesting showed up. On one occasion, it was writing. Odd scratch-mark-looking characters filled a wall with metered and intentional spacing. Several minutes later, and she came across three-dimensional portraits of robed birds. One of them even wore a monocle. She thought it creepy that someone would dress up a bird like that. But, she did not recall ever seeing holograms that sophisticated either. They were very high resolution and depending on the angle you took, you saw the appropriate side of the bird's head. Amazed, she recorded videos of them before continuing on. She knew that something even greater lay ahead of her.

The path continued for close to ten minutes before she arrived at a massive metal gate that was open. *I wish Dave was here*, she said to herself. Somehow, she just knew that she was making a mistake by continuing on. *But, she was a reporter and it was her job.* There was loose earth on the ground right at the opening of the gate. Kneeling down, she pinched the soil between her two fingers and brought it up to her nose. It was fresh soil. She could smell the life in it. Her grandmother was an avid gardener; and every summer she spent with her was filled with planting or uprooting various vegetables, so she was certain that someone or something had just been there. She prayed it was not one of the creatures that was displayed earlier in the hall. Standing up, she wiped the rich dirt on her pink pants and continued on. Up ahead, she could see that the wall ended and that there was a staircase similar to the one she just descended. At least she was almost there, but going in alone was not fun. *Damn it Dave, why couldn't you have followed me here. You follow me everywhere else?*

She stopped and decided to rest for a bit. Ahead of her was likely danger. *Could be the Chinese*, she thought. She sincerely hoped that whoever was waiting for her at the end of the giant stairwell would not kill her on site. Carol dropped to her knees again and meditated, breathing in slowly through her nose for four seconds and then holding it for four seconds before releasing it for another four. She refrained from breathing in for the last set of four seconds. Carol continued this for five minutes, calming her mind, body, and soul. Whatever lay ahead, she needed to be focused. Her muscles relaxed and brain calm, she stood up again fully refreshed. With the extra oxygen in the air, she felt alive and ready to tackle the large stairs.

Going down was not too difficult. Each four-foot step was just a hop down with only a mild thud, which fortunately, her hiking boots easily absorbed. Going up, though, would require real effort. Looking up, she counted thirty steps. It was not too big of a deal. Prior to easing down to spin class, she cross-fitted for nearly three years, where box jumps were a regular component. At the elevation she trained in, oxygen was a fraction of what it was in the room she was currently in. She looked at her first challenge, squatted down slightly and burst into the air and forwards, landing on her toes on the next step. She counted to twenty and then repeated, and again landed safely. On her third careful attempt, her toes were just beyond the edge of the step. If she fell, it would be twelve feet down onto a highly polished but still very hard rock surface. This time, she counted to thirty and slowly stretched her hammies at the same time. Her next attempt was better.

She did not want a repeat of her third attempt so she took a seat on the step and rested, keeping her mind elsewhere. Dave was on the forefront. He was not her type, so developing feelings for him all of a sudden was odd. But, he was very nice to her and thought of her in everything he did. It made her happy that a man looked at her as more than a piece of meat. Of course, she did work very hard to garner that attention, but it was never what she really intended. It was always about love of her body; and the wealthy slime balls that she dated only cared about loving her physically. Yes, they were cute, but always devoid of everything else. Dave on the other hand, was gentle, warm, and considerate. And, he was adorkable; when you looked past Cheetos stains on his printed tees, that was. Still, she realized that she needed him in her life for more than toting a camera around.

Twenty-six more steps were left. Gathering herself up, she tackled another four and rested. Then another four, and so on. Thirty minutes later, she arrived slightly winded at the top step. The staircase was wide enough so that she was able to cower to one side of it without being exposed to the large opening that was above her. Her future laid just four feet on top of her head. She would have to jump again, but only slightly. Her five-foot-four body just needed the boost to help her climb onto the floor just above.

"Come on kiddo. You can do this," she said whispered. With a gentle hop, she reached her light arms up to the edge and pulled strongly, moving her right hip up and onto a floor. She carefully wriggled her body and found herself on her back staring up at a cathedral-like ceiling. Images of constellations swam around it, but not the simple dots she was accustomed to from the local planetarium. These fireballs would zoom in whenever she stared at a particular one, revealing its planetary system, all in extreme high-definition.

Oxygen continued to fill her lungs as her mind took in the visuals. And that was just the ceiling. She got up onto her knees and then her feet, taking in what she saw. First the massive polished granite seats took her breath, then the tapestries, followed by the sheer grandeur of the massive room. *We are certainly not in Kansas anymore, Toto.*

CHAPTER 24

Waal

Waal was certain of Kiira's defeat when his co-conspirator, Dr. Mota walked in. Kiira may have been wearing armor but a direct tachyon burst would penetrate it, ending her life once and for all. How she survived the woods was beyond him, though still infuriating. Regardless, his own reinforcements had arrived, and soon his worries would cease. He casually walked towards the scimitar that Jaak had annoyingly tossed and picked it up as Mota kept her own weapon trained on Kiira.

"Silly girl. You should have never come back, least of all with a feckless oaf such as Jaak," he called out. "The woods would have been safer. Where is Saax, by the way? Did he die? Shot by bi-peds was it?"

Mota kept her weapon aimed on Kiira, forcing the deposed Chancellor to figure Mota could not be trusted after all. Now, she had two tachyon particle weapons trained on her.

"How did you know he was killed? That was never reported," Kiira said attempting to buy time, hoping Kiln was successful where Fugax clearly was not.

"Well, since you are going to die, I will clue you in. Not only did I plant your defective wristlets," he said reveling in the ingenuity of his plan. "I sent a signal to the bi-peds alerting them of your position. Of course, they thought it was just another one of their digital intelligence briefings, but all along it was my brilliant mind outwitting you stupid females!" he thundered with spittle flying from out his beak. "You never truly listened to Akeela. Never trust anyone!" he roared with a tinge of a laugh.

"You are sick Uncle. But, I guess you are not truly my uncle are you?"

"No, not that it mattered. It didn't when it came to my sister. I'm the one who poisoned her, just like I planned with your precious Akeela. She is somehow still in a coma, though. But, don't worry! I will be euthanizing her soon enough." Waal's eyes glowed like fervent suns.

"But if you didn't attempt to kill Akeela personally, who did?"

"Oh wouldn't you like to know? I could tell you, but the truth is you are simply stalling, trying to buy time for yourself. You should know this, though, before I kill you. Your little coup has zero chance of succeeding. I anticipated Jaak's return and locked up his soldiers replacing them with birds once loyal to you. Fitting don't you think?"

"What's fitting is that you are mad. You do realize that you will never be allowed to rule, right?" Kiira slowly stepped sideways, circling her old uncle. If he shot first, she would try to dodge him like she did before and hopefully manage to put Waal between her and Mota.

Waal caught what Kiira was attempting and fired a warning shot to stop her. The blast forced her to cease all movements short of her goal. The interim chancellor grinned largely.

"You can't win little one. Once I kill you, I'll move on to that ridiculous bird you called a sister."

Anger flared up inside of Kiira. But, she needed to remain calm.

"You forget that I am recording this very event. If the two of you surrender now, I will be lenient and ensure that you are not executed," she said hopefully. Kiira knew that the recorder was not activated yet when Waal made his presence known.

"Except, I deactivated all comms in this suite. So, you are clearly mistaken. You will have no such luck here. Anyway, I am growing weary of your pitiful attempt to stall me. Even with your armor on, you are dead. Goodbye Niece," Waal muttered.

"Hey Waal, you ball of flea-bitten feathers. Over here!" It was Akeela and she was tremulously standing on her own two feet. Waal roared and in anger temporarily forgot about Kiira, as he aimed his weapon at her instead. Before Kiira could react, a tachyon burst lased past her.

Waal lay on the floor immobile growling as his flesh disintegrated from the inside out, hatred flaring from his dying eyes. Mota lowered her weapon just as Fugax somehow managed to make his way into the room out of breath. Kiln followed shortly after with Valla and the young soldier. Mota spoke first.

"Sorry about that, but I needed evidence that Waal was behind everything before I could openly kill him. With Lün on his side, they would have countered you at every step," she said as she raised a wrist to show that she was recording audio as soon as she entered. "Hurry, go to Jaak. I will tend to Akeela."

Fugax aided Mota as Kiln and his team rushed towards their General who was dying before their eyes. Kiira joined them and dropped to the floor so that she could cradle his head.

"Get the bloody medics in here, now!" she roared.

As for Waal, all that remained was a pile of bio-dust beside an active scimitar that Valla picked up and turned off.

CHAPTER 25

Jaak

Mota and Fugax assisted Akeela back onto her nest and loosely covered her with a synth blanket. Before she could protest going back to bed, her eyes flickered, and she fell asleep. Mota eyed Fugax questioningly.

"Sorry," he said with eyes looking down at his feet. "I bumped into a baton by accident and had to fight my way over here, until the Draconem reached me."

"Of course you did. Dumb luck," she said smiling.

Kiira sat with Jaak's head resting on her red thighs hoping to provide him some comfort as his body decayed from within.

"Kiira," he uttered through a raspy voice.

"I'm here my General. Thank you for saving me."

"Of course. Anything for my Supreme Chancellor. Anything for my granddaughter," he uttered as his strength continued to fade.

"What? What do you mean?" Kiira's eyes teared up and immediately released a fountain of water, each connected drop damping her scarlet facial feathers.

"Eensul adopted you as a favor to me; and she loved you so very much. You may not recall, but I spent several hours in your quarters in secrecy. Your mother and I were never enemies. We were in fact childhood friends."

Jaak coughed roughly, forcing foamy blood out of his mouth.

"Save your strength. It's okay. I'll take care of you. I promise," Kiira pleaded as more tears barraged her face.

"You already have, by restoring my faith in our dying race. Kiira, my lovely Kiira. I did not appoint Akeela to be your guard. She appointed herself, as she is your mother. My son, Kaylor was her husband and your father; and he loved you so very much, even though we lost him before you were hatched. You see, he was murdered. Long I suspected it was Waal, but I could never prove it, until now."

Jaak's body trembled violently, Kiira scarcely able to control him. Kiln who was squawking orders at a medic team that arrived, rushed to assist her. Jaak ceased moving.

"Grandfather, I'm here and I did grow to love you. Please don't die on me now."

"Yes, grandfather. I waited so long to hear those words. May Spirit Terr continue to bless your mother Eensul for raising such a wonderful Quetz. And, learn about your grandmother, Rob'n. You are so much like…"

Jaak's eyes closed and his breathing stopped. The room was at once dead. Kiln helped Kiira off the floor as she carefully rested his head on her cloak. She had ripped it off, folded it carefully, and placed it underneath his head. Kiln removed his own purple robe and used it to cover his General in the colors of their warrior clan. Then in unison all present, sang the song of loss, their heads looking up to the ceiling towards Spirit Terr.

Little time was lost as the medics reverently raised Jaak to transport him to the infirmary where his body would be prepared for cremation. Valla, who was taking in a communication from her security team, rushed at the Major and Supreme Chancellor and spoke with urgency.

"Your Excellency. We are under attack. It's the humans. Their hovering crafts are having little affect on us, but intelligence anticipates that more powerful incendiary weapons will be on their way shortly."

"How did they get beyond our shields?" Kiln stared at his

second stoically.

"Their aircraft can penetrate if they move slow enough. Their new fighters are capable of hovering mid-air. I need orders," Valla implored.

"How much time before they reach us?" Kiira asked sternly.

"Your Excellency, we approximate their arrival in two hours," Valla responded.

"Major, give the order to expand the shield range by fifty percent. They likely believe that the perimeter is fixed," Kiira ordered. "Then, I want you to release an EMP in our vicinity. Knock down any bi-ped vessels by the mountain. If any other slow movers find their way in, have your team destroy them on site."

Kiln immediately spoke into his wristlet and gave the orders. Fugax and Mota, who were assisting in relocating Akeela into her daughter's quarters rushed over when they overheard the conversation.

Kiira looked at the two young military officers, assessing what she would do next. With her grandfather gone, they had no one to lead their military. Colonel Sharp was incapacitated and had proved too weak to lead as demonstrated by his troops being sequestered in their quarters. Kiln was also not of a royal bloodline so he could not lead an established clan.

"Our armies cannot fight without a leader. Major Kiln, for reasons you already know, I cannot appoint you as my grandfather's replacement. Captain Fugax, I hereby appoint you as General of our armies. Major, you will assist him until such time that the General can lead on his own."

"Yes, Your Excellency," Kiln said as he bowed, with Fugax following.

"Thank you for your trust in me Supreme Chancellor," Fugax said.

"There is one other thing. I still have at least one open adversary. Major, you are to arrest and confine Lün. I will formally charge her with conspiracy after we handle the bi-peds."

"Your Highness, Libur's brother, Ailer, may also move against you. He spent time with Lün and was to be appointed by Waal as his clan's elder," Mota interjected.

"Thank you, Dr. Mota. You saved my life. As a token of my appreciation, I appoint you as leader of the Seentia clan. I hereby execute my privilege in a wartime situation to enact such powers. I will figure out Lün's and my unc…Waal's replacement at a later time," she quickly corrected.

Thoughts of Saax rushed Kiira's mind. He would have succeeded his mother if not for Lün's and Waal's treachery. But, she continued with her duties.

"In order to ensure the safety of all future Supreme Chancellors and clan elders, I hereby establish a new clan, the Sang're. Kiln, you will be the first elder. Survey all the clans and select only the best to give the blood oath to. It is up to you, but I would suggest that you start filling your ranks with Valla and the young soldier, Private Stella. They acted with courage and honor today. They should be commended."

"I am deeply honored Your Excellency," Elder Kiln said.

"As am I," Mota said genuinely.

"Thank you. Dr. Mota. Please stand by me and help me draft a speech to the bi-peds. I'm going to send them a message."

CHAPTER 26

Kiira

Address to all Quetz across Terr by Her Excellency, the Supreme Chancellor, Kiira-Ave of the Draconem clan.

"War is among us. The bi-peds have attacked our home without cause and they took my best friend and betrothed from me, shooting him out of the sky like a common fowl. But, we will have our vengeance and will wipe this pestilent species off of the face of Terr forever. They pollute the sky, sicken the oceans, and even develop diseases to infirm themselves. We will help them along on that count.

For too long we have sat idle in our caves and mountains, watching these sub-creatures destroy our home. They once knew of us, fought beside us as our own clans battled one another. But, they forgot and relegated our existence to lore. Let us remind them of the sharpness of our talons and the bite of our ferocious beaks! Soon, I will give the order for all abled Quetz to don their armor and fill the skies! We will breathe fire upon them, and when they see us they will scurry like filthy rats into their obnoxious concrete dwellings! We will let them know that we are Dracons, the true rulers of this planet!

But, make no mistake; the hairless apes will fight back with animal ferocity. Their war machine will spew poisons and death. However, we have a secret weapon, one that they cannot counter, and that is our advanced intellect. We will use it to outwit and outmatch their every step. So, have no fear my fellow avians. Victory will be ours!"

CHAPTER 27

Carol

Ear-piercing chirping forced Carol to the floor. She quickly plugged her fingers into her ears and held her breath, praying the sickening noise would cease. When she looked up, a giant long-beaked bird was staring down at her. Across its shoulders a silk-like garment draped down to its feet.

"Who are you and why are you in my mountain?" it asked.

Shock was kicking in, and Carol felt like she was about to pee herself when the monstrous creature spoke again, slowly extending a wing.

"It's okay. I will not hurt you; but you do need to tell me who you are and why you entered."

"I, uh," Carol began before collecting herself. She was a reporter and she had a job to do. She steeled herself as she looked up at the red-feathered bird wearing a shimmery coppery-colored robe.

"I am Carol Rae Barton; and I am a reporter. I just happened to stumble across an entrance to a hallway that led me here, thinking it belonged to Chinese spies."

"Oh, yes. I remember you now. You are the human female that broadcasts herself across the electromagnetic spectrum, locally. Hmm. Your people are attacking our home. Do you know why?"

"No, but that is what I was investigating and how I got to be here. I am not a warmonger like those barbarians are."

"I see," the Quetz bird said, thinking. "I believe that you may be of great use to our leader. But, be warned. She is not at all happy with your race right now. Your people killed her betrothed."

“I don’t know anything about that. Though, my occupation has taught me to investigate thoroughly. I can infiltrate some of my people to figure out what happened and who is responsible,” Carol said shakily, with the weight of the bird’s left wing on her shoulder.

“Good. I am Dr. Mota, clan elder of Seentia clan; and I think we are going to become fast friends,” she said slyly.

CHAPTER 28

Saax

Through heavy eyes, Saax's vision slowly cleared up. Around him were archaic light fixtures dangling from a low ceiling. He heard soft noises from an adjacent room to the one he was lying in. He attempted to lift his body but found that the pain was unbearable. He also noted that thick synthetic cordage held him in place. Thin tubes with liquids coursing through them were attached to his body. He remembered flying away with Kiira before everything went dark. *Kiira! Where is she?* he thought through a still foggy mind.

He struggled but managed to only further tire himself. Seconds later, a team of humans poured in. Each wore a fully enclosed white body suit, with a clear polymer shield around their face, allowing him to see their bald simian faces. *Grotesque.* They spoke amongst themselves in a language he easily recognized, human English. It was his favorite of their idioms, as William Shakespeare wrote in it.

"Where am I?" he asked.

The team of men and women looked at each other confused. One individual, presumably the one in charge spoke, lowering his writing devices to his side.

"You are in a secret facility of the United States Army."

"Military, huh? Barbarians," he uttered as his strength continued to wane.

"Well, I can see why you might think that. But, let me assure you that we are not soldiers. All of us present are veterinarians, specialists in your type of physiology and anatomy. We saved your life and are here to restore you to full health," he stated.

"Right. And, then just let me go back home. No. You want to study me."

"Naturally, but we did save your life."

"Sure. So now let me go."

"Do you have a name, perhaps? I'm Doctor Daniel Thomas," he said with a wave of his free hand.

"If I can speak, don't you think I would have one?"

"My apologies," he replied. "I only meant that as an introduction. I don't know what to call you, that's all."

"Saax," he said. He thought of giving his full rank but thought better of it.

"It is my pleasure to make your acquaintance Saax. Oh this is my team, Drs. Carlson, Smith, Furgala, and Garza."

"Hello," they said in unison.

"When can I depart?" Saax asked.

"Well the U.S. Army will make that decision. We are only doctors. Besides, you still have a great deal of healing to do.

"Naturally," Saax whispered before passing out.

Dreams filled Saax's mind, of war and humanity. Though, Kiira too, was always in there. In his mind's repose, she laughed and danced about, calling him names as she always did. But sometimes, she was serious and gentle with him, with her wings around his shoulders as he wrapped his own around her body. There was never denying his feelings towards her. She was the love of his life; and, she needed him. He needed to break free of his prison.

The End

ABOUT THE AUTHOR

Dr. Maxsimo Salazar is a marine scientist and retired Naval meteorologist, physical oceanographer, and hydrographer. He began studying earth sciences at the undergraduate level while majoring in mathematics, which he continued while on active duty at the Naval Postgraduate School and the University of Southern Mississippi. His area of expertise is in the application of sparse basis functions.

Are you curious about the person behind the stories? Do you have questions about their writing process or characters? Maxsimo would love to hear from you! Whether it's to share your thoughts on their books or just to say hello, you can reach Maxsimo at authormaxsimosalazar@gmail.com. Join the conversation and connect with Maxsimo today!

www.ingramcontent.com/pod-product-compliance
Lightning Source LLC
LaVergne TN
LVHW091107080826
845145LV00008B/1837

9781953805027